Devil's Den

by Don Helin

Happy Birthday
Amber - Enjoy
Dev...

Don Helin

Publisher Page
an imprint of Headline Books, Inc.
Terra Alta, WV

Devil's Den

By Don Helin

copyright ©2013Don Helin

Publisher Page
P.O. Box 52, Terra Alta, WV 26764
www.PublisherPage.com

Tel/Fax: 800-570-5951
Email: mybook@headlinebooks.com
www.HeadlineBooks.com
www.DonHelin.com

Publisher Page is an imprint of Headline Books, Inc.

ISBN 13: 978-0-938467-55-7

Library of Congress Control Number: 2012947096

Helin, Don
        Devil's Den / Don Helin
        p. cm.
        ISBN 978-0-938467-55-7
        1. Mystery-Fiction 2. Gettysburg-Fiction 3. Ireland-Fiction 4.
Washington DC-Fiction

PRINTED IN THE UNITED STATES OF AMERICA

Dedication

To Elaine, for her love and support.

Acknowledgments

To my critique group – Carmen, Cathy and Laurie – and to Dennis and the members of the Pennwriters Fourth Wednesday Writers Group.

To my three readers – Marcia, Wade, and Dennis.

To Mark Nesbitt who started me on the trail of ghosts at Gettysburg.

To Cathy Teets and the staff at Headline books. Thanks for all your help.

1

Gettysburg, PA, Friday, June 3rd, 10:35 p.m.

He wandered along the curving path, the darkness covering him like a shroud. Hoofbeats echoed, then the sound of shuffling feet. Looking up, he saw moonlit monuments pointing to the sky as if they were the fingers of a hand.

Zack Kelly snapped back to reality and shook his pounding head. Where was he? Why couldn't he remember? Those damn hoofbeats again.

He stopped, then leaned against the wooden fence that paralleled the path around Little Round Top, and looked down at the boulders of Devil's Den. It hit him. Blake, where was Blake? He called her name, then called it again. No answer.

He recognized the Twentieth Maine Memorial, knew where he was, but had no idea how he got there or what happened to Blake. Why couldn't he remember? He had to find her.

Zack turned and ran down the path to his truck. He picked up a flashlight and retraced his steps, calling as he walked. Only the eerie sound of his own voice echoed back at him from the darkness.

As he reached for his cell to dial 911, a vehicle angled around the curve of Sykes Avenue from his right. First high beams, then red and blue lights flashed. The jeep pulled into the parking area and blocked his truck.

A tall, slender woman in a uniform stepped out and walked toward him along the winding path. Glancing up at Zack from under the brim of her hat, she pulled a ticket book out of her jacket pocket. "I'm Ranger Lee. You're here after hours and you'll have to leave."

Zack glanced at his watch. Ten forty-five. "I know the park closes at ten, but my friend's missing."

The ranger tapped the book against her hand. "What do you mean, missing?"

"We parked down there and my friend, Blake Lannigan, stepped out of my truck... said she hoped to maybe see a ghost out in Devil's Den."

"A ghost?" Lee chuckled. "Well, some say Little Round Top and Devil's Den are both haunted. Okay, what happened next?"

His head continued to pound. "I think I followed her up the path here to Little Round Top."

"You think?" Lee put her ticket book back in her pocket and watched Zack, rubbing her chin. "You'd better let me see some identification."

Zack pulled out his military ID and handed it to Lee. While he had his billfold open, the picture of his sixteen-year-old daughter smiled up at him. What would Laura think of her dad when she found out his friend had disappeared, and he couldn't remember what had happened to her?

"Did you see anyone else?" Lee asked.

"Not that I know of, but it was dark." Zack hesitated, then decided to blurt it out. "I thought I heard hoofbeats and shuffling feet."

Lee stared at him, then she smiled again. "Hoofbeats and shuffling feet? This is a joke, right?"

Zack swallowed his frustration. "No joke. Blake may have screamed. That's the last I remember."

Pulling out her flashlight, she held the ID up to the light. "Zack Kelly, active duty Army colonel." She flipped it over. "Six feet two and 195 pounds. Thirty-eight years old. Looks about right. Okay, I'll need a description of the young lady and what she was wearing."

He sensed her skepticism. Hell, he didn't believe it himself. "What? Oh sure. Her name is Blake Lannigan. She's tall, maybe

Shop Hours

Wednesday	12 noon til 8 pm
Thursday & Friday	12 noon til 6 pm
Saturday	11 am til 5 pm

Mechanicsburg Mystery Book Shop
6 Clouser Road • Mechanicsburg, PA 17055
Phone: 717-795-7470 • Fax: 717-795-7473
Email: mysterybooks@comcast.net
www.MysteryBooksOnline.com

Used Book Sale … Even Bigger!
12 noon until 6:00 pm • Wed - Sat

We're cleaning out even MORE used books. When we bought out Bryn Mawr Mystery Books a few years ago, we increased our inventory by 83,000 books.

We've sold approximately half of these to date. Averaging the number of books we've sold so far, I have it figured that I'll be one of the "bodies buried" before we sell all of these books.

These books will be 25¢ each. The only "hitch" … you have to go through the boxes to find the gems you want to buy.

Sale ends … when we've made enough space in our storage area.

We know where the bodies are buried…

five seven or eight, with long blond hair and blue eyes. Let's see, she was wearing black jeans, and a white blouse with a red pullover. Oh, yeah, she had on a pair of those low-cut black boots."

Lee jotted down the information. "You say this Blake ran down the hill toward Devil's Den?"

"I think so." Zack's mind flew over possibilities. He'd always been cool under stress, but he could feel the panic building. Couldn't show panic to Lee. "Look, we've got to find her. Maybe get some help to search."

"Okay," Lee replied. "Let's pull our vehicles down the road and turn right onto Warren Avenue. We can use our high beams to light the area."

Zack followed the ranger's jeep down the hill. They maneuvered their vehicles to face the battlefield and flipped the headlights on high. The beams cut through the murky darkness, revealing the large boulders of Devil's Den, appropriately named because on the steamy afternoon of July 2nd 1863, scores of Confederate soldiers died here attempting to breech the left flank of the Union lines. Zack called Blake's name again. Nothing.

Lee called. No answer.

Zack hurried onto the field, cutting between the boulders and calling, "Blake."

Lee leaned in through her jeep window. In a couple of minutes another jeep pulled up. Soon a police vehicle joined them, red lights flashing.

The ranger and a police officer got out of their vehicles. Lee whispered to them. The three stared at Zack. He knew what they thought. Some kind of nut. How could he convince them when he wasn't sure what happened himself. His head continued to pound. *What the hell was he into?*

The lights from their vehicles merged with Zack's. Zack hurried ahead of them, calling, listening, hoping, but hearing nothing.

The second ranger got into his vehicle and drove off.

"Where's he going?" Zack yelled at Lee. "We need all the help we can get."

"He's gonna circle around behind The Wheatfield, check the Peach Orchard, then come down behind Devil's Den. Maybe she got lost over there. We'll keep looking here."

The police officer walked over to Zack. Short, with no hat, the officer had black hair with a receding hairline. "Tell me everything that happened."

He raised an eyebrow when Zack told him about the shuffling feet. "How long has your friend been missing?"

"Since a little before ten o'clock."

"Tell me what you were doing before you got to the battlefield."

Zack tried to slow down. The guy was just doing his job. He told the officer about leaving Washington around mid-afternoon, driving to Gettysburg, looking around the town a little, then having dinner at the Pub and Restaurant on the town square. "After we finished eating, Blake wanted to see the battlefield at night. Said she hoped to see ghosts."

"Where are you staying?" the officer asked.

"The Cashtown Inn."

He made a note. "I think we'd better go to the station so I can fill out a report."

Zack had about enough of the bullshit. "Officer, I can't leave here until I find Blake."

Lee hurried over. "You best go with the officer. We'll continue searching."

Zack bit his lip. "Look, I work in the Pentagon. I'm going to call my friends in Washington. Maybe they can get a helicopter to help us search. We need to stay with it until we find Blake or work through every square inch of this area. Then, I'll go with you to the station. Make a formal statement. Whatever you want."

Zack stepped away and pushed in the number for his partner, Lieutenant Colonel Rene Garcia. A sleepy voice answered, "Garcia."

He told her what happened.

"Missing. Goddamn. Let me alert General Hightower. We should be able to get a chopper from Fort Belvoir. Be there fast as I can. I'll call you as soon as I figure it all out."

"Thanks, Garcia."

Zack disconnected. Turned to Lee. "I can't leave Blake out here alone. I can't do that to her."

Lieutenant Colonel Rene Garcia's Super Glide Custom Harley sped north on Route 270, the wind blasting past her. She loved the feeling of freedom on her bike, but shuddered when she thought about the tsunami that would engulf D.C. when the word got out that Blake Lannigan was missing.

The three of them had been partners on the national security advisor's special task force for the past eighteen months. Garcia thought the world of both Blake and Zack. She wouldn't just show up missing. Not Blake. Something crazy had happened.

The speaker in her helmet rang. "Garcia."

"Garcia, it's Hightower." The Vice Chairman of the Joint Chiefs of Staff, General Aaron Hightower, oversaw the task force that she, Zack, and Blake worked on. For task force purposes, he reported directly to the President's National Security Advisor, Darcy Quinn. "Where are you?"

"Just passing through Frederick," Garcia replied. I should be at Gettysburg in another half hour. Ah, have you talked to Quinn yet?"

"I just got off the phone with her. She's pretty upset. You know how close she is to her niece." He paused. "She told me she'd call her sister."

"Oh, man, this is going to get rough if we can't find Blake, like pronto."

"I'm working on the chopper," Hightower said. "We'll get it up there as soon as it's fueled and cleared. Maybe an hour. Not much more."

"I called the Pennsylvania state police," Garcia replied. "They're sending troopers and a forensics team if we need it. And, I've sent up some soldiers from Fort Myer. They should be on the way soon."

"Better contact the FBI and alert them. Don't you have a contact over there?"

"I'll get on it."

"After you mentioned Zack had trouble remembering what happened, I alerted his doc."

Another small shudder passed through her. "Right, sir. I'll call you once I talk to Zack."

She disconnected. *Blake was one great lady and smart as hell. And, oh shit, she had that top-secret clearance. The press would have a field day if they couldn't find her. The conspiracy theorists would go wild.*

2

Gettysburg, Saturday, 3:30 a.m.

Zack, the park rangers, police officers, and about twenty-five volunteers from the town of Gettysburg searched for Blake throughout the night. The state police K-9 unit arrived, pressing two dogs into the search. The park rangers located spotlights that helped illuminate the battlefield, but the searchers uncovered nothing but frustration.

Police made the rounds of motels and all-night restaurants with a description of Blake. So far, no luck.

A slim, dark-complexioned man with deep-set eyes walked up to Zack. Dressed in a blue jacket and jeans, he had the look of someone who'd seen it all. He held out his hand. "I'm Jim Munson, chief of police here in Gettysburg. I understand you've had an unusual night. Come over by my vehicle so I can see to write and tell me what happened."

Zack repeated his story, it seeming to be stranger and stranger each time he told it. *Shit, hoofbeats. Maybe he should drop that part. But he couldn't now. Too late.*

Munson watched him, making a couple of notes as Zack talked. "To be honest, Colonel Kelly, that's the craziest story I've heard since I joined the force twenty years ago. You expect me to believe that this Blake Lannigan ran out to Devil's Den and some guy on a horse picked her up?"

Zack struggled to hold his voice down. *Don't piss the guy off.* "Wait a minute, Munson, she's out there somewhere and could be hurt. We've got to find her before it's too late."

"All right, humor me and give me more background. How long were you eating at the restaurant before driving up here to Little Round Top?"

The question caught Zack off guard. He wanted to stay focused on the now. "I don't know for sure, probably an hour and an half."

"How many drinks did you have during that time?"

Munson probably figured he got drunk and lost his girlfriend. "What does that have to do with anything?"

"Just answer my questions."

"All right. I guess a couple of beers."

The officer who first arrived on the scene stood next to the chief. "I checked on you, Kelly. You had three beers and the lady two margaritas. According to your waiter, both of you seemed a little loud when you left."

"Well, pardon me for having fun. We are on vacation, for Christ's sake."

"Take it easy, Kelly." Munson leaned against the police car, took off his baseball cap, and ran his fingers through his hair. "What you've told me, Kelly, is that you came up here, had a few drinks, and your girlfriend ran off. You heard hoofbeats, then she disappeared. For the record, I'm having trouble believing your story. But, just to be sure, we're going to keep searching."

A motorcycle pulled up with a roar and a slender figure jumped off.

Zack waved, then yelled, "Garcia, over here."

Rene Garcia, dressed in her Army fatigues, ran up to Zack and pulled off her helmet. Short and slender, she'd clipped up her long black hair on the back of her head. Her gaze focused on Zack. "How are you doing? Tell me everything."

"Wait a minute," Munson said. "Who are you?"

Garcia glanced at him as if he were gum stuck on her shoe. She put her hands on her hips. "No, you wait a minute. Who the hell are you?"

Munson leaned back, obviously taken aback. "Chief Munson. Gettysburg police."

She held out her hand. "Okay. I'm Lieutenant Colonel Rene Garcia with the military police in the Pentagon. Colonel Kelly and I work together." She pulled out a tape recorder and clicked it on. "Now, Zack, I want you to go through step-by-step exactly what happened. Leave nothing out. As soon as I've got everything on tape, I plan to go out there and find Blake."

Garcia was painstaking in her approach to interrogation, more so today than normal. Zack appreciated it and summarized for her exactly what had happened.

She stopped him several times and made him repeat what he'd said or to double-check a particular time. It took about twenty minutes to go over everything. He didn't want to own up to not being able to remember everything that happened, at least not yet, and Garcia didn't push it. She would later when they were alone.

Garcia switched off the tape recorder. "I talked with General Hightower right before I arrived. He's authorized a squad of soldiers from Fort Myer, and a helicopter from Belvoir to assist in the search. They should be here any minute."

"Has Quinn been notified?" Zack asked.

Garcia nodded, then turned to Munson. "Blake Lannigan is the president's national security advisor's niece, plus she is the diplomatic program at the State Department."

Munson's eyes widened. "This woman is the niece of Darcy Quinn? Oh, man, this is going to be a nightmare with the press."

Zack swallowed, trying not to think of Quinn's reaction. "You bet your ass."

Garcia turned toward Munson. "Anything else before we get moving?"

"Kelly, you told my officer you were staying at the Cashtown Inn. Yet you hadn't checked in. Why is that?"

"We didn't have a chance. I hope that's not a crime too."

"Oh, for Pete's sake," Garcia said, "can we do this later? There's a woman wandering around out there somewhere and you're playing word games."

An Army van pulled up and seven soldiers jumped out from

the back. A sergeant climbed out of the front seat and saluted. "Colonel Garcia?"

"Yes."

"I've been told to report to you."

"Who's in charge of the search?" Garcia asked.

Munson motioned toward Park Ranger Lee and called, "More recruits for you."

"Great," Lee replied. "We can use all the help we can get. It's a big area."

The soldiers followed Lee toward the field, but the sergeant hung back. "Uh, we've got some mechanical problems with the van. Started acting up on the way up here."

Garcia glared at him. "Goddamn it, when's the last time you did a TI on that vehicle?"

"Wait a minute, Sarge," Zack called. "Get out there and organize your men to help the ranger. I'll take a look at it later. Maybe I can jerry-rig something long enough to get you back to D.C."

The sergeant saluted. "Thanks, sir."

"Okay," Garcia said, "let's get going."

Headlights and spotlights lit the field. Zack counted at least thirty townspeople who had arrived to help. The baying of bloodhounds sounded from across the field. Had they found a scent?

A jeep pulled up and a tall, sandy-haired male stepped out. "Zack, I heard what happened and hurried over."

"Goddamn, Cliff, all this shit came down right after I saw you at the restaurant last night. Oh, Cliff, this is Colonel Rene Garcia. She works with me on the Pentagon's task force." He decided not to mention that Garcia was an MP.

Henderson shook hands with Garcia. "Cliff Henderson. Zack and I served together in Afghanistan before I got out of the service. Had enough of all that crap."

"Cliff ran our interrogation unit," Zack said. "Good at what he did."

"I've been circling the battlefield in my jeep," Henderson said, "but found nothing so far. I remember from last night at the restaurant that Blake is a striking woman. She should be easy to spot and hard for people to forget."

For the next hour, they searched every inch of Devil's Den and the adjacent area. Major T.J. Wilson, another member of Quinn's special task force, landed a helicopter on the field and received a quick briefing from Zack. As Wilson headed back toward the chopper he called, "I'm connected in with the police radio band. We'll find her."

Zack got encouraged when one of the state police dogs picked up a scent, but then lost it at a point along the road.

Garcia and Zack climbed into his truck. "I called my contact at the FBI," Garcia said, "and told him the story. Because of who Blake is, he agreed to hustle some agents up here. There's been so many shoes tromping around here it's probably not going to do much good to bring in a forensics team. But, we'll do it anyway."

The sun peeking over the emptiness of the field ate away at Zack. He put his head back on the seat and shut his eyes, trying to think what else they could do. "This is impossible."

"No one disappears into thin air," Garcia replied. "She's here somewhere and we'll find her." She pulled out her cell phone. "I'm going to call and update General Hightower."

When she disconnected she said, "Quinn's flying up here by chopper. Hightower expects her to land in about three hours. He wants us to set up a place to brief her."

Zack tried to stop the pounding that started again in his head. He had to concentrate. Stay calm. "I'd better call my aunt. See if she can keep an eye on Laura for another day just in case."

Sean Lannigan stood at the door to his closet, gazing at the row of suits, trying to pick out just the right one. He yawned and glanced at his watch. Six-thirty. Time to get moving.

At a press conference the past Wednesday, the president announced that he would appoint Lannigan to the Supreme Court.

His meeting with the chairman of the judiciary committee was scheduled for ten o'clock that morning. He studied position papers all day yesterday and stood ready. Hell, he'd been practicing for years. The time to finalize the deal had arrived.

The old fart liberal judge he was to replace had finally hung it up. Lannigan would step into the chair and help erase the damage the bastard had done. He had the support of the chairman of the judiciary committee. Fucking senator better come through with his support since Lannigan had set up the old man with all the cute broads. He had enough on the esteemed senator to hang him by the nuts from the nearest tree and watch the press have a field day. He'd better not screw with Sean Lannigan.

The phone rang. Lannigan reached over to answer it.

"Sean, it's Darcy."

"Not now. Holly is on her way upstairs."

"Sean, this is business. There's a problem at Gettysburg. Blake is missing. You'd better get Holly on speaker."

"Missing? What the hell do you mean my daughter's missing?"

"All I know is that something happened and they can't find her."

"Just a minute. Here's Holly. I'll put you on speaker."

"Holly, it's Darcy. We have a situation, but I don't know much about it yet."

"Is it Blake?" Holly asked, her voice rising.

"Yes. I've been notified that Blake is missing in Gettysburg."

Holly screamed. "What the... ?"

"Let me finish. Apparently Blake and Zack Kelly arrived there last night. After dinner, Blake ran out onto the battlefield by Devil's Den. She seems to have disappeared."

"That's impossible," Holly yelled. "No one just disappears."

"I'm trying to get more information. When I do, I'll call you right back."

"She's with that military punk," Lannigan said. "I told her to stick with her own kind. Not get involved with his sort."

Quinn's voice hardened. "I'll let that go, Sean, because I know you're upset. Zack Kelly is an outstanding officer. I don't know what happened, but we'll get to the bottom of it."

"I want the FBI involved," Lannigan said. "Now."

"We've already done that. One of my people notified them this morning. We've got helicopters, troops, volunteers all searching. So far, not a trace. I have to go. I'll call you back as soon as I know more."

"I want to meet with that military guy," Lannigan said.

"I'm planning to fly to Gettysburg in a little while," Quinn replied. "I'll let you know a time." Darcy Quinn is the one flying to Gettysburg. She invites the Lannigans to go with her.

Lannigan slammed down the phone. "I told her not to run around with fucking scum."

"Now, Sean, let's not jump to conclusions until we know more." Holly pulled out a handkerchief. "My baby, missing."

"I'll bet he did something with her. And I've got my interview with the chairman today." Lannigan turned back to his row of suits in the closet. "I'll probably have to cancel the damn thing. And after all my work."

"You asshole. That's all you care about. Your fucking nomination." She stormed out of the room.

Lannigan glared after her. He'd worked his whole life to put the slums of Boston behind him. *Why hadn't Blake listened to him? She had a Harvard master's degree, great-looking woman. Hell she could have any guy she wanted. But then she goes off with that military jackass.* He'd never understand his daughter.

3

Gettysburg, 1:00 p.m.

A military staff car pulled up to the Gettysburg Park Visitor's Center. An aide jumped out and opened the back door for National Security Advisor Darcy Quinn. Her short brown hair lay perfectly styled, her makeup fresh as always. She wore a white blouse under a navy blue suit. Zack didn't know the other two in the car. He assumed they were Blake's parents.

Zack and Garcia saluted and stood at attention. Quinn brushed past them. "Let's go inside where we can talk."

General Hightower stepped out of the back seat of the second staff car along with Travis Plank, Quinn's press secretary. The two were stark opposites. Hightower, tall and slender, looked sharp in his pressed Air Force uniform. Plank, on the other hand stayed slightly heavy, his curly light brown hair sticking straight up. He reached into his pocket for a tissue to clean his small round glasses. Plank drove Hightower crazy with his smoking. Hightower had told him at several task force meetings that he always smelled like a damn furnace.

A slender, black-haired woman, wearing a dark suit with a long jacket and a short skirt that showed off her legs, stepped carefully out of the front seat. Zack caught himself watching a flash of thigh. Great looking lady.

General Hightower walked up to Zack. "Any news yet?"

Zack saluted. "Nothing yet, sir. My friend, Park Ranger Cliff Henderson, has set up for us to use the Ford Motor Education Center inside the visitor's center."

"Lead away." Hightower hurried off to catch up with Quinn, Zack right behind him.

When they entered the visitor's center, Zack directed Quinn toward the conference room. Zack had been assigned to Quinn's special task force since his reassignment from Afghanistan a little over eighteen months ago. Their goal was to help her cut through the red tape and bureaucracy in the Pentagon.

Quinn's task force reminded Zack of his ranger battalion back in Afghanistan. The men of the battalion had to be vigilant and work together. Now, Zack had screwed up and lost one of his teammates. He wouldn't blame Quinn if she booted him off the task force.

When they reached the conference center, Quinn took a seat at the head of the rectangular table, motioning for the others to sit around it. "First I'd like to introduce my sister, Holly, and her husband, Sean Lannigan."

A tall woman, Holly Lannigan's silver hair draped to her shoulders, but her face looked young enough to give the impression the silver might be premature. Her manner impressed Zack.

"I wanted to give them a firsthand opportunity to hear what happened and what we've done so far," Quinn continued. "I also would like to introduce my friend, Shelia O'Donnell. Before this is over, Shelia may be able to help. And I think you all know General Hightower and my press secretary, Travis Plank."

Quinn pointed at Zack and Garcia. "This is Colonel Zack Kelly and Lieutenant Colonel Rene Garcia. They are key members of my task force. Zack, why don't you tell us what you know about last night."

Zack looked down at the floor for a moment to compose his thoughts. "Blake had never been to Gettysburg before and this is one of my favorite places. I told her about all of the things to see, and she really wanted to drive here." Her parents squinted at him when he told them about her running onto the battlefield, particularly when he mentioned hearing hoofbeats and shuffling feet.

"Let me get this straight," Sean Lannigan said. "She jumped out of your truck and ran onto the field. She may have called for help, then you heard hoofbeats and marching feet. Is that what you're trying to tell me?"

Zack swallow hard. "Yes, sir. Sounds crazy, but that's the truth."

"Did anyone check nearby stables to see if any horses are missing?" Lannigan asked.

"Sir, that's a good question," Garcia replied. "I'll follow up on that."

Quinn stood and moved toward a counter. "Let's fill our coffee cups before we proceed any further."

After they were reseated, Zack told about the arrival of the park ranger. "Then a police officer arrived and I told him what happened. He obviously didn't believe me. Must have thought I was drunk and maybe even pulling his leg when I told him about the hoofbeats."

"I can't say that I blame him," Lannigan said.

Holly Lannigan pushed hair back from her face. "What you're telling me is that my daughter could have been wandering out there alone for hours. Could still be."

Zack needed to phrase his answer carefully. "I don't believe so, Mrs. Lannigan. We've spent hours searching for her. I called and called. She never answered."

Garcia leaned forward. "We've had a helicopter, soldiers from Fort Myer, the state police, and a host of civilian volunteers aiding us in the search."

Sean Lannigan stood and paced over to the window. A federal judge, he looked impressive dressed in a dark-blue, pin-striped suit. He stood over six-foot-four with wavy gray hair combed straight back, and dark-framed glasses accented his blue eyes. Heavy bags hung under those eyes.

"I don't know what else to tell you," Zack said, "other than I'm sorry for what happened."

Garcia raised her hand.

"Garcia," Quinn said, "something else?"

"At five o'clock this morning, I called in the FBI. They're rechecking everything. We won't rest until we find Blake."

Mrs. Lannigan pursed her lips. "But what if they don't find her? If the search has been thorough, where is she?"

Lannigan turned from the window and glared at Zack. "I can't believe you have the gall to show your face here. I hold you responsible for the disappearance of my little girl." His voice quivered. "I want you out of my sight."

Mrs. Lannigan started to rise. "Wait a minute, dear, he's here to help us understand."

Lannigan's face darkened to a beet red. "You'd better find her... or else."

Quinn walked over to take Lannigan's arm, then turned back toward Zack. "Zack, I think it's best if you and Colonel Garcia wait outside."

Fifteen minutes later, Blake's father stormed out of the conference center, ignoring Zack and Garcia. Mrs. Lannigan walked behind him, nodding briefly to Zack. General Hightower poked his head out. "Zack, Garcia, you can come back in now."

Quinn motioned toward the conference table. "Please."

When they were seated, she said, "Zack, I'm sorry for what Sean said. He's distraught about Blake. He'll come around as things unfold. I do, however, expect results."

"I can't say that I blame him. If it were my daughter, I'd be frantic. I understand exactly what's going through his mind. I wish I could change what happened, but I can't."

Quinn motioned toward O'Donnell. "I introduced Shelia earlier, but didn't tell you that she's a medium."

Zack watched her with renewed interest. *Mediums. Weren't they involved with ghosts? Hell, they talked to dead people.* He'd never met a medium before.

Quinn took a sip of coffee. "I don't know what each of you think about mediums, but I've known Shelia for much of my life, and I can tell you that she's the real deal."

Garcia didn't move. Didn't say anything.

"When you told me what happened, I called Shelia and invited her to sit in on our meeting, she knows Blake. I don't mean to say that I believe there's some sort of paranormal activity going on here, but I think it's worth exploring every alternative."

O'Donnell had long black hair and milky white skin. She watched Zack. He couldn't help but stare at her, then he dropped his gaze.

"Shelia," Quinn said, "are you familiar with Gettysburg?"

"I've visited here before during my trips to the States," O'Donnell replied. "Gettysburg is without a doubt one of the most haunted places in America."

"Where do you live?" Garcia asked.

"I'm going to Trinity College in Dublin, hoping to start law school next year. I travel to the United States about four times a year to attend conferences. I happened to be in the Washington area when Darcy called me."

"Thank you for coming," Quinn said. "What are your thoughts?"

She took a deep breath and pushed a strand of hair back from her face. "You may not agree with everything I have to say, but please give me your attention. There are a number of reasons why spirits remain on the earth. A violent or sudden death is at the top of the list."

"Gettysburg would certainly qualify on that score," Zack said.

O'Donnell watched Zack for a moment. "Unfortunately, yes. Another reason might be their fear of judgment. If they happen to be religious and haven't been to church, or meant to spend more time in church, they may fear they won't get into heaven."

Zack enjoyed listening to the lightness of her accent. "What you're saying, is that if a young person dies suddenly and violently, he—or his spirit, may stay bound to the earth?"

"I didn't say that. I said a violent or sudden death is at the top of the list."

"Oh, right," Zack replied. "Do you really believe a spirit captured Blake?"

"I have no idea, Colonel Kelly. Please don't try and extract things I didn't say. Blake is my friend. I plan to explore all the possibilities I can think of to find out what happened to her."

"That's enough for now," Quinn said. "Next, I'd like to hear what the press is going to do to us."

Travis Plank stood. "We need to organize a press conference as soon as possible. They're going to be all over us if we don't get ahead of it."

Zack hated to think of the public chewing on all this. "What are we going to say?"

"Tell them what we know," Plank replied. "Go over what happened, what we've done so far. Otherwise they'll drive us crazy."

"I agree with Travis," Quinn said. "Where can we hold it?"

"We can hold it right here," Zack replied. "This room is big enough, and the Gettysburg Foundation has been kind enough to set it aside for us."

"I'll set up the press conference for four o'clock. That way the reporters can meet their deadlines." Plank looked at Quinn. "With your permission, I'll notify everyone."

Quinn nodded and stood. "I've got to head back to Washington, but Travis I expect you to take the lead on this and keep me advised."

Plank gave her a thumbs-up.

"Okay," Quinn said, "let's get with it. Remember, I want to see results."

On her way out the door, Shelia O'Donnell put her hand on Rene Garcia's arm. "Excuse me, Colonel, did I hear that you're from Austin, Texas?"

Garcia watched her a moment before answering. "Yes."

"Are you related to the writer, Emilia Garcia?"

Garcia had been through this many times before. The reputation of her mother, an internationally known best-selling author on women's issues, particularly meditation and spirituality, followed Garcia wherever she went. "Emilia Garcia is my mother."

O'Donnell's face lit up. "I've read all of her books. She's such a great writer and so intuitive on meditation. I bet you've learned so much from her."

Garcia's mother had taught her how to meditate and how to close her mind to unwanted thoughts. She tired of all the attention. Being Colonel Rene Garcia was hard enough. She had carried her mother's reputation around her neck like an anchor her whole life. *Enough*, she thought, and turned to leave. "Yeah, I guess."

4

Gettysburg, 3:50 p.m.

Travis Plank waited for Zack and Garcia at the front door of the conference center. He pulled them aside and motioned toward the room next door. "In here, Colonel Kelly. We need to talk."

Zack took a deep breath and followed Plank. *Don't let the press make you out to be a nut.*

Plank led them into the room and shut the door. "We don't have much time before the press conference starts." He handed Zack a folder. "The top page lists the key points we want to emphasize."

"Who'll conduct the conference?" Zack asked.

"I'll lead it," Plank replied. "I contacted the mayor's office and because of who Blake is, the mayor wanted to make opening comments and conduct the conference."

"Typical politician," Garcia said. "He wants to bask in the reflected bright light."

Plank chuckled. "All too true. This thing could spiral out of control if we're not careful. I'll open by welcoming everyone and tell them there's a fact sheet on Blake and other information in a folder in the back of the conference room."

"What do you want me to do?" Zack asked.

"Sit there and look pretty. I don't think we want you to do any talking."

"That doesn't make sense," Zack replied. "She came here with me. I should tell them what happened."

"And what was that?"

Zack started to say something, but realized that Plank was right. He needed to keep his mouth shut and stay out of the way.

"I want you on that stage so I can turn to you if there's something particular that you can answer. Remember what they tell you about an inspector general inspection. Don't answer the unasked question. Be honest, but give short answers. And don't volunteer a damn thing. If you can't remember, don't say anything. Any questions?"

Zack hated to be smothered like this. "All right, Father, I'm ready."

Plank looked about ready to say something else, then glanced at his watch. "Okay, four o'clock. Let's go." He opened the door, then turned to Garcia. "Best if you wait in the back of the room for us."

Garcia touched Zack's arm. "Good luck," she whispered, "you can do it."

A man who could have played right tackle for the Washington Redskins stood at the door to the conference center. Plank shook hands with him. "Oh, Zack, this is Special Agent Henley Spitz."

"Colonel Kelly," Spitz said. "I'll be leading the FBI investigation into the disappearance of Ms. Lannigan. I've got to tell you that something seems really wrong here. I'm going to find out what."

Plank stepped between the two men. "We can talk about all this later. Right now, it's time to go inside."

Zack and Plank took seats in the front of the room, Spitz stood off to one side. The Gettysburg Foundation logo hung on the wall behind the podium.

Reporters filled all six rows of chairs and a number leaned against the back wall. Four cameras had been set up in the rear. Noise from the reporters chattering to each other and on their cell phones resounded around the room, making it difficult to hear.

Plank stepped up to the podium and tapped his finger on the microphone. His navy-blue blazer covered his paunch, and the white shirt, plus red-and-green striped tie, made him look every bit the media professional. Zack wished he'd brought a sport coat with him.

"May I have your attention, please?" Plank said into the microphone.

Conversations stopped. Faces turned toward the front of the room.

Four men rose from chairs in the back and switched on cameras. Zack squinted at the lights. The heat hit him and he started to sweat. Or, maybe he was sweating because he had no damn idea what he'd say about the memory lapse.

Plank cleared his throat. "First of all, I'd like to thank you all for coming on such short notice. We plan to provide you with everything we know in time for you to make your deadlines for the evening news. There's a press release in the back. Be sure to pick one up on your way out."

He looked down at a piece of paper. "Let me tell you a little about Ms. Lannigan. Blake graduated from the University of Pennsylvania and holds an MBA from Harvard. She's a member of the national security advisor's special task force along with Colonel Kelly. A State Department diplomat, she's been assigned to the embassies in France and China. On a personal note, she loves tennis and golf and has the goal of running a marathon in every state. So far she's completed seven marathons. There is additional information about her in your packet."

A woman called from the back. "Is it true that her father has been nominated by the president to become a member of the Supreme Court, and her aunt is the president's national security advisor?"

"Yes, both of those statements are true." Plank took a deep breath and looked down at his notes. "Now, please let me finish before you ask more questions. Ms. Lannigan and Colonel Kelly left the Pentagon after work yesterday and drove here to Gettysburg."

A reporter shouted out, "We know all that. What about... ?"

Plank stopped him with a wave of his hand. "You may know it, but not everyone else does. Please let me finish before you start asking questions. The two ate dinner at one of the restaurants on the square in town, then drove out to the hill overlooking Devil's Den."

"Is it true Kelly heard hoofbeats and shuffling feet?" a voice called. Some chuckling.

Zack sighed, relieved that Plank stood out in front. But he had an idea where this was headed. *Could he backpedal? Maybe say he only thought he heard hoofbeats? Screw it. Tell the truth and let it fall wherever it would.*

Plank continued. "After they were parked, Ms. Lannigan ran up the hill to the overlook around Little Round Top. We believe she then ran out toward Devil's Den, excited to maybe see a ghost. That's the last anyone has seen of her. Teams searched from shortly after her disappearance at ten-thirty last night until just before this conference started. The state police and FBI are involved. The Army has provided a search and rescue team as well as a helicopter. We will not rest until we find out what happened to her. I will continue to update you as things change."

A number of reporters raised their hands.

Plank waved them away. "Before I take your questions, let me introduce FBI Special Agent Henley Spitz. Mr. Spitz, would you like to say a few words?"

Spitz walked to the podium. "Thank you. First of all, let me say our hearts go out to the family of Ms. Lannigan. I want you to know that the FBI will do everything in its power to find Ms. Lannigan and arrest whoever is behind this mysterious disappearance."

He pulled notes from his sport coat pocket. "Upon notification at approximately five o'clock this morning, the FBI immediately dispatched a team of agents to assess the situation. Our mobile crime scene lab arrived around ten o'clock this morning and conducted a thorough physical investigation at the site. Unfortunately, the area had been so badly trampled by the searchers, it was impossible to find her footprints. We have found some items of physical evidence that we are reviewing."

That comment caught Zack's attention. Maybe they had something that would help.

"We appreciate the support of local law enforcement," Spitz continued. "Chief Munson has shared the results of his initial investigation. As yet, we have no substantive information as to what may have happened. Now let me turn it back to Mr. Plank."

Plank moved back to the microphone. "All right, who has the first question?"

"How can someone just disappear?" a voice shouted from the back of the room.

Plank squinted and shaded his eyes. "Good question. The lights are bright up here so I'd appreciate it if you'd call out your name and organization. Now, to your question. To be frank, we don't know what happened. Agent Spitz, can you help us here?"

Spitz stepped forward again and leaned over the microphone. "In cases like this, there are normally three possible scenarios. First of all, Ms. Lannigan never arrived at the site. However in this case, we have Colonel Kelly's statement that they arrived about nine-thirty Friday evening."

"But... ," a voice called out.

"Let me finish," Spitz said. "The second alternative is that she left the truck as Colonel Kelly said, ran onto the battlefield, and someone, as yet unknown, kidnapped her. Perhaps Kelly and Lannigan had been followed. The third alternative is that for some reason she ran out onto the battlefield and kept going, perhaps picked up by someone she knew. I can't think of any other alternative that makes sense to me."

A man called out, "Johnson, *Harrisburg Patriot-News*. Colonel Kelly's original statement said that he heard hoofbeats and shuffling feet. Does that mean a ghost kidnapped her?"

"We are not as yet eliminating any possibilities," Spitz replied.

"Wait a minute. Are you saying a ghost could have taken her?" The man smirked. "I want Colonel Kelly to tell us exactly what he heard."

Uh-oh, Zack thought, what should he say? He stepped to the microphone, ignoring the concerned look on Travis Plank's face. "Blake Lannigan and I work together in the Pentagon and are good friends. I love visiting the Gettysburg battlefield, and Blake told me she wanted to see if the battlefield was haunted."

Nervous laughter sounded from the audience.

"After I parked the truck, she jumped out and ran toward the battlefield. Yes, I thought I heard hoofbeats and shuffling feet. I may have been mistaken. Maybe it was the wind. Maybe it was something else. But that's what it sounded like to me."

Zack turned back to his seat and sat down.

"Wait a minute, Colonel. Myron Kutz, *Carlisle Sentinel.* What happened next? You were there. What happened?"

Zack stepped back to the microphone, head pounding. The lights almost blinded him. It hurt to think. "As I told the investigators, Blake ran out onto the battlefield. I followed her. She disappeared. I can't believe it anymore than you can, but that's what happened."

Plank stepped up to the microphone. "Thank you, Colonel Kelly. I know this is very trying."

"Peart, *Lancaster Intelligencer.* Blake Lannigan is a member of this super task force in the Pentagon that works directly for the national security advisor. She also is a senior staffer in the State Department. She must be cleared for all sorts of top secret information. Are you concerned about the possible compromise of this material?"

"Excellent question," Plank replied. "Any time there is the possibility of a security breach, it's a matter of utmost concern. We are reviewing the material Ms. Lannigan had access to and trying to determine if there is any possibility of a compromise."

"Herbert Manley, *Washington Post.*"

Holy shit, Zack thought, *the* Post *is here. Gonna be a big story.*

Manley stood. "Is it possible that some foreign government kidnapped her and is pumping her for information as we speak?"

"That's a tough one," Plank replied. "As Special Agent Spitz has said, we're not eliminating any alternative. For your information, her father has established a $100,000 reward for information leading to the safe return of Ms. Lannigan. Now, I thank you all for your time and attention. We'll continue to update you as the investigation proceeds."

Plank stepped back from the microphone and motioned toward the door. Voices yelled for his attention. He raised his hands. "That's all the time we have for questions. My business cards are on the back table. Call me with any additional questions you may have. Thanks again for coming."

Plank led Zack into the small room off the auditorium. "I think that went as well as we could have expected. We bought ourselves some time. But, just so you know, the questions are going to get much tougher as the investigation proceeds."

The door opened and Agent Spitz entered the room. "I didn't say anything on that stage out of respect for the Lannigans, but I'm going to be watching you, Kelly. If you did something to Blake Lannigan, you'll make a mistake and I'll be there to nail you."

Spitz turned and stepped out, banging the door shut behind him.

5

Gettysburg, 6:30 p.m.

After the press conference, Shelia O'Donnell told Zack she wanted to spend one more night in Gettysburg to determine if she could pick up any vibes on Blake. Zack doubted the effort would be successful, but he agreed to stay with her. Secretly, he wanted to find out what a medium could do.

Garcia decided to ride back to Washington as it appeared further searching for Blake would be fruitless. The FBI, state police, and local police had interviewed merchants along the main drag and handed out pictures of Blake. The FBI lab continued to evaluate possible forensic evidence, but so far none of these efforts had produced any tangible results.

Zack and Shelia sat in Zack's truck outside the visitor's center. "Blake and I made reservations for two nights at the Cashtown Inn. Let me see if we can stay there tonight."

"Zack," Shelia replied, "no way can I afford a place like that."

"Blake insisted on picking up the tab. I don't think she'll mind if we use the two rooms for another night."

Zack called to confirm the reservations. After talking to the clerk, he clicked off his cell. "We have a problem. They gave away the reservation for the General Lee room, but we still have a reservation for the General AP Hill suite. Do you mind sharing a room? I'll sleep on the floor."

"We're adults, Zack, at least I think we both are. We'll make it work. Quit acting like you're a fifteen-year-old kid going to his first prom."

Zack had to chuckle as he drove to the Pub and Restaurant. Point taken.

Shelia had swept her black hair into a ponytail and silver hoop earrings framed her long slender face. When they entered, men watched her. Zack could understand why. Shelia made quite an impact.

As they sat in a booth, a chill descended on Zack. "I can't believe I was just here with Blake."

"Were the two of you having a tumble together?" Shelia asked.

Zack squinted at her. "What?"

She leaned forward and whispered, "Were you shagging her?"

"You don't beat around the bush do you?"

"Dammit, Zack, just answer me. It matters. The depth of your relationship matters to the spirits."

"I'm not sure if I believe that or not," Zack replied, "but no, I wasn't 'shagging' her. We're good friends and partners. That's all."

"Okay. Now, tell me a little about yourself, Zack."

"Isn't it more important that we talk about Blake?"

"I've known Blake and her parents all my life." She turned as the waiter arrived at the table. "I'd like a Guinness, please."

"I'm sorry but we don't have Guinness."

"No Guinness. How do you survive without Guinness?" She sighed. "All right, I give up. What Irish beer do you have?"

The waiter gulped. "Sorry, no Irish beer. We've got English beer."

"Oh, God, no. I'm not going to drink any beer from those fucking Brits."

The waiter stared at her, then he started to laugh.

"Let me see your beer menu." She glanced at the list. "I'll take a Foster Lager. Guess that's as close as I'm going to get to what I want."

"Make that two," Zack said.

After they ordered, Shelia leaned toward Zack "Now, let's hear your story."

Loud laughter from a woman talking on her cell phone in the next booth caused Zack to turn. "Damn, I hate those things." He glanced back to Shelia. "Let me give you the abbreviated version."

"Good, not everyone does that."

"I was born in New York City, then moved to Minneapolis when I was five."

"Why did your parents move?"

"My dad was a cop and got killed in a shootout during a drug bust." Zack wasn't going to tell her that even though his dad was buried a hero, there lingered suspicions in parts of the department that his father was a dirty cop and had it coming to him.

She watched him for a moment, then said, "Is that why your mother moved?"

"Yeah." Zack had to look away. He had the uneasy feeling that Shelia somehow could tell the true story by watching him. The memories were tough. Even though he was so young, he remembered hearing his mother cry herself to sleep. She worked two jobs to keep her three kids in food and clothes. Plus she hated the looks of those who suspected the worst of her husband.

"Did you like Minneapolis?" Shelia asked.

Relief swept through him as they moved to a safer subject. "It was all right. I graduated from high school, then attended the University of Minnesota on an Army scholarship."

"Do you have any children?"

Zack really didn't want to get into all this. "Ah, one daughter. She's almost seventeen and lives with me in Washington." *Could he trust Shelia? Could she be involved in what happened to Blake?*

"Teenagers can be a challenge. I know, believe it or not, I was seventeen once."

Zack decided to give her a few more details as she could check the information on the Internet. "Once I graduated from the university and entered the Army, I went to Airborne and Ranger school. I've been an officer in the Rangers ever since. Oh, I did manage to get a master's in history along the way."

The waiter brought their dinners. Shelia cut into her steak and took a bite. She closed her eyes. "Oh, my, that is good. And your wife?"

Be careful Zack thought. "I don't want to talk about her. What about you?"

She chewed on her steak for a minute. "I was born and grew up in Galway. It's located on the western coast of Ireland. I worked in Dublin for a few years before I started back to school at Trinity."

Zack looked away for a moment, thinking how to proceed.

"Go ahead, ask," she said. "There aren't any questions I haven't heard."

"Okay. When did you first realize that you had this, ah, special gift?"

Shelia laughed. "Oh, yeah, a gift. Well, as a little girl, I heard voices and communicated with spirits. I assumed everyone did. When I started school, I realized that I was different. No one else seemed to hear the voices that I did."

"Did you feel weird?"

"Sure. Every kid wants to belong. I didn't. It was particularly bad for me because my parents were devout Catholics. The Catholics don't look kindly on people who talk to the dead."

"Do you really talk to the dead?"

She smiled again, a beautiful, full smile. "Come on, Zack, what do you think? But I prefer to call it communing with spirits."

"How did you get to know Darcy Quinn?"

"Darcy's parents moved to America when she was a little girl and mine stayed in Galway. The Quinns came back to Ireland for visits so we stayed in touch. She's hosted me on several visits to America. I'm not as close to Blake's mother, but I really enjoy Blake. She's one great lady. That's why I want to help."

Zack swallowed a bite of scallop. "Damn, these are good. What do you want to do first?"

"I'd like to go to the Jennie Wade house after dinner."

Zack finished chewing. "Why there?"

"Why do you think, Zack? I'm a medium." She held up her beer mug in a toast. "I've got friends I need to talk with."

6

Jenny Wade House, Gettysburg, 10:45 p.m.

Zack and Shelia entered through the side door of the Wade house and sat on a long wooden bench in the basement waiting for the midnight tour to begin. Zack had to duck his head so he didn't bang it on the low ceiling. He didn't believe they would actually run into a ghost, but figured that it would ease Shelia's mind if he accompanied her through this place. Besides, he was sorta interested in what might happen. *Who knew?*

Their female guide, dressed in a period costume, opened by saying, "The only civilian killed during the Battle of Gettysburg was twenty-year-old Jenny Wade." She pointed around the room. "With only minor changes, things are much the same as they were when Jenny Wade lived here 150 years ago."

Zack's gaze followed where she pointed. The room consisted of a low wooden ceiling and stone walls. A fireplace stood in one corner. All in all, the room appeared to be in pretty good condition.

"Her sweetheart," the guide continued, "Corporal Johnston H. Skelly, was wounded in the Battle of Carter's Woods and died on July 12, 1863. Before his death, he asked his boyhood friend, Wesley Culp, to deliver a message to Jenny Wade. Culp, who was actually born in Gettysburg, had moved to the South years before, and ended up fighting against his friends from the North."

She paced around the front of the room, hands folded in front of her. "A union soldier killed Culp before he could deliver the message. Skelly died never knowing of his girlfriend's death. Some say he visits the house late at night, looking for her. Others are convinced that it's Wesley Culp who visits, still trying to deliver the message to Jenny Wade from Johnston Skelly. You'll have to decide for yourself which you think is true."

Zack glanced at Shelia, an eyebrow raised, trying to hide a smile.

She leaned over and whispered, "Quit looking at me like I'm some nut. For your information, I haven't heard from either one of them yet, but the evening is young."

Well, no shit, Zack thought, but he didn't say anything. She knew he was a skeptic. Instead he raised his hand and asked the guide, "Why didn't she leave town when the Confederate soldiers first arrived?"

"Good question," the guide replied. "Jenny Wade's sister had given birth four days before the battle. The two women stayed in the building to care for the baby and because of her sister's weakened condition.

"The first day of the battle they both did okay. The second day an artillery round landed nearby but didn't hurt either of the women or cause any damage to the house. Unfortunately, on the third day while Jenny Wade stood in the kitchen making biscuits, a shell burst through the wall and killed her. We'll be able to see the bullet hole when we go upstairs."

"How do you know the house is haunted?" a woman asked.

"We've seen chairs moving, doors closing, and heard various sounds."

"Do you think it's Jenny Wade doing that?" the same woman asked, her voice pitched slightly higher.

"Now that's a tough one. Some people believe it's Jenny Wade and some think it's her sister. The prevailing view of our mediums is that the young boys who lived across the street in an orphanage and were abused by the staff are responsible for the sounds and the moving of furniture."

Shelia whispered, "I've seen the little boys."

The guide must have heard Shelia and gave her a funny look. "Before we leave on our tour of the house, I'd like to introduce Mary Ann. She's a medium and will tell you a little more about the house and some of the things that she's observed and felt."

A heavyset woman with long red hair stood and turned to face the group. "Good evening. First, I'd like to address the issue of spirits from the other side trying to reach you as often happens in what we call a haunting. If you walk through a haunted building, like the Jenny Wade House, you'll sometimes feel chills. That can mean that someone from the other side is trying to contact you."

Zack stayed skeptical of this crap. *Who were these guys trying to kid?*

Shelia put her hand on his arm and whispered, "Don't be so judgmental."

It surprised him that she seemed sensitive to his thoughts. *What else did she know about him?*

"Have you actually seen spirits here?" a man called from the back.

"I've seen a woman at one of the side windows looking out. Often I feel emotion and energy in the upstairs rooms. Chairs may rock on their own, and once two chairs felt as if they, too, were full of energy. The last time I visited here, I smelled bread baking. Other members of the tour smelled it, too."

Holy shit, Zack thought, *wouldn't that be something?* He leaned back. *What am I thinking? Who's going to believe that?*

"Why are the spirits here?" the same man asked.

"I believe they're asking me to help their souls cross over to the other side. They need energy to help them cross over."

"What about all the soldiers people claim to have seen here in Gettysburg?" Zack asked.

The medium's gaze froze on Shelia for a moment before she continued. "Soldiers are a special case. They may not cross over because they don't want to leave their buddies. We have to convince them that it's okay to catch the light and leave. Sometimes spirits who have crossed over may come back to tell their story. Sometimes these souls come down to help loved ones solve problems."

"How can you tell the difference?" another woman asked.

"If they haven't crossed over they tend to feel warm, if they have then they tend to be cold." Mary Ann walked to one side of the room. "Be very careful of any negative energy that may weigh you down. It's important that you protect yourself if your house is haunted."

"How do you do that?" a woman asked.

"There are a variety of ways. Protecting yourself with prayers is normally the best. I suggest that you ask a knowledgeable person to help you with your specific case. Don't try and contact spirits on your own. It could be dangerous."

"Good advice," Shelia murmured. "Very good."

The tour guide stood again. "Thank you, Mary Ann. I always enjoy having a medium here to help us understand some of these issues. Now if you'll all follow me, we'll head upstairs to the kitchen. Look closely and you can see the holes in the door from the shell fragments that killed Jenny Wade."

Shelia leaned closer to Zack. "Mary Ann is good. Her advice could help people who might encounter spirits. I agree with her."

Zack didn't say anything. He was tired of the whole thing and couldn't shake his concerns about Blake. That's where he should be. Out on the battlefield searching for her rather than sitting in here listening to some medium. He almost left, but then decided to go along. *Couldn't hurt, could it?*

The group shuffled up the narrow stairs, Zack having to duck a number of times to keep from bumping his head. "Good thing I've got a hard head."

Shelia patted his arm. "Looks like you're just tall enough."

The guide led them into the kitchen. Ropes blocked off most of the cabinet tops and the tables, but still everyone could see the bullet holes. Zack thought about the probabilities of those bullet fragments hitting Jenny Wade and marveled what had happened to her. Today's modern high-velocity bullets could travel considerable distances. But one hundred and fifty years ago? *Wow.*

They followed the guide out of the kitchen, through the living room, and up the creaking, wooden stairs to the two bedrooms. As they moved through the house, ropes guided visitors away from the various pieces of furniture and along a narrow path.

Upstairs, the tour guide grouped them in the two bedrooms. "In a few minutes, we'll shut off the lights. You'll have about ten minutes to commune with the spirits."

"Good," Shelia said, "this is what I've been waiting for."

When the lights went out, Zack stood back against the wall and waited. Flashbulbs popped as people took pictures, hoping to catch a ghost moving around.

This is a crock, he thought. *Isn't it?*

Shelia took his hand and put it on the rope separating them from one of the beds. "If you hold on tight, you can feel a spirit tugging on the rope."

Zack didn't want to admit it, but he did feel pulling on the rope. After a minute, he moved back against the wall.

He wasn't sure how long he'd been leaning against the wall, probably only a couple of minutes, when he felt something touch the back of his head, as if someone were playing with his hair. It felt so real, he moved his hand to brush away what ever it was. Probably a fly. The damn thing stopped, then started brushing his hair again.

When the lights came back on, Shelia walked over to him and leaned in close. "Did you feel something on the back of your head?"

Zack looked at her, not wanting to admit that he had.

She smiled that bright smile of hers that made Zack smile back. "I asked one of the little boys I met on my last tour of the house to brush your hair so you'd know he was here."

The smile froze on Zack's face.

7

Gettysburg, PA, Sunday, 2:15 a.m.

Zack drove five miles west from Gettysburg on Route 30 toward the Cashtown Inn, then curved left onto Old Route 30. The darkness that surrounded them on the winding road matched his mood. He couldn't help but think about whatever had touched the back of his head. *Could it be? Hell, no.*

Shelia, ever chipper, chattered about what she'd seen and heard at the Jenny Wade House.

"Any leads from your friendly spirits on what happened to Blake?" Zack asked.

Shelia shook her head. "I know you're a skeptic, Zack. But, I want to walk the battlefield where Blake disappeared. I need time to stand and listen. Time to meditate and feel the energy."

"Okay, your call." Shortly after they passed the Cashtown Fire Department, Zack pulled into the asphalt parking lot of the Cashtown Inn.

"We made it," Zack said. "Man, I'm really beat."

The red building loomed in front of them in the darkness. Three stories tall, it stretched from the road back to where a hill rose behind the building. Air conditioners pointed out from most of the windows. A sign at the front of the building read, Cashtown Inn 1797. Flowers lined the parking lot and the sidewalk leading toward the building. Zack leaned back. "I could fall asleep in the truck."

"Have you stayed here before?" Shelia asked.

"No, my first time, but this is an important historical place. Maybe you'll get a lead about Blake. Should be lots of energy here."

"What's so special about it?"

"Well, Cashtown Road provided the main artery for the Confederates as they marched into Gettysburg on that afternoon. Much of the Army camped near here the night before the first day of the battle. Sometimes, it's almost like I can sense their presence."

"Be careful, Zack, you're beginning to sound like me." She stared up at the old building for a long minute. "You're right. I can feel the energy pulsing from the building."

Zack shut off the engine. "People say it's haunted."

"Come on, Zack, smile. Look on it as a chance to make new friends."

Zack opened the door and stepped out of the truck, stretching. He led Shelia up the three steps to the porch, and shuffled around the cluster of rocking chairs. Feeling to the left of the door, he came up with the door key and room key in the box as the landlord had promised.

Zack unlocked the front door. Shelia followed him up the wooden stairs to the General AP Hill suite. It took Zack a few minutes to get the suite door unlocked. He pushed it open and stepped inside. "I hope one room is okay with you."

"Damn it, Zack, don't get your knickers in a twist. We're only going to stay here for a few hours."

"Okay, okay."

A queen-sized canopy bed stood in the center of the room. Zack figured he'd spend all of his time sleeping on the floor. If it didn't bother Shelia, it wouldn't bother him.

Shelia circled the room, looking everywhere. "Oh, my, this is beautiful. Look at that canopy bed and is that a Victorian vanity? And that dressing table. This is really nice."

"It's one of the original guest rooms in the Inn. General A.P. Hill used the Inn as his headquarters. It's actually kind of exciting to stay in the room where Hill planned his strategy."

"Great selection, Zack, thank you." She carried her overnight bag into the bathroom and shut the door behind her.

Zack stripped a cover from the bed and pulled off his clothes while Shelia was in the bathroom. He wrapped himself in the cover and dropped to the floor, wearing only his boxer shorts, immediately drifting into a deep sleep. He didn't even remember her coming out of the bathroom.

Later, he wasn't sure how much later, he heard three raps on the door. *Oh for Christ's sake,* he thought, *am I going to spend the night haunted by some ghost?* He got up and opened the door. Peeking out, he saw nothing other than empty hallway. That gave him a jolt. He looked out again, then shut the door and decided to try and forget it.

He lay down, pulled the cover over his head, and fell back asleep. Later, three more knocks on the door woke him. No damn spirit was going to get him up again. He tried to go back to sleep. Three more knocks. Maybe Shelia would get the door this time.

Tired of it, Zack threw back the cover and pushed himself up off the floor. As he walked to the door, he said, "All right, general whatever your name is, you've got me."

He jerked the door open.

Shelia stood in the doorway, hand raised to knock again. She looked up and down the hallway. "I thought you'd never answer the door. I couldn't sleep and thought I'd look around, see if I could make any contacts. Forgot the key. Sorry to wake you."

"Did you knock on the door before?"

"No, why?"

"Ah, no reason."

Shelia smiled at him. "No reason, huh?"

Only then did Zack realize that Shelia wore only a sheer white robe with a nightgown underneath. All that was under the nightgown appeared to be Shelia. Her robe had fallen open to reveal her smooth throat and the swell of one breast.

She walked over and slipped into the bed. "You know, Zack, you've got to take things as they come. Don't over-think so much."

Zack lay back down. He'd maybe turned down an invitation from this beautiful woman. *Was he some sort of nut? Maybe, maybe not. No complications. Not now.*

He shut his eyes, taking a long time to fall back asleep.

Rangers stormed the house, Zack directing the operation. On his right, one soldier tossed a grenade through the window of the old house, blowing out a wall. The soldiers rushed through the smoke toward the damaged wall. Two of his men waited downstairs and three charged up the stairs.

Zack shot and killed a guard who had taken a position in the window, then followed his troops inside. He reached the bedroom door in time to see a tall man with a long dark beard reaching for his rifle. One of Zack's troops shot the man, spinning him around and dropping him to the floor.

A woman screamed. The interpreter yelled at her to stand aside and not to move. She threw herself on the floor. Zack ducked around the bed to see her pulling a rifle out from underneath the bed. He shot her in the arm, the round throwing her against the wall. She screamed again.

The clatter of machine gun fire sounded from outside. A grenade exploded.

Three children ran out from another room and fell to the floor next to the woman. She pulled the children to her, covering them in her blood.

Zack told one of the rangers to keep an eye on the woman and children while he lifted the bearded man to his feet. Intelligence reports showed this man might be one of the top Taliban commanders in the region. Cliff Henderson would interrogate the man. He'd get the information. Cliff was good at it.

As Zack moved forward to pat him down, the bearded man pulled a knife from behind his back and threw himself at Captain Michael Sullivan. Sullivan fell to the floor gripping his chest. Zack lifted his rifle, fired. Zack shot him in the face and again in the chest. The man slipped to the floor, once more stabbing Sullivan as he fell.

Henderson ran into the room. Seeing Sullivan, he

dropped next to him on the floor, cradled Sullivan's head in his hands. "No," he called, "no, not you, Michael." Henderson looked up, his eyes focused on Zack. "He's dead. Why didn't you kill that Taliban bastard?"

Those eyes continued to stare at Zack in his dreams, piercing, searching Zack's face. Why hadn't he killed the bearded man before the man knifed Sullivan again? Why?

———————

Zack heard his name. "Zack, Zack, wake up. Zack, you're dreaming."

Zack shook himself awake, wrapped in a pile of sheets on the floor, his face dripping in sweat. Shelia stared down at him, eyes wide, mouth open, calling his name. "Zack, are you all right. You were yelling about some Taliban commander. It must have been a terrible nightmare."

He looked around, head pounding. Held his head, trying to clear the pain but it wouldn't leave him. The throbbing made it tough to think.

Shelia grabbed her robe and slipped it on, then reached down to help him up off the floor. "Say something, Zack, say something to me."

Zack couldn't get his mouth to form words. Finally he managed to mumble, "Yeah, I'm all right. Another damn dream."

Shelia watched him as he struggled to sit on the bed, then hurried into the bathroom. She returned with a wet washcloth and placed it on his forehead.

He pushed her hand aside. He didn't need anyone babying him. "Don't ... ."

"What do you mean, don't? You're drenched in sweat. You were yelling something awful about killing a man. Did you kill someone?"

What the hell did she think soldiers did? During the raids, he and his teams had killed people. Raids every night, sometimes two times a night. They needed intelligence, killed to get it. But this night haunted him. He should have been able to prevent Sullivan's death. Should have prevented it. "I can't tell you about what we did."

"Zack, look at me."

Zack turned to stare at her, then looked away. Checking his watch he saw that it was six-thirty. "I need to get up and take a shower."

She took both his hands. He tried to pull them away.

"No." She pulled his hands back to her. "Wait a minute, Zack, let me hold your hands. Look at me. Dammit, look at me."

Zack stared at her again.

She held his hands. "Just relax and look at me."

He did as she told him. Her eyes seemed to pierce into him, her lips moving slightly. Zack lost track of time, staring into those eyes. He heard her say a prayer, a prayer for the dead. A prayer to help dead people find rest and move into the light.

She dropped his hands. "Zack, you've killed a number of people."

Goddamn, what did she expect. He was an Army Ranger. He'd spent three tours pulling intelligence out of hard-nosed Taliban commanders. "Maybe a few."

"They're here," Shelia said, "standing around you in a circle, watching you. We need to figure out how to make them leave or they'll continue to haunt you."

"What?"

"You heard me. The spirits of the men you've killed surround you, refusing to leave. We need to help them find the light. Find rest for their souls."

"How do you know that?"

"Zack, it's what I do. And believe it or not, I'm very good at it."

8

Cashtown Inn, Sunday, 8:15 a.m.

The hostess greeted Zack with a hot cup of coffee as he stumbled down the stairs. "Hello, Colonel Kelly, my name is Maria. I hope you slept well last night. It's been quite a while since any spirits have haunted our guests."

Zack didn't reply. Damn, he needed coffee. No need to mention the knocking on the door or the beautiful ghost in a sheer white robe who entered his room.

Footsteps sounded as Shelia skipped down the last three stairs, dressed in a pair of black slacks and a white long-sleeved blouse. Damn, Zack thought, how does she look like that on so little sleep?

Walking over to the square wooden table, she sat across from Zack and pulled in her chair. "Coffee, I need coffee."

Maria hurried over to the pot and poured Shelia a cup. "Here you go."

"Oh, sorry, I didn't see the pot. I could have picked up a cup myself."

"Relax," Maria said. "You're on vacation. Enjoy it."

Shelia laughed. "Now that's something, Lassie, I could get used to."

"Lassie? My name is Maria."

"Sorry, Maria, I'm from Ireland and sometimes everyone is a lad or lassie to me."

"I thought I recognized your accent. Welcome to Gettysburg. Is this your first time visiting us?"

Shelia placed a napkin in her lap and spread it out. "I've been to Gettysburg before, but never to the Cashtown Inn."

"Well, welcome back. Eggs, bacon, toast?"

"Wonderful," Shelia said. "I'm starved."

Maria walked to a side door and called into the kitchen, then returned. Classical music played softly in the background.

"Could you tell me a little about your inn?" Shelia asked.

"We're very proud of our history. It's likely that more Confederate generals passed through these doors than any other building in America. Here at the inn, they could get food, water, whiskey, and information."

Zack placed his cup down with a clink of the saucer. "Whiskey was especially important the night before a battle."

Maria laughed. "I'm sure that was the case. Way too many men didn't live past those fateful three days."

"Zack told me they arrived here at the inn the afternoon before the battle."

Maria walked over to pick up the coffee pot again. "We know that General A.P. Hill met here with General Lee, and also that Hill gave the okay for General Heth to lead his troops into Gettysburg the next morning. And, of course, that decision started the entire chain of events."

Zack took a sip of coffee. "I understand you've have a number of hauntings."

She refilled their cups. "Our guests have seen a man in uniform standing in the hallway. We've heard footsteps in the attic and the scrapes and thumps of things being moved around. Of course, when we climb up into the attic, we don't see anyone and nothing has changed."

Zack winked at Shelia. "Recently?"

"It's been a while. Not much has happened since we finished the renovation of the inn."

"That makes sense," Shelia said. "Building projects tend to stir up spirits. Increases energy. Makes them more active."

A slender woman brought out two plates of eggs, with three strips of bacon and toast. "The jelly is special," the woman said. "It's homemade right here in Gettysburg."

"Wonderful," Shelia said. "My mum used to make all of our jelly when I was growing up."

"Are you Irish?"

"Aye. I grew up in Galway, Ireland."

Maria picked up a photograph wrapped in cellophane from the sideboard. "Let me show you this picture. We believe it was taken around 1890."

She brought it over to their table and pointed. "At the left hand corner, you'll see the image of a man. It looks as if he's wearing a floppy hat, similar to what the Confederate soldiers wore. No one has ever been able to verify if he stayed here as a guest or not."

Zack stared at the photo, then handed it to Shelia. "Wow, that's something."

Shelia looked at it for a long moment, glanced at Zack, then handed it back to Maria.

"What brings you to Gettysburg?" Maria asked.

Shelia stayed silent, probably waiting for Zack to take the lead.

"Just a short vacation," Zack said.

Maria picked up her own cup of coffee. "Did you hear about the woman who disappeared on the battlefield Friday night?"

"Where did you find out about that?" Zack asked.

"It's front and center in our morning paper. Apparently she's the niece of the president's national security advisor, and her father has been nominated to be on the Supreme Court. Newsmen from Washington descended on our town yesterday. They held a press conference at the visitor's center. Really a big deal. Here's the paper if you want to read about it."

Zack saw a picture of Blake on the front page with a headline, "Have you seen this woman?"

Maria took another sip of coffee. "I bet that guy did something to her. Now he's trying to cover it up. They ought to hang him up by the testicles."

Shelia put a hand over her mouth to stifle a giggle. Glancing at Zack, she lifted her coffee cup in a toast.

Zack swallowed hard. "Has anything like this ever happened before?"

"Not that I can think of." Maria walked over and picked up their empty plates. "Bet we'll find out the guy is a no-good bastard."

Shelia looked down, twisting the fork in her hand. "You can never tell about some people."

Zack pulled his truck into the asphalt parking lot a short distance down from the summit of Little Round Top and shut off the engine. "This is where Blake and I parked Friday night. I'll have to tell you that I don't remember everything that happened."

"You had a flashback didn't you?"

"I'm not sure what happened." Probably dumb to admit anything to her.

"Zack, I can read you like a book. But it's okay, I'm on your side."

Zack didn't know about that. He liked Shelia, liked her a lot. Smart, funny, good looking. But maybe she was involved with Sean Lannigan, hoping to get Zack to admit to something. He thought back to Friday night. "We must have spent about ten minutes in the truck talking, then I think Blake got out and started walking up the path to the top of Little Round Top."

"Tell me exactly what happened as best you can remember. It could be important."

The frustration boiled up inside him until it threatened to explode. He couldn't remember. Damn, he couldn't remember. "Okay, I'll try. Blake said she wanted to see a ghost and ran out onto the battlefield. I must have tried to follow, but couldn't find her. I wandered along the paved walk around Little Round Top, calling her name but she didn't answer. As I started back down the path to the truck to get a flashlight, the park ranger drove up."

"How did you know where she went?" Shelia asked.

Zack had to think about that. How did he know? "Where else could she have gone?"

"You said that you heard hoofbeats and shuffling feet?"

Zack's head started to pound again. "I did, damn it, I did."

Shelia put her hand on his arm. "Take it easy. Zack. I believe you. Others may not, but I do. Trust me, I want to help you figure this out."

"Easy for you to say. I can tell by the way people look at me, they think I'm some sort of nut case. It's driving me crazy. I'm not nuts."

"I don't want you to get all crazy on me, so let's get with it and look around." Shelia hopped out of the truck and walked up the curving path to the memorial at the front of Little Round Top. Zack followed her.

She stopped along the sidewalk, next to the Pennsylvania monument. Her eyes closed. She stood there for a minute or so, then turned to Zack. "I'm picking up vibes of Confederate soldiers from Alabama and Texas. There are Union soldiers from New York and Maine."

His eyes widened. "That's right."

"Don't be so surprised, Zack, I'm not some nut either. You don't want others thinking you're a nut. Well guess what? I don't either so knock it off."

"Sorry. I'll try and do better."

"That would be nice." She put her hands on her hips. "All right, now tell me what happened during the battle here so I can sort out what I'm hearing and seeing."

Zack paused a moment to think about the fighting that had occurred here 150 years ago. "It was day two of the battle. General Lee had ordered General Longstreet to attack the left flank of the Union forces."

"What happened next?" Shelia asked.

"The Union Army anchored the left end of its line here at Little Round Top. General Meade instructed General Sickles to hold Little Round Top at all costs. But Sickles was afraid he'd miss all the action stuck up here, so he ordered his troops forward into Devil's Den. His action left Little Round Top undefended. When two Texas regiments came out of the woods over there from Big Round Top, they outflanked Sickles."

"Outflanked?"

"That means General Longstreet's soldiers circled around behind General Sickles. It would have been a rout except that General Meade's engineer arrived and saw what had happened. Too junior to order Sickles back, he called in a regiment from Maine. They arrived just in time to block the Confederate advance."

"I sense a lot of fighting."

"A blood bath on both sides," Zack replied. "That's why they call this area the 'Valley of Death.'"

Shelia stood silent, looking across the field, the breeze rustling her hair.

"Hundreds of soldiers died before it was over. The 20th Maine ran out of ammunition. Their commander ordered his men to fix bayonets and charge the Texans. That action broke the back of the attack, forcing the Confederates to withdraw."

She started to cry.

Zack hurried over to her. "What's wrong?"

"I can hear the men's screams. Oh, Zack, and I can hear their cries for help and water. It's terrible, Zack. Those poor men... ."

Zack put his arm around her shoulder. "I'm sorry."

She straightened her shoulders and started to walk along the path paralleling the edge of the hill, passing a few visitors. "Let's drive over to Devil's Den. Can we do that?"

"Sure. We'll curve around the back of Little Round Top, then drive over past the Wheatfield."

When they reached Devil's Den, the two walked in circles around the point where Shelia started, the circles getting larger with each turn they made. Finally Shelia reached the road. She stood there for another moment or so.

"Anything?" Zack asked.

Shelia shook her head.

Disappointed, Zack took her arm. "Come on, let's go. I hate to leave here, it's like leaving Blake, but we've got to get back to D.C." The two walked back the path toward Zack's truck. He opened the door for her. "Blake couldn't have disappeared. No one just disappears. There has to be a logical cause."

"I agree, Zack. There must be a reason."

"But what?"

"I don't know but we'll find out. For Blake's sake we must."

9

Falls Church, VA, 2:30 p.m.

Zack pulled up in front of the white-stucco rancher and walked up the sidewalk, careful to step around the chunks of broken cement. Gordy Hale was one hell of a therapist, but not worth a darn when it came to taking care of his property.

An ex-Special Forces doc, Hale had seen it all. He'd set up his practice in the quiet suburb of Falls Church, rather than at Walter Reed because he saw so many high-ranking officers, officers who didn't want anyone to know they were being treated by a mental-health guy.

As Zack reached the front porch, the door swung open and Hale stood there, filling the doorway. At six foot six and who knew how many pounds of solid muscle, he'd been one hell of a football player before he went to medical school. 9/11 changed everything for Gordy, and he entered the service shortly there after."

Zack shook his hand. "Thanks for seeing me on such short notice."

"You said it was important. Come on inside. How about a beer?"

"Thanks. I need one."

"Let's go out on the back deck. My wife's shopping with the kids."

He led Zack through the house, stopping at the fridge for two Rolling Rocks, then slipped out the sliding glass door and down three steps to the two lounge chairs on the lower deck.

Hale lowered his bulk into the chair, a loud squeak testimony to his weight, and took a sip of beer. "All right, what's going on."

"Friday night, I drove my friend, Blake Lannigan, to Gettysburg to show her around."

Hale looked up from under his dark bushy eyebrows. "Zack, you don't need permission from a shrink to go out on a date... overnight at that. You're a big boy."

Zack tried a half-hearted smile but failed. "Yeah, yeah." He told Hale what happened.

"She disappeared?" Hale snapped his fingers. "Wait a minute, I read something about that."

Zack took another sip of beer. Hale would probably have him committed when Zack told him about the hoofbeats and shuffling feet. Fortunately he didn't, but shot Zack a funny look.

"The worst part, Gordy, is that I don't remember what happened."

"Go over that first part for me again. Try to come up with whatever you can."

"She stepped out of the truck and ran up the path toward Little Round Top."

"You definitely remember that?"

Zack thought for a moment. Did he? "Hell, I think so. And I might have heard her shout something like 'stop that.' I'm pretty sure I ran toward the sound of her voice." Zack lowered his head. Looked at his feet. "But goddamn, I'm not sure."

"And?"

"All of a sudden bombs were going off, the Taliban bastards were shooting at me." Zack stopped. Swallowed. "So real... I was there, Gordy, damn it, I was back in Afghanistan."

Hale took a sip of beer, rolled it around in his mouth before swallowing. "You feel pretty weird about that?"

Zack didn't know what to say.

"Don't. Not one bit. What you're experiencing is perfectly normal. You're having flashbacks brought on by stress. Maybe from being tired, maybe from the beer, maybe from the darkness, maybe all of that."

Makes sense, Zack thought.

"Those flashbacks are compliments of your government sending you to Afghanistan for three tours and putting you through what you went through. Every night a fucking mission to root out another Taliban leader. Your own soldiers getting killed. You taking that bullet in the shoulder. For god's sake, man, give yourself a break."

Zack waited.

"We've talked about this, Zack. You've got post-traumatic stress disorder from the continuous exposure to the threat of death or serious injury. And you know what... ?"

Zack shook his head.

"This is what pisses me off. There are some one hundred-seventy thousand Iraq and Afghanistan war veterans diagnosed with PTSD. You, my good friend, are trying like hell to deal with the mess you've got and stay on active duty. You can do it. And you know what, I'm gonna help. But goddamn, don't be so hard on yourself."

It was Hale's turn to wait.

Finally, Zack said, "But... but what about Blake?"

"Now, that's another issue." He chugged more beer, rolled it around in his mouth again. Swallowed. Took another sip. "She's still missing?"

"Yep. I met with her father. He's pissed as hell at me."

"Can't say I blame him."

"Lannigan says it's my fault. That his daughter shouldn't be mixed up with a military puke."

"Well, fuck him. I heard that he put out a big reward for finding his daughter and bringing the person responsible to justice." Hale paused. "Do we know she was kidnapped?"

Zack shook his head. "We don't know anything."

"Okay. What you need to do, Zack, is to separate the two issues." He held up one finger. "You had a flash back. That's normal after what you've been through. Not much you can do about that." He held up a second finger. "But, you need to work like hell to find Blake Lannigan. That's what you can do. And when you do that, you won't feel like such a shit about the flashback. Do what you can do, man, don't sweat what you can't."

Hale watched Zack. Waited. Hale was a pro at waiting.

"Thanks, Gordy." Zack pushed himself up out of his chair. "I'd better get rolling. Laura's already pissed cause she thought I was going to be home last night."

"Don't be a stranger, Zack. We need to keep working on your flashbacks."

As Zack walked down the front sidewalk of Hale's house, he thought maybe he should apply for disability compensation, take Laura and head west. Find someplace where the two of them could do things together. Some fly-fishing, settle near a great school. Then he thought about his friends—Blake, Garcia, Wilson, General Hightower...hell, Quinn. They depended on him. Nope, he'd see this through.

10

When he opened the back door, Zack called out Laura's name. A headache had formed as his mind whirled trying to pull together too many loose threads. Hightower had called a meeting at the Pentagon for later that evening. Garcia was checking with the FBI to see what they had found out about Blake and would have an update at the meeting. Zack didn't expect anything. At least not yet.

His daughter sat in front of the television, her long brown hair curling over the collar of her jersey, head bent over a book and bobbing to some beat blowing into her ears from her iPod.

Zack stood at the opposite end of the living room and waved his arms.

"Huh?" Laura looked up. "Oh, it's you." She pushed a button on the iPod and pulled out the earbuds. "I didn't hear you come in."

Zack laughed. "No kidding. It's a wonder you can hear anything with that music. Where's Aunt Mary?"

"Today's her bridge game so she won't be back for another hour or so."

Mary loved her bridge. Called it her one vice although she loved all kinds of games.

Zack leaned over and kissed Laura on the top of her head. "How's school going?"

"Okay. Algebra's a pain in the butt but everything else is cool."

"I remember when I was in eleventh grade. Algebra was a problem for me, too."

"I'm surprised you can remember back that far. Wasn't that around the Ice Age?"

"How did you get to be such a wise ass?"

"Now, now, watch your language. There are impressionable youth around."

"Yeah, right." Zack found himself still trying to sort out living with a sixteen-year-old girl, hell, almost a woman. When his ex-wife had been sentenced to a prison term for possession and sale of drugs, General Hightower had helped Zack receive a compassionate reassignment back to Washington, D.C. from Afghanistan. Then he got Zack assigned to Quinn's special task force in the Pentagon.

Zack understood that Laura was pissed at leaving her friends in Minneapolis and being forced to move to Washington. The crazy hours that Zack worked at the Pentagon didn't help.

"Hungry?" Zack asked.

"I was just getting ready to raid the potato chips. Maybe have a beer or two."

"Sorry, friend, no beer. Not until you're thirty. How about something a little more substantial, like spaghetti, meatballs, and a salad?"

"Got something for my sweet tooth?

"I'll pull those brownies out of the freezer. Baked them last Thursday. You liked those."

"All right," Laura said. "Spaghetti it is."

Zack walked into the kitchen, grabbed a beer out of the refrigerator. He made sure he still had spaghetti sauce and a few meatballs left over in the freezer, then took a box of linguine out of the pantry, put it in a pan of boiling water and added some salt. He set the timer, then put the meatballs and sauce in the microwave. Thank God for microwaves.

While the pasta cooked, he washed lettuce, cut in tomatoes and green peppers, then added some croûtons to the salad. Laura wouldn't eat a salad without lots of croûtons. He couldn't blame her. He'd been like that as a kid.

Laura had disappeared into her iPod again, so Zack walked over and tapped her on the shoulder. "How about setting the table?"

"Huh?"

"How about setting the table?"

"Oh, sure." She got up and went to work.

Time to finish his beer. "Hey, any news on the boyfriend front?"

"Matt's still in my orbit. He's being really nice to me." She laughed. "Must want something. I wonder what that is."

"Well, if you don't know by now all of my long, boring lectures have been for nothing."

"Don't worry, I got it. Just kidding. I got it."

"I sure hope so." Zack heaped a portion of spaghetti on each of their plates, added sauce and a couple of meatballs, then two pieces of garlic bread. Not great, but okay for twenty-five minutes. "Will you get the ranch dressing and Parmesan cheese out of the fridge?"

Laura twirled a few strands of pasta onto her fork and stabbed half a meatball. "Got an 'A' on my English test."

"Good job. I'm really proud of you."

She got a faraway look in her eyes as she chewed. "Yeah, I suppose."

"Thinking about your mom?" Zack asked.

Her lips straightened into a line. "No."

"We could make a copy of your report card and mail it to her. Show off a little." Silence for a minute as they both chewed. "Where's Friday's mail? Anything of importance."

Laura pointed. "On the desk."

Zack walked over, picked it up, then came back to the table.

He spotted an envelope from his aunt's doctor. Uh-oh, he thought. His aunt had retired after thirty years in the Foreign Service, two months before her husband died. The two had all those wonderful plans about retirement, then he had to go and die on her before they could live them out. Now she had been suffering heart pains. Didn't complain, but Zack made sure she saw a doctor on a regular basis.

He glanced up at the muted television and changed the channel to CNN.

"Hey," Laura called.

"Just a quick peek." The picture showed a burning building with the announcer saying that twelve had died so far in the explosion of a chemical plant in North Carolina. Then another forest fire in California. He muted the set. "Never much good news."

Laura's face brightened. "What say we take in that flick we talked about? I haven't been out on the town for a few days. I'm going stir-crazy."

Zack took a deep breath. "I can't tonight."

Laura glared at her father. "Wait a minute. You promised."

"I know and I'm sorry, but something's come up at work. Besides, you've got school tomorrow."

"You were gone the last two nights but told me on the phone we'd do something together tonight. Now you're going back on your word? You do that all the time."

"I feel terrible, honey. But there's a woman missing, and I've got to go back into work tonight. We think she might have been kidnapped."

"It's always something. That's what mom said. Why you two got a divorce in the first place. Now you're doing it to me." She stood and dropped her fork on the plate with a loud clang, then stomped over to the chair in the living room. "I'm not hungry anymore."

Zack walked around to stand in front of her. "I'm sorry."

She glared up at Zack, then reached down to put the earbuds back in. "Whatever. Knock yourself out. Maybe Aunt Mary will go to the movie with me if she ever gets home. At least she loves me."

There wasn't much more Zack could say. He'd promised Laura a night out and had to go back on his word. He stumbled around the kitchen, cleaning up the dishes and trying to figure out what he could say. Couldn't come up with a thing that would help make it right.

Moving over to stand in front of Laura, he motioned for her to take the earbuds out. "I know you're mad at me and I'm sorry, but I honestly can't help it. A good friend and one of my partners on the task force is missing. We need to find her before it's too late."

Laura stared at him, eyes red.

Leaning down, he squeezed her hand. "I love you."

"Bullshit, you never loved me. All you love is the Army."

Anger built up in Zack, threatening to blow. "Don't you dare say that." He stared at Laura who glared back at him. Thought of all the things he'd done for her. No, that wouldn't help now.

Zack turned and let himself out the front door, still steaming. Damn, he hadn't handled that worth a shit.

A tall stranger arrived at Dulles Airport via Aer Lingus, cleared immigration using the passport provided to him, then continued on through the terminal. He liked to travel light, only a small overnight bag with a change of clothes. On the red-eye over, he'd reviewed the dossier containing the target's personal and professional history, a number of surveillance photos, and the man's address.

He'd been told that he was to follow his target, take care of him, then hop the night flight back to Ireland the following day. The sort of job he liked. Easy in and easy out.

He stopped at the rental car desk, signed for a car using his alias and phony ID, then rode the bus out to the cars.

Once at his car, he pushed in the number on the cell he'd been given. A voice provided him directions to a hotel in Arlington as well as a location where he could pick up a pistol. He'd been assured it was a Glock, his favorite.

Looking around once more, he started the car and pulled out of the lot. Aye, this was the way he liked it. Easy in and easy out.

11

Arlington, VA, Monday, 8:30 a.m.

Waking up at a leisurely six o'clock, Zack shook Laura out of bed, no small task, and hustled her out of the house in time to catch the bus. She still wasn't talking to him.

At last night's meeting, Darcy Quinn had told him to stay home and get his head straight, so he hadn't rushed into work. He had to push himself to take on a five-mile run after Laura left, but knew he'd feel better once he finished.

When he returned home, Zack brewed a pot of coffee and cooked a ham and cheese omelet, then carried his breakfast outside and sat on the back deck. A wooden fence enclosed the rectangular lot. He had planted a cherry tree last fall and the blossoms this year had been terrific. Not like the ones around the Tidal Basin, but still pretty darn good. And it was all his.

He thought about all that had happened in the last two days and puzzled over his next steps. Shelia had told him to stay focused on the problem and something would come up. Well, he kept focusing and all he got was a headache.

He cleaned up the kitchen and started upstairs to take a shower when the phone rang. An anxious voice said, "Oh, Zack, it's awful."

"Is that you, Aunt Mary?"

"Yes, of course it's me. It's Laura."

Zack's heart started to beat rapidly. "Laura. Is she hurt?"

Mary was obviously trying to talk through her tears. "The assistant principal at her school called me a few minutes ago."

"What?" Zack asked, fighting to stay calm and not succeeding worth a damn. "Why did they call you and not me?"

"I guess they have both our numbers and for some reason called me."

"Tell me what's wrong?"

"Wait a minute. Let me catch my breath."

The fingers of his right hand almost strangled the phone cord. "For god's sake, tell me what's wrong."

"All right, let me try and explain. The assistant principal called to say that Laura has been in an altercation."

Zack leaned back against the wall. Laura in another fight. Got the same hot temper as her old man. Probably with the same kid who kept giving her a bad time. "Was it with that Samuelson bitch?"

"Zack Kelly, please don't use that awful language."

Zack coughed to cover a chuckle. He should have expected that. "Did she get in a fight with that same girl?"

"I believe so."

"All right," Zack said, "settle down and tell me what the principal said. Exactly."

"Apparently they were getting off the school bus, and all of a sudden Laura started hitting the other young lady."

"All right, call the principal and tell her I'm on the way."

"Thank you, Zack. Be sure and tell me what happens. I'm so worried about her."

Zack took one of the fastest showers of his life and threw on some clothes. He called Garcia to let her know he'd be extra-late, then ran out to his truck. Firing it up, he drove over to Washington Lee High School, trying hard not to speed.

———————

Zack pulled into the school parking lot and hurried up the front sidewalk. He could hear kids yelling from the gym class outside.

Opening the front door, he showed his ID to security, then cut across the tiled hallway to the office. He knew the route. When he stepped inside the office, Laura sat with her back to one of the walls. The other girl sat across the office from her. They glared at each other.

Zack remembered all the times he had ended up in the principal's office, and had to thank his lucky stars that his mother interceded when she did. He'd spent his youth thinking about his father and how much he missed him.

The story went around that his father had been a dirty cop. That he was shot because he got caught between two drug lords. No one could prove the rumors, but still they persisted.

Zack's mother packed up Zack, his kid brother and sister and moved to Minneapolis. They had to scrounge to get by, but get by they did. What had really happened to his father remained a mystery.

In high school, Zack hung out with a group of toughs and had to fight to defend himself. If it hadn't been for the mentoring by his high school football coach, Zack probably would have ended up in jail. All that came crushing down on him as he stood there, watching Laura.

Laura looked up at him, eyes red, and mouthed, "I'm sorry."

Zack walked over and put his hand on her shoulder. "I'm here, now. Let's go in and talk to the principal."

When Laura got up, the Samuelson kid blurted out, "I hope you get expelled."

Zack looked over toward the girl. Saw the black eye. He had to duck his head to hide a smile.

When they entered her office, the assistant principal, a tall, angular woman with too many sharp features, looked up. "Colonel Kelly, I'm sorry you had to come in, but it seems your daughter can't stop fighting."

She gave Laura a chance to tell her side of the story.

"Look," Zack said, "I can't condone fighting, but you and I both know that the Samuelson kid egged it on by yelling at Laura about her mother. It's not Laura's fault that her mother's in jail. She gets good grades, is active in sports, and this one kid won't leave it alone."

"While I understand what you're saying, I can't allow one of our students to fight with another one. I'm going to suspend both girls for one day."

She pointed her finger at Laura. "You need to learn to control that temper of yours, young lady. If this happens again, I'll have to take more serious action. Is that clear?"

Laura looked down at her feet and whispered, "Yes, Mrs. Johnson."

"Look at me. I want to make sure you understand what I just said."

Laura looked up. "I understand, Mrs. Johnson."

"Okay, just so we're clear with each other. You can get one of your friends to bring your homework to you." She looked at Zack. "Colonel Kelly, I'm sorry this was necessary, but I hope Laura learns from it."

"I'm sure she will," Zack replied.

When they stepped into the outer office, the Samuelson girl whispered, "Jail bait."

Laura started to move toward her, but Zack held his daughter's arm. He almost walked over and told the kid to bug off, but he couldn't fight Laura's battles for her. As they walked down the hallway, Zack leaned over to Laura. "What say we go out and get something to eat? Maybe a good, greasy burger."

Laura smiled, the smile that always penetrated straight to Zack's heart. "Really?"

He put his arm around her. "Yeah, really."

12

Zack picked up Shelia at her hotel, then the two headed for a restaurant in Pentagon City to meet Garcia for an early dinner and a strategy session. Since he'd missed the Pentagon meeting, Garcia had promised him an update on what happened and the proposed path forward.

He parked his truck behind the restaurant and the two walked inside. The waiter seated them and handed out menus. "Something to drink?" he asked.

"A Guinness." Shelia gave Zack a thumbs-up. "Try it, you'll like it."

The waiter made a note on his pad. "The lady has excellent tastes."

"I'll take a Guinness, too," Zack said. "Oh, and we're expecting another party. She should be here any minute."

After the waiter left Sheila said, "Tell me a little about Colonel Garcia. I'm fascinated that her mother is Emilia Garcia. I'd love to meet her mother one day."

Zack thought for a minute. He still wasn't sure if he could trust Shelia. Maybe a little information wouldn't hurt. "Garcia and I have been partners on Darcy Quinn's special task force for about eighteen months. She's a military police officer and a good one. Garcia grew up in Texas and has been in the Army about sixteen years. Lady has a black belt in karate. I've watched her knock around some pretty big guys. Impressive. A super officer and a good friend."

"A good friend?" Shelia asked.

Zack could tell what she was asking, and he wasn't even sure of the answer himself. "Yep, a good friend."

The waiter brought their beers and Zack took a sip. "You're right. It's good." He checked over his shoulder. "I'm going to see if Garcia's here yet. She may be waiting outside."

He took another swig of beer, stood, then walked toward the front door. A stocky man with a slight paunch stood outside, next to the doorway. He sported a wisp of a mustache and a scruffy beard. Partially bald in front, the remaining black hair was long in the back and gray at the temples. His eyes were a penetrating blue, his skin so pale and white it caught Zack's attention.

The man pulled a Glock from behind his back. Eyes fixed on Zack, he raised the gun.

Reflexes kicked in. Zack sprang forward, driving his shoulder into the man's waist. He grabbed the shooter's wrist. Forced his arm up in the air. Two shots fired. The blast reverberated.

Grabbing the man by the hair, Zack pivoted him around using the man's own weight to keep him off balance, and punched the shooter in the chest. Heard a loud whoof. Beads of sweat broke out on Zack's brow.

The two fell to the sidewalk, nearly knocking over an elderly woman. Zack jumped up and hit the man in the face with a solid right hook. Should have been enough to send him flying, but he shook it off and raised the pistol again.

A woman screamed. Someone fell to the sidewalk. Zack hit the man's arm again. Snatched at the pistol. Missed.

Two more shots. The shooter brought down the weapon. Smashed Zack in the face. The blow staggered Zack. He fell to one knee. Launched up again and tackled the shooter. They tumbled to the sidewalk, knocking over a man moving past them.

The shooter kicked Zack in the head, momentarily stunning him. Jumping up, he lifted the weapon. Zack threw himself at the shooter, this time hitting the man in the legs with his best tackle. The man went down. His head hit the sidewalk. The gun flew toward Zack. He kicked it away.

The shooter tried to pull himself up. Zack kicked him in the head. The man fell back again, shaking his head. Zack forced his weight against the man's arm, keeping the wrist in his grasp. He pushed as hard as he could until he heard the crack of the man's arm. A loud scream.

Zack hammered him in the face. The man fell back again. Zack reached down, grabbed the gun, stuffed it in his belt. He pulled the shooter to his feet. Smashed him in the face, once, twice, three times.

The shooter fell. Zack locked in. Started kicking him. He'd show this Taliban enforcer not to mess with Army Rangers.

In a blur of images, Zack grabbed him again. Pulled him to his feet, yelled, "Where are you hiding the IEDs? Tell me." Smashed him in the face again. Again. "Tell me. You've killed three of my men. Tell me, you bastard, or I'll cut your balls off."

Arms grabbed him from behind. Garcia's voice knifed through the haze. "Zack, stop it. Zack, stop. You'll kill the guy."

"He's killed three of my men. I need to find where the IEDs are."

"Zack, it's all right. There are no IEDs. You're safe now."

Zack shook his head. Saw Garcia. "What are you doing here? Thought you were back in Washington."

"Zack, you're in the Pentagon City Mall. This guy tried to shoot you. You've stopped him. Let him down. Zack, drop him."

Zack turned back to the bloody face. Looked around at the crowd that had gathered. No military guys. He remembered he was in the mall and let go. The shooter collapsed to the sidewalk. Bleeding from the face, mouth and nose.

Garcia glanced down at the still body stretched out on the sidewalk. "Zack, Zack, my God, are you all right?"

Zack put his hand on his forehead, shook his head to clear the ache. "Goddamn, I think so."

Shelia ran up behind him. "What happened?"

"Guy tried to kill me."

Shelia looked down at the bleeding mass of humanity on the ground. She took a sharp intake of breath.

"What's the matter?" Zack called.

Shelia put her fingers to her mouth and shook her head, tears forming in her eyes.

————————

The next two hours passed in a haze of screaming people, flashing red lights, yellow crime-scene tape, and intense questioning.

The first police officer on the scene required Zack to tell his story three times. He led Zack, Shelia, and Garcia into a back room of the restaurant where two detectives joined them. The taller of the two, Lieutenant Myron Fox, seemed in charge. He motioned for them to take a seat at a circular conference table in the corner.

Zack explained to Fox what had happened, repeating much of what he'd told the other officer.

Fox watched him. "You know the man is dead."

A sharp pain hit Zack in the chest. My God, did I kill the guy? "No, that's not possible."

"Yeah," Fox replied. "He was beaten so badly he died."

Everyone in the room looked at Zack. The pressure built up on him, closed in. He'd killed the guy with his bare hands. "Bastard tried to kill me."

Fox looked down at his notebook. "Doesn't give you the right to kill him."

Zack wasn't going to put up with this bullshit. "Listen, Fox, I walked to the front door of the restaurant, looking for Colonel Garcia. I saw this guy with a Glock. He aimed it at me. For some reason, he wanted to kill me. Do you understand that? He wanted to kill me. If he'd succeeded, he'd be gone and you'd be looking at my dead body. Wouldn't be any sweat off your nuts if he'd succeeded, but I wouldn't have cared for it worth a damn. I defended myself and the guy died. End of story."

Zack almost told Fox to go fuck himself, but he thought better of it and lapsed into silence.

"Do you know martial arts?" Fox asked.

"Martial arts? Hell no, I don't know any martial arts."

Fox watched Zack for a minute. "All right, let's move on. When's the first moment you saw him?"

"Let me repeat my story for you. I was sitting at the table with Shelia and got up to go outside to see if Colonel Garcia had arrived yet. She'd planned to meet us at four o'clock and it was about four fifteen."

Fox made a note. "Was that the only reason you got up. Maybe you saw the guy? Recognized him? Wanted to get to him before he got you?"

"Never saw the guy before in my life. When I got to the front door, something made me notice him. Pale skin and his eyes. Something about the eyes. But I didn't really think much about it until I saw the Glock pointing at me. Then I had to react. If I hadn't, well... ."

"Is there anything in your work at the Pentagon that could have led to this?"

"I suppose it's possible, but I can't come up with anything right now that makes sense."

"Come on, Colonel, no one walks up to the front door of a restaurant and tries to shoot a guy without some reason. There must be something."

"I might as well tell you this because it's bound to come up. There is a case I've been working on the last couple of days." Zack shared with Fox what had happened in Gettysburg during the past forty-eight hours. "To be honest, I can't see any similarity between these two cases."

Fox turned to Shelia who sat watching the officer at the door. "Ms. O'Donnell, can you think of any reason why this might have happened?"

She shook her head but kept her tissue over her mouth.

Garcia stood, almost pushing her chair over backward. "Look, Detective Fox, Colonel Kelly and Miss O'Donnell have just been through one hell of a traumatic event. Do you think you could cut them some slack?"

"All right." Fox turned a page over in his notebook. "Now I need to talk with you. You say you're a military police officer?"

"That's right. Colonel Kelly and I work together in the Pentagon."

"And you just happened to come by?"

Garcia forced a smile. "You don't make it sound so good. As Colonel Kelly has repeatedly told you, we had an appointment to meet for an early dinner. We needed to develop some strategy on this case we're working together. When I arrived, I saw the two men fighting. I heard shots and ran to try and help Zack."

Fox looked at his notebook again. "Yeah, the guy had probably died by that time."

"Why don't you get off that beat, Fox, it's getting boring. Look, I ran forward and tried to get behind the man to hit him on the back of the head. I saw Zack on the floor, the guy taking aim at him. Then Zack launched up and started hitting the man, trying to disarm him."

"Trying to disarm him by beating him to a pulp."

"I know you need to investigate all that," Garcia said, "but I believe you'll see that if Zack hadn't defended himself, he'd be dead. And the damn shooter would have waltzed off down the street. Not a great picture. This was a clear case of self-defense, pure and simple."

The questioning continued for another twenty minutes. When he finished, Fox asked each of them to fill out a written statement then told them they could leave.

He glanced at Zack. "Give me your address and phone number so I can contact you if necessary."

13

The White House, Washington, D.C., Monday, 8:00 p.m.

Zack looked out the side window as the staff car streaked across the Memorial Bridge from the Pentagon. The driver maneuvered behind the Lincoln Memorial, down Constitution Avenue toward Seventeenth, then left to Pennsylvania Avenue. He weaved through traffic, heavy in spite of the fact that it was late on a Monday evening.

They turned off Pennsylvania Avenue into the northwest gate of the White House. Zack and Garcia showed their identification to the sentry, then passed through the security gate and pulled up in front of the basement entrance to the White House on West Executive Avenue.

Zack pushed open the car door and slid out, Garcia right behind him. A side door to the White House opened and a Secret Service agent Zack didn't recognize motioned with his hand. He wore the standard dark suit, crisp white shirt with a bland tie, and sported an earbud. "Follow me, Colonel Kelly, Colonel Garcia. Ms. Quinn is expecting you."

The agent escorted them down the marble hallway past the Roosevelt Room, staffers rushing by, papers in hand. Zack had been at the White House to see Darcy Quinn a number of times, but these visits still put him in awe.

From the west wing reception area it was only a short distance to the office of the national security advisor. The agent opened the door, and when they entered, two secretaries were typing on computers. A small room off to the right held a printer and copy machine. Quinn's senior secretary, Evelyn Brady, rose and motioned to Zack. "Right this way, colonels, Ms. Quinn is expecting you."

When Zack and Garcia entered Quinn's office, Shelia already sat in one of the chairs in front of the desk. The office had windows on two sides. Bookshelves lined the wall across from Quinn's desk. A round table stood off to the side with six chairs around it. Zack could smell the coffee brewing. Smelled good. He needed a cup.

Darcy Quinn hurried into her office from a second door, followed closely by General Hightower. Hightower wore his Air Force dress uniform, an anxious look clouding his face. Quinn, as always, looked immaculate in a pair of black slacks and a red blazer.

"Zack, are you all right?" she asked. "You could have been killed."

"No doubt the shooter's idea," Zack replied.

Quinn moved to the conference table and motioned for them all to sit. She fluffed up her brown hair which she'd combed back on her head. "I'm so glad none of you were hurt."

"Zack got pretty bruised up from the rumble with the shooter," Shelia said.

Quinn reached for a phone, hanging on the wall next to the table. "Do you need to see a doctor? I'll call the White House medical office."

"I'm fine," Zack replied. "A couple of aches is all. Moving a little slowly."

Evelyn Brady brought in coffee and sandwiches. Zack realized he hadn't eaten anything for hours. Sandwiches looked good. Ham and cheese. His favorite.

"All right," Quinn said, "tell me everything. Leave nothing out."

Zack repeated the story from the time he'd left Laura with his aunt until he finished with Detective Fox. Shelia and Garcia interrupted to add a few points as he went along.

"Do you think this has anything to do with Blake's disappearance?" Quinn asked.

"I've been trying to fit the whole thing together," Zack replied, "but I can't. None of this makes sense."

Quinn glanced over at Shelia. "Did you find out anything of interest at Gettysburg?"

"Nothing concrete that would help find Blake. But I plan to keep looking."

General Hightower leaned forward, hands folded. "Let's take a moment and think this through. Is there any reason you can think of why that man tried to kill you at the restaurant?"

"That's what's been bothering me. Not only that he tried to kill me, but how he even knew I was at that restaurant at that particular time." Zack paused. "I've been racking my brain, but I don't have any answers. Garcia?"

"I can't help but think the assassination attempt is somehow tied to Blake's disappearance. But I don't see the connection. At least not yet."

Quinn glanced at Shelia. "You've been pretty quiet. Can you think of any link?"

Shelia bit her lip and rubbed her fingers together. Tears streaked her cheeks.

Darcy Quinn walked around the table and put her hand on Shelia's shoulder. "I'm sorry. This must have been very traumatic for you. I should have been more thoughtful."

Shelia squinted at Quinn, then she frowned.

"What is it, Shelia? We've known each other for years. You can tell me."

Shelia looked down at her hands and clenched them into fists. "His wrist. His right wrist."

"Who's wrist?" Quinn asked.

"The shooter had a tattoo on his right wrist."

Zack finished a bite of sandwich. "What's important about the tattoo?"

"It's a symbol of the Irish Mafia. I'm afraid that somehow I've brought them here, and they almost killed Zack. Oh, God, how could that have happened? All I wanted to do was help."

Zack sat up straight, the trace of a headache forming. *Why would he come after me? Was it a mistake? Could that damn*

Lannigan have something to do with this? "You're saying the Irish Mafia sent that shooter? This is a contract on me?"

"The tattoo is something the members from my part of Ireland all wear. It's a source of pride to all of them."

"The Irish Mafia? Incredible. Did you recognize him?" Garcia asked.

Shelia shook her head.

"We need to figure a link," Zack said. "Something that makes sense. I don't want to sit here while Irish hit men are coming after me and I don't even know why." He leaned forward. "Think, Shelia, think. What can we do with this information?"

"There's only one possibility I can come up with. I could talk to my cousin. He may know the shooter and have an idea why he came here."

Quinn thought about that a moment, finger pointing at her chin. "Is this Terry you want to talk to?"

Shelia nodded. "I expect he'll be honest with me. If he knows something, it could be valuable."

"All right," Quinn said, "what's our plan from here?"

General Hightower stood and walked to the window. "Let's go over the key points again. We're missing something. First, Blake disappears and while she was with Zack then she comes up missing. Second, seventy-two hours later a hit man from the Irish Mafia tries to kill Zack. No way that could be a coincidence. These killers don't walk around shooting someone they happen to see."

"I agree with the general," Zack said. "This was carefully planned. He must have been following me or someone tipped him off where I'd be."

Zack tried not to glance at Shelia. Could she be the plant? She knew his schedule. If she's working with Lannigan that would explain a lot. "I still don't see why he'd come after me. Unless someone thinks I'm to blame for what happened to Blake."

"Or," Garcia said, "Blake had some sort of link to the Irish Mafia, and they're responsible for what happened to her."

Silence descended on the group as they thought about that possibility.

Zack rubbed his chin. "An interesting idea."

Garcia leaned forward, elbows on the table. "Here's what I plan to do. First, I'll meet with Lieutenant Fox and tell him what Shelia shared with us. Second, I'll get with my contact in the FBI antiterrorist division and find out what he knows about the Irish Mafia. Maybe there's something cooking that we've stumbled on to."

"I like Garcia's idea about talking this through with Fox," Zack said. "We owe it to him. If he finds out I've been holding out on him, and he will, he'll slap me in jail. Then I agree we need to involve the FBI. If Shelia's right, and we've got an Irish Mafia shooter on our hands, the FBI has got to know about it. See if this fits into some case they're working."

Quinn glanced over at Shelia. "What about you?"

"I can help the most by talking with my cousin, but I don't think I should do it on the phone. It needs to be done face to face. Of course, that requires a trip back to Ireland to meet with Terry."

"Will he level with you?" Zack asked.

"I think so. We've been through a lot together."

Quinn glanced at General Hightower. "Aaron?"

"I agree. Seems logical."

"I'd like to go with Shelia," Zack said. "If some hit man is after me, I want to do something about it and pretty damn fast."

Quinn tapped her pen on the conference table, the sound echoing in the room. "I don't think so."

"There's nothing for me to do here right now. Garcia can handle the cop end. The search for Blake goes on. Shelia may need my help."

"I'd feel better with Zack along," Shelia said. "Terry is in the gangs, and I'm never sure how he'll react. Or for that matter, how others will react to my queries."

Quinn walked to the window and looked out for a moment. She turned back to face them. "All right, I'll approve the trip. Now, we've all got our tasks."

"What about Laura, Zack?" Garcia asked.

He hated to even talk about Laura in front of Shelia. "My aunt will keep an eye on her."

"Not what I mean. My point is that if someone is after you, maybe they'll go after her."

"Holy crap." Zack banged himself on the forehead. "You're right. How did I miss that?"

"I can ask Major Wilson to keep an eye on her," Hightower said. "No one's going to get past him."

Zack liked the idea. T.J. Wilson had grown up in the ghettos of Washington, D.C. and led the Black Diamond gang for years. He'd made a reputation as a highly decorated chopper pilot in Afghanistan supporting Zack's Ranger Battalion. Zack knew he could trust T.J. to protect his daughter. "Thanks, General. I'd feel a lot better if T.J. stayed at my house to watch over Laura and my aunt."

Quinn reached for the intercom. "I'll get Evelyn to book a flight for Zack and Shelia to Dublin. I think the red-eye is probably the best. That'll give you both time to get your stuff together and for Garcia to make some preliminary inquiries."

Zack stood. "That works for me. I need time with Laura anyway. She's already angry with me because I've been gone so much."

Garcia caught up with Zack on their way out of Quinn's office and pulled him aside. "I know what you're up to, Kelly. Using yourself as a damn target to smoke out the bad guys. If you go and get yourself killed over there, I'm gonna personally grab you by the stacking swivel and kick your ass all the way around the block a dozen times."

Zack had to laugh, but he got the message. "I don't want that."

"Just remember what I said. Now, I've got another idea. You'll need a pistol while you're in Ireland, particularly after what happened today. I've got a friend who's an assistant military attaché at the American embassy in Dublin. Let me see if I can set it up."

Garcia looked at her hands for a moment, obviously thinking. "Hopefully she can get you a contact in the Garda and set up a briefing with them."

"The Garda?"

"The Irish have a national police force. You'll need to meet with someone in the Special Branch, which is like our FBI. Some really good guys, and they deal with toughs every day. Best to be prepared if you run into a bunch of bad asses."

Garcia stepped closer and put her arms around him. "Take care of yourself, you big sack of shit." She turned and hurried back into Quinn's office.

Zack's gaze followed her. "I will, partner," he murmured.

14

Falls Church, VA, Tuesday, 10:00 a.m.

Zack walked up the sidewalk to Gordy Hale's house, sidestepping around the same bits of cement he had the other day. Hale had agreed to see him early since Zack needed to catch a plane at five-thirty that evening out of Dulles.

The door opened before Zack knocked and Hale stood there. "Come in, Zack. I'm sorry that I don't have much time. I've got to be up on the Hill to testify in a a couple of hours."

They ended up on the porch again, both settling in their chairs for a few minutes to talk, minus the beers. "I heard about what happened outside that mall restaurant," Hale said. "Why don't you give me the details?"

Zack summarized the incident, highlighting the point that he'd lost himself in a flashback during the fight with the shooter. "I killed him, Gordy, God help me, I killed him."

"Zack, the guy tried to kill you. You defended yourself."

"I think the cop was right. I had him down and kept beating on him. Garcia's even worried about me on this one."

"What do you want me to say?"

Zack looked down at his hands, flexing them. "I don't know."

"I can't give you a short answer to all this, Zack. There is no answer. Your mind is damaged from what you went through in Afghanistan. I can tell you this. A person's relationship to a traumatic event can change as well as the way it affects him. People with PTSD continually re-experience the traumatic event. Maybe they can avoid individuals or situations associated with the event. But I've got to emphasize that forgetting a trauma is not a healthy reaction."

"I can't forget it, Gordy." Zack looked away at a cardinal on the feeder. A small touch of reality. "I just can't."

"Let me finish what I was trying to say. Forgetting traumas like you experienced in Afghanistan is not a healthy reaction, so the goal is to not feel dominated by those memories."

"What does that mean?"

"We've got to continue working on your problem. Medication is often used, you know antidepressants and antianxiety medications."

"I'm not... ."

"Zack, let me finish. I know you're not a big fans of pills, so I suggest we use behavior therapy."

"Which is...?"

"You need to focus on learning a variety of relaxation and coping techniques. We need to increase your exposure to a feared situation as a way of making you less sensitive to it. I think some group discussions may work. This helps because it makes you realize that others are going through the same damn things that you are."

"I don't know."

"Zack, we've got to do something. You don't want medication. I can understand that. Cognitive therapy has you take a closer look at your reactions to events and learn to be less negative and eliminate nonproductive thinking. That should help you. You need to quit being so hard on yourself. You've got a problem and you need to deal with it. Not your fault, but you're the only one who can come up with the solution."

Zack thought about that.

"You're stuck with your memories. You've got to figure out a way to live with them. Don't let those memories dominate you. Remember, the guy tried to kill you. What did you do when guys in Afghanistan tried to kill you?"

"I fought back."

"What did you do today?"

"I fought back."

"Roger that. What you have to do now is to learn to measure

your responses. You took the gun away. Now, learn to stop. Gonna be tough, but not impossible."

Hale stood and patted Zack on the back. "Gotta go. Zack, you're a good guy. Been through a lot of bad shit. We're going to figure this out. But you can start by measuring your response to things. Try not to get too angry. Don't overreact. One thing to ponder. If you got in a different line of work and quit running into shitheads trying to kill you, then it might be easier."

Zack thought about that. But he loved the Army. Loved belonging to the Army Rangers. This was his life and he didn't want to leave it. "Yeah, I guess that would help."

15

Dublin, Ireland, Wednesday, 5:30 a.m.

After a six-hour flight from Dulles Airport, Aer Lingus Flight 2242 dropped through the heavy clouds and settled in for a bumpy landing at Dublin Airport. A light rain splattered the windows.

Zack enjoyed the flight, something he didn't do that often. Aer Lingus was a far better ride than any of the American carriers he'd flown, and certainly better than traveling in the back of an Air Force jet. The Irish stew they'd been served tasted great, and he washed it down with a couple of Guinnesses.

He stayed alert and awake during the flight, watching other passengers, particularly the men and their right wrists. One male passenger, two rows back, seemed to watch them, but Zack guessed he probably just enjoyed looking at Shelia. Zack couldn't blame him.

The plane taxied to a stop. Zack stood and stretched, then plucked his two bags from the overhead rack, a small overnight grip with a change of clothes and his laptop. He wore a blue blazer, a light blue dress shirt, and khaki pants. The blazer would cover the M-9 and give him pocket space to slip in an extra fifteen-round magazine.

He still wondered if he could trust Shelia. That would be critical here in Ireland when he met her cousin. He didn't think she was in on the plot but... .

The two followed the line of passengers into the customs and immigration queue, Zack keeping an eye on the people around them. His paranoia had been useful and helped keep him alive during those three tours in Afghanistan.

After they cleared customs, Shelia led Zack to the bus that would take them to long-term parking. "Remember, you're in Ireland now," Shelia said, "and we drive on the opposite side of the road. Got that from being under the damn Brits for eight hundred years. I still hate the bastards for what they did to my family. But that's a story for another day."

"I've got my international driver's license," Zack said. "No problem with pitching in with the driving if you need me."

When they got to the lot, the Chevrolet Malibu sitting there surprised Zack. "Wow, a Chevy. Didn't expect that."

"American cars are big here, Zack. I love mine." She smiled. "Great hunk-pickup wagon."

Zack stopped her from unlocking the car. "Let me check under the body first." He bent down and checked for any wires or tubes that didn't belong, using his experience from Afghanistan. He'd seen too many good people blown up by bombs. "You can unlock the door now."

She opened the car and started to slide in behind the wheel. "Wait a minute," he called. "Pop the hood." He traced a few wires. "Looks okay. Start it up."

"You are careful."

"Damn straight. I live by the motto, 'Don't trust anyone but your own mother and never turn your back on her.'"

"Not a bad philosophy. Works well here in Ireland. I'll use it, too."

It took about forty-five minutes for them to drive from the airport into the center of Dublin. The Irish Sea lay to their left, and the heavy gray clouds begin to lift so Zack could enjoy the view.

As they entered a long tunnel, Shelia said, "Dublin's right on the water. Great during the summer, but cold as a witch's tit in the winter when the wind gets to howling."

Zack had to laugh and even felt a trace of heat.

When they exited the tunnel, they came upon Dorset Street, which headed straight into the heart of the city. It took about another fifteen minutes to fight their way through the traffic before they turned left onto Capel.

Shoppers strolled the streets and bikers whizzed past them as they stayed locked in the traffic. Zack watched the bikers and the cars wheel around them, never knowing if someone would toss a bomb or pull a pistol on them. He wasn't armed yet and would feel better when he was.

Based on Shelia's recommendation, Evelyn Brady had made reservations at the Montclair Hotel, one of the nicer hotels in Dublin and located right in the center of town.

Once they checked in, Zack called through the open doorway between their two rooms, "I hope you don't mind adjoining rooms. Don't want to impose on you."

Shelia started laughing again. "I can always lock you out if necessary. But Zack, when are you going to quit analyzing things and just go with the flow? That's what I'm doing. We'll see where the *flow* takes us. I like you being nearby in case I get into trouble. Besides, we're got bigger things to worry about than a little harmless shagging along the way. Who knows, you might like it."

Her comment gave Zack a little more heat. Shelia would take some getting used to, but he was ready to work on that.

"Now," Shelia said, "if you're quite through organizing things, I need to get out my mobile and call my cousin. See what I can find out."

Shelia pushed in some numbers and paused, tapping her foot, then she said, "This is Terry's cousin, Shelia O'Donnell. Is he there?"

She listened then said, "Yes, his cousin, Shelia. Maybe this afternoon? Let me give you the number of my mobile." After she disconnected she asked, "Now what?"

"I need to make a call."

"Who are you calling?"

"A contact Garcia gave me."

———

They walked down the stairs and out through the ornate lobby of the hotel, receiving a wave from the clerk at the desk who happened to know Shelia. Was that a coincidence? No, he didn't believe in them.

She'd parked her car in a spot along the street not too far from the front door. Crowds swirled by them, talking, laughing, some with pinched faces carrying briefcases.

"How about taking this girl out for breakfast?"

"Great idea. Do you know a place?"

"Aye, lad, I know just the place."

When they entered the Dublin House, the warm smell of fried breakfast filled the air and made Zack's stomach growl. Enough people around so he felt safe in dropping his guard a little.

Steam rose from the teapot on the table. After they ordered, the waitress brought a plate heaped with scrambled eggs, sausages, and bacon including fresh bread with butter and jam.

Zack dug into the eggs. "Now this is what I call a breakfast."

Shelia chewed for a moment and swallowed a bite of egg. "Welcome to Ireland, Zack. I hope you like it."

Zack took another forkful of eggs. "Do you know where the American embassy is located?"

"Aye, I had to go there and fill out a ton of paperwork the first time I traveled to the States."

"Garcia told me the colonel would be expecting us at eleven-thirty."

Shelia looked at her watch. "That gives us about an hour. Should be about right, mate, if you get busy and eat up."

After breakfast, they drove south from the restaurant on West Grafton, then turned left onto Lesson Street Lower.

Zack looked across the river. "Isn't that Trinity College?"

"Pretty, isn't it? I worked for a few years, then went to Trinity. Managed to graduate in pre-law last year. I've decided to hold off on graduate school until I see where my medium skills take me. I hope to attend law school one of these days." She giggled. "Gotta figure a way to make a living other than marry some rich old guy and wait for him to tank."

Zack checked around them, then glanced forward. "What's that ahead of us? I can see mountains."

"That's the Wicklow Mountains. They run north and south

across County Wicklow. You can just barely see Lugnaquilla through the clouds, the highest peak at about three thousand feet."

Shelia had to downshift her Chevy because of the traffic. "If we had time, I'd like to show you the Monastic settlement of Glendalough. Founded by Saint Kevin in the Sixth Century, the monastery became one of the most important learning centers in all of Europe. It's beautiful."

Right now, Zack had other things on his mind than some old monastery.

She put her hand on his arm. "I'd love to show you my country, Zack. It's so special."

"Maybe one day."

"I know," she said, "but not today."

16

American Embassy, Dublin, Ireland, 11:30 a.m.

The American Embassy stood on the right side of the road, a four-story gray building with a circular drive. The Marine guard raised his hand to halt their vehicle. Zack flashed his military ID and Shelia showed her driver's license. The guard stepped into the guardhouse and made a call, talked for a moment, then waved them in.

Zack glanced around the lot. "Not much security."

"The American Embassy doesn't need high security," Shelia said. "The damn Brits, now that's another story. Their embassy is a fortress and with good reason. It's only a few doors down the street."

Colonel Reilly met Zack and Shelia at the front door and led them upstairs to her office. She had brown hair, done up in a bun, and a melodic southern drawl. She stood trim and fit in her military dress-green uniform.

Their footsteps echoed in the tiled hallway. A number of smudges and dirt marks dotted the walls. Zack thought he caught a whiff of stale smoke and it surprised him.

When they reached her office, she introduced Detective Sergeant Powell. He had dark hair, with a receding hairline and long sideburns. A thick mustache covered his upper lip. His eyes watched Zack, alert and direct. "Welcome to Ireland, Colonel Kelly, and welcome back Ms. O'Donnell."

Reilly offered coffee, then organized a stack of papers on her desk. "Colonel Garcia called and said that you'd need some help while you were here. Specifically she asked if I could get you a concealed weapons permit and an M-9 pistol. I met Garcia when she was in Ireland on a liaison trip last year and have a great deal of respect for her. I agreed to help you, but first, I'd like to hear why you need the M-9."

Zack glanced over at Powell, eyebrow raised.

Powell took the hint. "I'm with the Garda. We're the national police force here in Ireland."

"Let me add a little," Reilly said. "Detective Sergeant Powell is with the Special Branch of the Garda. That's like our FBI. I've worked with him before and thought it critical that he be involved."

Zack took about twenty minutes to summarize for Powell and Reilly what happened the night of Blake's disappearance in Gettysburg, then he discussed the shooting outside of Washington. Powell's eyes got wide when Zack noted the tattoo indicating the shooter to be a member of the Irish Mafia.

"Are you sure about the tattoo?" Powell asked.

Shelia set her coffee cup on the round table next to her, a slight tremble to her hand. "I've seen the marking before and recognized it right away."

"That's quite a story," Reilly said. "I can see why Colonel Garcia thought you might need a weapon."

Zack took a sip of coffee. "A story I'm not quite sure I'd believe if it hadn't happened to me. What can you tell us about the Irish Mafia?"

"The Mafia has been broken up not only by solid police work here and in the States, but also by their own infighting," Powell said. "What we have now are several groups of rival gangs who operate in Dublin and routinely have shootouts with one another."

Colonel Reilly handed Zack a packet of papers. "I have some unclassified material for your reference. If you need more, I can get additional summary sheets." She glanced at Shelia. "I hope I can trust you to be discreet in what you tell others."

"Of course. I'm in the middle of this mess myself. Zack and I are planning to meet with my cousin this afternoon."

"What's his name?" Powell asked.

"Terry McHugh," Shelia replied. "Do you know him?"

Powell shook his head, then made a note.

Reilly turned. "All right, Sergeant Powell, go ahead."

"We were on standby yesterday in northwest Dublin after one of the gang members was fatally shot outside a pub. Punk had a long record. Somehow he'd managed to get acquitted for murdering another man with a sawed-off shotgun a few years back. Something like the twenty-fourth murder this year. A statistic we're not proud of."

"The Garda is doing everything it can," Reilly said, "but Dublin is a tough area."

"Bastard was acquitted earlier for the attempted murder of the Garda officer who arrested him. Two officers were shot and wounded in that battle."

"You see, Zack," Shelia said, "some of our streets are like your Wild West."

"Fortunately, not too many," Reilly replied. "I don't want you to get the wrong idea. Most of Ireland is a wonderful place to visit. You do have to be careful in certain parts of Dublin."

"Thank you, Colonel Reilly, I appreciate that," Powell said. "We think this is all tied to the feuds going on in the city. We anticipated there would be attempts on people's lives and to be honest, we look for more."

"Any suspects?" Zack asked. "Perhaps someone we may run into?"

"We're looking at enforcers for one of the Dublin gangs. Someone as yet unknown killed the head of the gang a couple of years ago. Believe me, these guys can carry grudges for a long time."

"Zack, we're Irish." Shelia laughed. "It's part of our makeup."

Powell chuckled also. "Ms. O'Donnell has a point. For your information, the Garda district that covers Finglas, Blanchardstown and Cabra is one of the worst areas in Ireland. We expect more killings before the end of the year." Powell took another sip of coffee. "Also, we expect more attacks on the Garda. We were able to defuse a plot a couple of weeks ago. Our officers stopped a car that we suspected was headed to firebomb the home of one of our Garda officers."

Colonel Reilly handed Zack an M-9 pistol with a holster he could clip onto his belt.

"Why the M-9?" Shelia asked.

Zack smiled and said, "It's the standard weapon for the U.S. Army and for our special operations forces. Beretta modified it so the M-9 fires the standard NATO 9mm round. Plus, it's got a 15-round magazine."

"Don't give me that smiley-smirk like I'm some dumb dame, Colonel, or I'll go home and be back to shoot your ass off with my Sig-Sauer 9mm pistol. You forget, I'm an Irish lass who's lived through some pretty tough times."

Zack bowed to her. "I keep underestimating you. I'll be more careful in the future. You can count on it."

"Much better. You're forgiven." She flipped her pencil in her fingers like it was a cigarette and said, "Don't let it happen again."

Zack set the M-9 back on the desk. "Wow, you sound just like Humphrey Bogart."

"My hero," Shelia replied. "I loved all of his movies."

Zack turned back to Reilly. "Now before I get in any more trouble, how about ammunition?"

Reilly reached back into a gun safe and brought out two magazines. "I ask that you exercise extreme caution. If you shoot up the town, I'll be in big trouble."

"Don't worry," Zack replied. "I don't plan on using a weapon unless there's no other recourse. Now, you think this is all from feuds among rival groups. Could any of these battles spill over to the United States?"

"These feuds are constantly evolving," Powell replied. "After one dispute ends, another starts. Often these gangs split, then turn on one another."

Shelia leaned forward. "The tensions simmer for years, then one little thing happens and the battle turns violent."

"She's right," Powell said. "The roots of some of this go back a number of years. We know that a senior official in the Provisional

IRA during the period we call *The Troubles* passed information on bombings and targets to the Garda."

"Money?" Zack asked.

Reilly nodded. "You can always follow the money. The story goes that he was having a cash crisis and got 15,000 pounds for the information. This enabled the Garda to arrest members of the gang as they were boarding flights for Belfast. You understand this didn't go over very well with some of the other members of the IRA, and they do have long memories."

"You asked about spillover to the United States," Powell said.

Reilly leaned forward and in her best Southern drawl said, "I invited Sergeant Powell to join us because we're working together on a number of cases."

"The Garda has received intelligence that one of the crime families is operating a prostitution racket that may be headed toward your shores. If you get any indications of what may be going on, I'd appreciate a call right away." He provided Zack his mobile number.

"Will do," Zack said. "And thanks for the information."

Reilly stood and shook hands with Shelia and Zack as they moved toward the door. "You need to return for a debriefing before you leave Ireland. And please try to stay in one piece." She smiled. "Dead American officers make it very difficult for our marketing efforts."

17

Gettysburg, PA. Noon.

Rene Garcia rode her Harley along High Street, dressed in her Army field uniform, watching the reaction of people probably trying to figure out who the hell she was. She always seemed to attract attention wherever she went. Surprise, surprise.

Housed in a three-story white building, the borough offices spread over about a quarter of the block. A sign in front indicated visitors should enter on the left side. She pulled into the parking lot, shut off the engine and walked to the stairs. Two white pillars framed the entryway. The pillars made the building look official.

She stopped by the door. What did she want from the mayor? Probably nothing more than an update on what he'd learned so far. She needed a feeling for any like-incidents in the recent past. After her appointment with the mayor, she'd drive to the Visitor's Center to meet with Cliff Henderson. She'd learned over her career you never know what you might find out. Keep digging and pushing.

As she reached to open the door, her cell rang. She answered, "Colonel Garcia."

"What is going on, daughter? I read in the paper that you were involved in a fight where a man was killed."

Oh, no, not now. "Hello, Father."

"I told you you should have stayed in Austin to get your Ph.D. You could be teaching now. No one is going to shoot at you here."

Her father never adjusted to Garcia joining the Army. Her mother, a well-known author on women's issues, didn't like her joining the Army either, but she knew her daughter needed to do her own thing. Garcia appreciated that and loved her for it. She taught Garcia how to meditate and close her mind to the outside world. Focus and meditate. She needed that now.

Her father wanted her to teach with him, get married to a nice Hispanic boy, and have lots of babies. Well, bullshit, that just wasn't her.

"I was never in any danger, Father."

"What do you mean you were never in danger? The paper said this man tried to kill Colonel Kelly. What did this Kelly do? Why is he being shot at?"

"It's part of the job, Father. We don't know yet why the shooter tried to shoot Colonel Kelly. I arrived after the incident started and had to try and help him."

"Why? What are you in the middle of? Your mother has been crying all afternoon."

Oh, damn, Garcia thought, pulling the mother-is-crying-card out of his vest pocket. "I'm getting ready to go into a meeting and I can't talk now. I'll call you later."

"Wait. I want you to come home right now. We need to sit down and talk this out."

"I must go, Father. I'll call you later."

"Wait a minute, young lady, don't you dare hang up on.... ."

She disconnected. Guilt surrounded her like a dark cloud for hanging up on her father, but he left her no choice. If only he could learn to let her lead her own life.

She stood there for a moment, using her mother's techniques for deep breathing to get centered. Finally, pushing the door open, she walked into the building. At the information desk, a slightly plump, balding man looked up at her. "May I help you, Colonel?"

"I have an appointment to meet with Mayor Sampson."

He looked down to check the calendar. "Oh, yes, that's right. He's expecting you." Pushing in a number on his phone, he said, "Sir, Colonel Garcia is here to see you."

The mayor hurried down the hall toward her. A short man, he wore a slightly wrinkled brown suit with a blue tie. He looked comfortable, like he'd been the mayor for a while. Maybe a long time. Maybe too long.

He flashed his best baby-kissing smile at her and offered his hand. "Colonel Garcia, I'm Gregory Sampson. It's very nice to meet you. Please come back to my office. Would you like some coffee?"

"Thanks, Mr. Sampson, that would be great." She followed him down the hallway. In a moment, the man from the front desk brought in a cup of lukewarm coffee. She took a swallow. "Thank you for seeing me on such short notice."

"You said it was important."

Garcia took another sip of coffee, trying to determine how much to share with him. "As I mentioned on the phone, I work with Colonel Kelly on National Security Advisor Darcy Quinn's special task force. Ms. Quinn has asked me to go over everything again to try and make sense out of what happened Friday evening. And more importantly, find Ms. Lannigan."

"Yes, of course. Anything I can do to help."

Garcia figured it wouldn't hurt to drop Quinn's name a time or two. "Can you update me on what you've found so far in the disappearance of Ms. Lannigan?" She pulled a tape recorder out of her pocket, set it on his desk, and pushed Record. "I like to gather everything on tape, then I can pore over it later and eliminate what I don't need." Also, she thought, I can nail your ass if I find out you lied to me.

"I understand about the tape. Sometimes I do that myself." He laughed. "My memory isn't all it used to be."

"Yes, too many facts." *Who knows, maybe it's time for you to retire Mister Mayor.*

"Sadly, you're probably going to be disappointed with what I have to tell you. The police chief has been coordinating with the FBI. He told me earlier today he even talked this morning to a representative of Homeland Security. Since Ms. Lannigan is the daughter of a potential member of the Supreme Court, as well as Ms. Quinn's niece, her disappearance has made quite a splash in our local community. I'm sure you know about the press conference Saturday. The newspapers have been playing it up big."

"I attended the press conference before I headed back to Washington." Garcia didn't comment on the number of times she'd seen the mayor on television, smiling big for the audience. "Has anything like this ever happened before?"

He thought for a moment, rubbing his double chin. "We've had people disappear for short periods of time, but they always show up after a day or so. Usually it involves a fight, you know a child mad at her parents or a husband and a wife who had a argument. Some guy gets drunk. Hits his wife. But, no nothing like this. Ms. Lannigan seems to have disappeared into thin air."

Time for the key question. She watched his eyes to gauge his reaction. "How long has Munson been the chief of police?"

"I'll have to check our records to be sure, but I think about seven years."

"Is he doing a good job? I know that might be a tough question for you to answer, but I'd like to know as much as I can about him."

"He seems to be doing fine. I've lived in Gettysburg all my life and have known him for a long time." The mayor stopped for a moment. "He's due to retire from the police department at the end of the year."

"Is that like a forced retirement?" Garcia asked.

"Not exactly, but after the extended period he's been chief, the city council believes it's time to appoint a new chief. You know, insert some fresh blood into the force."

Garcia leaned forward. "Is there something you're not telling me?"

"Not really. I think the chief has done a good job, but you know we all get tired after awhile. The city council and I felt that it was time for a change."

Garcia let the silence draw out. She'd found that was the best way to get extra information.

"Now," the mayor continued, "what can you tell me? Is this part of some national security thing? Did those two just happen to come down here for a visit or were they on some sort of inspection or special trip? Ms. Lannigan works in the State Department. I find it hard to believe all this came about just from a simple visit. Maybe some sort of secret mission?"

"When the Defense Department is involved, everyone immediately thinks of a conspiracy. But as far as I know, it's exactly what I've told you. They came up here to do some sight-seeing and she disappeared." Garcia took another sip of coffee, thinking how best to handle her next point. She decided to come right out with it. "There's another item for us to consider. Someone tried to shoot Colonel Kelly yesterday afternoon outside a restaurant in the Pentagon City mall."

"Tried to kill him?" The mayor's eyes got big. "Wait a minute. I read about a shooting in Pentagon City, but didn't realize it involved Colonel Kelly. I understand the shooter was beaten so badly that he died. Did Colonel Kelly beat him up?"

"Zack only defended himself from someone trying to kill him." Garcia decided to keep the rest of the concerns to herself.

"Do you think this has anything to do with the disappearance of Ms. Lannigan?"

Garcia shrugged. "To be honest, I'm checking out every possibility. What do you think?"

He looked at her over his glasses. "She disappears into thin air while they're at a parking place overlooking Devil's Den. Kelly hears hoofbeats and shuffling feet. It's been three days now and no trace of her. Then the next day someone shoots at the colonel. Come on, Colonel Garcia, you can do better than that."

"I wish I could. Believe me, I wish I could. I find it just as weird as you do. But having said that, I plan to find her and bring to justice whoever is behind this." She leaned forward and shut off the tape recorder. "Oh, one more question. Do you happen to know Ranger Cliff Henderson over at the park office?"

"Not really. He's been here about a year. I believe he left the Army and applied for a job as a park ranger. As far as I know, he does his job well. I've certainly never had any problems with him myself. Why do you ask?"

"Just looking at every possibility." She paused. Here was her chance to follow up. "Anything else you can share with me about Chief Munson. Anything at all? Maybe an extra woman in his life, a drinking problem, a gambling problem. Colonel Kelly's life may depend on it."

Garcia waited as the mayor took a moment to look out the window. He turned back toward her. "I believe the chief is frustrated that he has to leave at the end of the year. He's told me he would like to stay on for another couple of years."

"Do you have any idea why? Maybe money problems?"

"No, no, nothing like that. I think he's wedded to his job and doesn't want to leave it. You know, not sure what he'd do with himself."

Garcia wondered if he wanted to keep the job badly enough to kidnap Blake. Being an MP, she knew that cops had special powers. After all, who'd check on the police? She rose and extended her hand. "Thanks so much for your time. I'd better get moving."

The mayor stood and shook her hand. "Anytime, Colonel Garcia. If I can help you, please let me know. I want this awful thing to be over."

On her way out, she thought about where Munson might fit into the puzzle. *Did she need to meet with some members of the city council? Was there anyone else to consider? Anyone who could help her?* She'd have to listen to the recorded interview with the mayor. Maybe something would click.

Garcia didn't believe in ghosts. But if she found that no one else was involved...

18

Dublin, 5:00 p.m.

When they reached O'Donegans at Merion Square, Zack checked his watch. Five o'clock. They were right on time. Reaching under his coat, he felt the reassuring lump of the M-9 holster on his belt.

He nudged Shelia's arm to halt her. "Before we go in, tell me a little about *The Troubles*. Was your cousin involved?"

Shelia leaned against the wall and shook her head. "Terry's too young for that, but his father stayed active with the IRA for much of his life. *The Troubles* began around the end of the 1960s. The border between the north and south was heavily fortified with checkpoints manned by British Security Forces. The damn Brits sent men to jail without trial in an attempt to stop the IRA."

Zack looked around, saw no one watching them. "Go ahead."

"In January 1972, the second Bloody Sunday happened. Following what they thought to be an agreement, the IRA didn't bring any weapons to a protest rally. British soldiers fired on protesters who were listening to speeches and they killed and wounded a number of people."

"Terry's father?" Zack asked.

Shelia shook her head again. "But it angered people throughout the entire country. The hatred continued to build and has lasted for years."

"Isn't it pretty well settled by now?"

"It took another twenty years and too many lives before the warfare ended. Now some of the remnants of the IRA hang together in gangs. That's who you're going to meet."

"Okay, thanks." Zack looked around once more, then pushed open the glass door and the two entered. To his right stood a five-foot-high wooden bar with more than a dozen men sipping their Guinness. Each of the men had a shot glass by their beer. Lots of whiskey going down, too.

He followed Shelia toward the back where a solid-looking man sat at a four-foot round wooden table sipping a glass of whiskey. Short, burly, and wide-shouldered, he looked like he might have been a great rugby player. The man wore his flat cap down over his forehead, covering much of his bushy brown hair. When they reached the table, he tipped his hat. "Top of the evening to you, Cousin Shelia, and who might this lad be?"

She leaned over and kissed his cheek. "Terry, this is my friend, Zack Kelly. Zack, my cousin, Terry McHugh."

Zack reached down and shook hands with McHugh.

"Any friend of Shelia's is a friend of mine. They serve a decent pint of dark Smithwicks Ale, Kelly, or you might want to try a Paddys whiskey. We call it the water of the gods." He pushed his cap back on his forehead. "With a name like Zack Kelly, do you have any Irish blood flowing in your veins."

Zack pulled out one of the wooden chairs for Shelia and one for himself. "Not that I know of. I come from a long line of Norwegians and Swedes, but I suspect a number of my ancestors might have landed here before me. They may even have left a little of themselves before they departed."

"Aye. The Vikings arrived in the mid-800s. Spent a number of years dumping their crap all over my Irish ancestors."

"Yeah, let's not go there." Shelia glanced at the menu. "I think I'll try a Smithwicks. Little early for an Irish whiskey. Why don't you try one, Zack?"

A tall, slender woman in a black skirt and white blouse hurried over. She looked at Zack, eyebrow raised. "Sir?"

"How about a couple of Smithwicks?"

"Yes, sir." She hurried off, her ponytail bobbing behind her.

McHugh sipped his whiskey. "Now, lovely lady, what may a poor Irishman do for you?"

"Don't give me that poor Irishman blarney, Terry McHugh, I know better. We need your help with a wee problem." Sheila told McHugh what had happened at the restaurant back in the States and that she had spotted the tattoo on the man's right wrist. She stopped when the waitress brought their beers and set them down.

Zack and Shelia raised their bottles in a toast to McHugh and each took a swig.

Zack brushed his arm across his mouth. "That is good."

"It is that," McHugh said. "Okay now, on with your story."

After she finished, McHugh got a puzzled look on his face. "Do you happen to know the name of the shooter?"

"I don't know his name, but I saw the tattoo and knew right away where he came from. I'm betting that someone here sent him. But my question is, why?"

"Did you mention it to the Garda?" McHugh asked.

"The Garda?" Zack figured he'd better play dumb and not let McHugh know he'd already met with the Garda. "Your police force?"

"Aye, lad, we call them the Peelers."

"The Peelers?"

"You'll get a wee bit of education tonight from my cousin," Shelia said. "Not the sort you'd receive in the classroom."

"True enough," McHugh replied. "We don't have local police forces here in Ireland, but rather a national force. Now you need to know that it's bad press for our group when one of our own doesn't finish the job assigned."

"He came too fucking close," Zack said. "That better count for something."

"Sorry, but it's true. The man had been hired to do a job. When he misses, it's bad for business." McHugh stood. "I need to ring up a contact on my mobile. Sit back and enjoy your Smithwicks. I'll be back in a flash."

Zack and Shelia nursed their beers and waited. About ten minutes later, McHugh returned. He took another sip of whiskey. "For some reason, it appears you may have made an enemy. But I don't know the details. I explained that you were a friend of Shelia's.

My competitor is willing to see you. Now Tuohy can be a difficult sort."

"Tuohy?" Zack asked.

"Tuohy O'Toole," McHugh replied. "Be careful, friend, he doesn't take to cunts."

"Cunts?" Zack asked.

"You know," McHugh replied. "Stool pigeons."

"I was afraid of that," Shelia said. "Tuohy is based in my home town of Galway. That man is terrible bad news."

McHugh nodded. "Aye, he is that, but hopefully he'll be reasonable. I'd go with you except I have other pressing business that can't wait. I told him you'd be available to meet tomorrow evening."

"I hope you set up the meeting in a public place," Zack said.

"Aye, a wise lad you are. You'll need to stop at a house along the way to get the actual directions. O'Toole doesn't let anyone know where he'll be very far in advance." He smiled. "What is it you Yanks say? That can be dangerous to one's health and longevity."

Zack took another swallow of beer, the smooth liquid flowing easily down his throat and cooling his mouth. Pondering for a moment, he decided to take a chance and try to bring out McHugh. "Is this O'Toole part of the Irish Mafia?"

McHugh's eyes hardened for a moment, then the easy grin returned. "I don't like to use that term. We prefer to talk about the IRA and our continuing battle to free the bonds around our country from the fucking Brits."

"I thought that was over," Zack said.

McHugh took another sip of his Paddys. He put his hand on Shelia's arm. "You'll have to give this poor young colonel a little history lesson."

Before Shelia could say anything Zack said, "She told me about *The Troubles.*"

"Goes back farther than that. Way back to the time of Oliver Cromwell. Heartless bastard. He crushed all opposition. Bastard killed over 3500 men, women and children."

"We've had our own frustration with the Brits in the United States."

"I know that, but you came out on top. They kept their foot on our neck for centuries. In the late 1700s, only five percent of the Catholics owned land here even though they were seventy-five percent of the population. Bastards wonder why we hate 'em."

Shelia finished her beer, stood, giving McHugh a kiss on the cheek. "I think that's enough of a history lesson for tonight, Terry. We'd better get going since we have to be across the country by tomorrow."

"Aye, that's true."

"Let me ask you one more question," Zack said.

McHugh took another sip of his Paddys, and raised his hand to motion to the waitress.

"I saw in the paper the Garda is on alert because of the shooting outside of a pub a day or so ago."

"You must be talking about David, the poor lad."

"Is he one of yours? The paper said the Garda is on the outlook for more retribution."

He stared at Zack, then smiled again. "I can't answer that. Not good for business."

"Didn't think you would."

He leaned forward and motioned for Zack to lean in. "But I can tell you there are a number of gangs here in Dublin. And they don't always agree."

"Like some of our bigger cities back home."

"That is true and more tied together than you might think. Now, let me give you directions to the contact who'll provide the meeting's location." He pulled a sheet of wrinkled paper out of his jacket. "Remember, the lad will expect a little reimbursement. He's not going to help you out just because he thinks you're a fine sort."

Zack wondered what McHugh meant about these gangs being tied together with gangs back in the States, but decided to let that go for now. "Reimbursement shouldn't be a problem so long as it's reasonable."

"Aye, that's good," McHugh said. "But you may disagree on what's reasonable, so be careful. Anyway, be sure and give my best to O'Toole."

"If I do that, will he shoot my ass?"

McHugh laughed, a long laugh, and pounded his glass on the table. "Aye, lad, he may do that. Perhaps it's best if you leave me out of the conversation."

Zack glanced over at the band in the corner of the pub. It consisted of a woman playing a flute, and two men, one playing a banjo and the other a guitar. He enjoyed the music and started tapping his foot to the beat.

In a moment he turned back to McHugh. "Seriously, thanks for your help."

McHugh watched the band, humming along. "Be careful, lad. This could be tricky. You don't want to get in the middle of a major ruck."

"Don't I know it."

"Good lad, and off you go. Be sure to take care of my cousin. It would be very bad if something should happen to her."

Zack picked up on the implied threat. Great. Now he had it coming at him from all sides.

19

Gettysburg, 2:30 p.m.

Rene Garcia parked along the edge of the asphalt parking lot, locked her bike, and sat down on a bench in the shade. She pulled out the military file on Cliff Henderson her assistant had given her and paged through it.

Henderson entered the Army after 9-11. Following basic training, he attended ranger and jump school. He did well in training, scoring high on all the tests, and got selected for Officer Candidate School. After graduation from OCS, he shipped out to Afghanistan.

Now this is interesting, she thought. Upon his return from his first tour overseas, the Army assigned him to Quantico for a short course on prisoner interrogation. She could find no record of how he did in the course, but upon graduation, Henderson served three six-month tours in Afghanistan, then one in Iraq. She'd need to push him on that course. What did he learn? How did he use it?

Putting the file back in the envelope, she followed the winding sidewalk up to the front door and entered the Gettysburg Visitor's Center. The cavernous center had been open for a couple of years and it still had the smell of fresh paint and new furniture.

A rush of activity greeted her. Groups of people milled around in the bookstore off to her right, while visitors interested in a tour waited in line ahead of her. An orientation video ran every few minutes in the large auditorium to her right front. She debated watching the video but looked at her watch. No time. Maybe later.

She spotted a Starbucks next to the front door of the dining area. On her way over to get a much-needed caffeine hit, she stopped at the information desk along the left wall. A gray-haired man with a tan vest over his blue shirt walked over from the far side of the counter. "May I help you, Colonel?"

"Yes, thanks. This is my first time in Gettysburg, and I'm not sure what the foundation does."

His smile seemed genuine. "That's an easy one. The park service coordinates the rangers and many of the educational programs. We manage the building, the museum, bookstore, and other things like that."

"Did you hear about the woman who disappeared last Friday?"

"Who hasn't? It's the talk of the town."

"Any ideas what might have happened?" Garcia asked.

He leaned in toward her and whispered, "Some people think a ghost took her."

"Do you?"

"I've lived here all my life and seen some pretty goofy things. Honestly, I don't know what else to think unless she ran off." He leaned in closer and whispered, "Maybe that military guy killed her. He seemed a little weird to me."

"Well, thanks for the information. I'd better get going."

"Wait a minute. I haven't told you about the foundation. Maybe you'd like to join."

"No thanks, not now. Maybe later."

She turned from the counter to watch a number of young people hurrying toward the auditorium. A clock on the wall counted down the minutes to the next presentation.

Garcia enjoyed watching the kids playing with their family or arguing with their siblings. It made her wish for her own family.

She walked over and stood in front of Starbucks, looking at the menu. Something made her turn. Ranger Cliff Henderson walked across the room toward her. A tall, well-built man with shaggy blond hair, he extended his hand. "Colonel Garcia, nice to see you again."

She wanted to smile at him but her upbringing kicked in. It wasn't polite for a Hispanic girl to be too forward. "Ranger Henderson."

"Welcome to Gettysburg. I see you found our secret weapon, Starbucks."

She shook his hand, pulling it away quickly. She didn't like men she didn't know touching her, but decided to let it go. "Ah, thanks for seeing me."

"My pleasure. May I buy you a coffee?"

"No, thanks. I've got it."

They picked up their coffees and walked into the dining area, actually more of a place for visitors to bring their bag lunches and eat in air-conditioned comfort on a hot, sultry day.

He pulled out a chair for her. "I didn't notice the other day that you were so attractive. Zack has been holding out on me as usual."

She sat down. "Henderson, if you'd tried all that stupid, adolescent bull crap when we first met, I would have brought an M-80 Rocket Launcher with me to get your attention. Now, can we talk business? You know, like mature adults. I have some questions for you."

He leaned back, obviously shocked at her reaction. "I'm sorry. Can we start again?"

"It seems that I don't have any other choice, so let me update you on what happened yesterday." She told him about the incident at the restaurant, deciding to withhold the information about a possible Irish Mafia connection.

"Do you think it has anything to do with the disappearance of Blake Lannigan?"

"I don't know. I thought that maybe you could tell me."

"I've been racking my brain trying to figure out what could have happened to her. People don't disappear into thin air, but that's exactly what she seems to have done. I've driven around the entire park a number of times and out to the highway. Stopped at most of the fast-food places and motels with a picture of Ms. Lannigan. No one has seen her. It's really weird. Almost like she meant to disappear."

Garcia took a sip of coffee, giving herself a moment to organize her thoughts. "I know Blake, and I know she didn't just disappear.

Despite what Shelia O'Donnell may think, I don't believe spirits were involved."

"I wouldn't discount it," Henderson said. "We've had a number of unusual occurrences happen over the years. Some of which have never been explained."

"You can't be serious."

"Deadly serious." He smiled that fetching smile again. "Pardon the pun. You know, part of the reason paranormal experiences go unreported is that people will be asked if they've ever seen a ghost. They have to answer no. So they figure they haven't had a paranormal experience."

"Ranger Henderson, what are you trying to say? Spit it out."

"Let me explain. And please call me Cliff."

"Ranger Henderson, please go on."

"According to what I've read, only about ten percent of paranormal experiences are visual. Two thirds are auditory and the rest are experienced by either touch or smell. So you see, you don't have to see a ghost to have one present. But first, let me tell you a little about Gettysburg."

Garcia took out her tape recorder. "Do you mind if I record this to refer back to it later?"

"That's fine. The battle lasted three days and the two armies together totaled about 175,000 men. In addition to the horrible fighting conditions, soldiers were wandering through town looking for food and who knows what else. Imagine what that did to the town."

Garcia swallowed hard. Must have been a bitch.

"When the two armies departed, they left behind around 50,000 casualties to be cared for by a handful of doctors, nurses, and the few people who remained in the town."

"Are you trying to tell me this is what led to all of the paranormal activity?"

"Could be. There are two incidents that seem the most realistic to me. One of the re-enactors told me about hearing the sound of soldiers marching through distant woods. Are you familiar with the term re-enactors?"

"Ranger, I wasn't born yesterday."

"Right. I'm sorry. Anyway, this guy said he saw a fog rolling across the field and from inside the fog he heard the sound of hoofbeats, shuffling feet, and moving equipment. Apparently others heard it, too."

Garcia got a shiver up her spine. "Sounds like what Zack heard. Do you have a name and address for this re-enactor? I'd like to follow up with him."

"I'm not sure if I can locate him or not. I'll see what I can do."

"Yes, please do. Now, go on."

"Another incident happened over on Culp's Hill. Apparently a doctor and his family were staying at a campground. From the woods one night, he heard the sound of someone yelling, '*Help me.*' He heard it several times, and the campground manager heard it, too."

"What about any park rangers?" Garcia asked.

"Since the doctor and his family were on the park grounds, a ranger happened by because it was after the time for the park to close. When the ranger listened, it was silent for a few minutes, then '*help me*' sounded again. The ranger called for backup to see if they could find and help the individual. The group searched, but finally around 1:30 in the morning they called it off."

"What did they do?" Garcia asked.

"The rangers logged it in as another unexplained incident."

"This sounds like a bunch of bull crap to me."

"Sorry, but I don't think so. And I didn't mean to scare you."

"Takes more than that to scare me. The person responsible for Blake's disappearance is someone with motive and opportunity. That's the way I've been trained to think about incidents."

"Who has motive and opportunity?"

Garcia thought for a moment. "I have to meet with the ranger who first came upon Zack. It was only a few minutes after Blake disappeared. Maybe she was involved or saw something she didn't figure was important. Often people don't realize what they saw until they talk it through later."

"She's off today but will be back tomorrow."

"What about Chief Munson?" Garcia asked. "How well do you know him?"

"Why do you ask?"

"I'm trying to figure out who might have a motive to help Blake disappear."

"I don't know him very well. As far as I can tell, he's an all-right guy."

Garcia looked around. A group of girls had come in and were throwing wads of paper at one another. Kids. She took another sip of coffee. "Anyone else that you can think of who might have a motive to do something like this? Someone who also is strong enough to carry Blake. I think that eliminates most females and smaller men." She decided to push a little. "How about you?"

"Now wait a damn minute, Garcia. Zack's my friend. Why would I do something like that to him?"

Keep pushing. Put him on the defensive. "You knew Zack through the Army. Maybe he did something you didn't like."

"Don't be silly. We were close. Ask him."

Garcia decided to push ahead with questions. "What did you do in the Army?"

"I'm sorry, but my job was classified."

"Is that because you were one of those guys water-boarding Taliban captives?"

Henderson squinted at her. "Why do you say that?"

"Look, Henderson, I didn't come down here unprepared. I read your file. I know your training. So you can drop the bull. You're outed now, and I've got every clearance in the book."

Henderson stayed silent for a moment.

"Ranger Henderson?"

"I'm a trained interrogator. Special Operations Command attached me to Zack's unit to insure we got all the intelligence out of the Taliban that Zack's soldiers captured."

"Did you like your job?"

Henderson stared at her. "No, but it was important. I obtained intelligence that helped our guys. I liked that part. I didn't like what it sometimes took to get the information."

"You used torture?" Garcia asked.

"No comment."

She decided to let that go for now. "You held an important and necessary job. Why did you leave the Army?"

"I got tired of running all over the world on a moment's notice. And a close friend of mine got killed. I didn't want to be involved in all that killing anymore."

"What were the circumstances around his death?"

Henderson looked away for a moment. "I don't like to talk about it."

"Maybe you could humor me. It might be important."

"We were on a night maneuver to capture a Taliban leader. My friend led one of the patrols. When we hit the area, one of the Taliban commanders knifed him. A young captain, he should have never been out in front like that."

"Who was in charge?"

"Zack led the operation."

"Maybe you blame him."

"No. Shit happens in war." Henderson looked away again. "Colonel Garcia, I don't want to talk about this. I really don't."

"All right. Where all were you assigned with Zack?"

"We were at Fort Bragg together, then again twice in Afghanistan."

Garcia stood. "I'm trying to consider all possibilities. That's what I do best. There always is a logical explanation for everything that happens. I intend to find it with or without your help."

He stood. "I understand. You're doing your job. When you mentioned Munson, you got me thinking. I heard through the rumor mill that his job could be in jeopardy. Tight budget and all that. Maybe he decided he needed to stir up a little crime on his own."

"Keep thinking of possibilities." Garcia stood. "I'm going to find out what happened to my friend. Heaven help the person who hurts her."

"I wouldn't want to be that person. How about if I walk out to the parking lot with you?"

"Be my guest."

When they got to the Harley, Garcia unlocked her bike.

"Pretty big bike for such a little lady."

"Goddamn it, Henderson, that's the second time you've acted like an asshole. You're now zero for two on my list. I bought my Super Glide Custom Harley four months ago and I love it. It's got tank-mounted gauges, a leather fuel tank panel, a solid stainless steel pull back handle bar, mid-mounted controls and low rear suspension. It's 93 inches long with a 96 cubic inch displacement and gets me 53 miles per gallon on the road. Now if you don't like it or think I'm too cute for it, you can get out of my way or I'll run your ass down."

Henderson held up his hands in mock surrender. "Wait a minute, please wait a minute."

"I'm waiting."

"Before you make the drive back to D.C., how about having dinner with me? I'm sorry for the way I acted at the beginning of our conversation. What I said was juvenile. I do enjoy talking to you and would like to kick around some more possibilities. Maybe between the two of us we can come up with something that makes sense. So far, nothing does."

Garcia thought about that for a few minutes. Henderson was a good-looking enough guy and seemed fun to be with. Maybe between the two of them they could come up with something. As usual, she had nothing waiting for her back in D.C. She thought about her job, she thought about her father, then she figured, what the hell? "All right. I'll give you one more chance to act like a guy I want to spend time with and not some juvenile jerk."

20

When they arrived back in her room, Shelia said, "I'm a mite hungry. I was hoping we could get a bite of something to eat before I die of starvation."

Zack stayed silent for a moment. "Well, now, we don't want that to happen. But first, give me a few minutes."

He pulled his laptop from its bag, adjusted the screen, and powered it up to check his e-mails. One e-mail from Garcia read that she planned to meet with the Gettysburg mayor, then with Cliff Henderson. Maybe she'd come up with something to lead them to Blake. He shut it down. "How much do you trust McHugh?"

Shelia frowned. "I've known him all my life. He's been like a big brother to me."

"That doesn't answer my question. Do you trust him?"

"I trust him, but I know he's got other pressures from the gang he runs with. What is it they say? Trust but verify."

Zack figured the same way. Something told him that McHugh could give him up and not think another minute about it. "I think we should pack up and get out of here."

"But, we've got these rooms for the night."

"That's exactly what McHugh will think. And we're not sure who else knows we're here. If he's going to pull something, he'll assume we'll be here until morning. If we leave now, we can get to the place early to meet the contact. Be ahead of where they think we'll be."

She rubbed her palms on her thighs. "Makes sense, but I was

thinking forward to a couple of drinks, dinner, and a chance to relax before we begin our travels."

It would be easier if he were running alone, but he had to watch out for her. "Something tells me we should get the hell out of Dodge."

"Dodge?"

Zack laughed. "It's one of our American sayings, means let's go. We can stop once we're out of Dublin and find someplace to eat."

Shelia walked over and pulled her suitcase out of the closet. "I've got a friend from college who's about to graduate and go to law school. She told me she could be headed to the States later this summer. I'd like to check with her before we leave town."

"Once we're out of here, you can give her a call."

After they packed, the two headed for the elevator. Zack then reached over and stopped Shelia. "I think we ought to go down the back stairs."

"You are being careful."

"Hopefully unnecessary, but I don't think so. Something tells me... " He turned toward the stairs. When they reached the first floor, Zack peeked into the lobby. He saw two men standing at the desk, both wearing watch caps and long coats. Coincidence? He whispered to Shelia, "Come on. Let's sneak out the back door."

They ducked into the corridor and made for the rear entrance. Outside in the parking lot, Zack checked to make sure no one watched their car, then they threw their stuff in the trunk and got in. "Why don't you call your friend before we get moving?"

Shelia drove through the late-evening Dublin traffic until they reached the outskirts of town, Zack watching behind them in the rearview mirror. McHugh knew Shelia's car and had her license number. Too bad they didn't have a rental car they could change once in a while.

Forty-five minutes later they sat in Mary McGregor's apartment. A petite woman, McGregor's hair was as red as Shelia's was black, and the freckles on her face highlighted her round blue eyes. She had the same musical laugh. Zack immediately liked her.

After the two women talked briefly and caught up on what each had been doing, Zack asked, "I understand you may be headed to the States for the summer. What do you plan to do?"

"It's part of a summer internship that's been established for pre-law students between Trinity College and the U.S. government. All expenses paid. My friends send me glowing reports. They're having a ball. Met a bunch of fun blokes. I leave tomorrow."

That comment rang a bell with Zack. "Don't you have to apply for a visa?"

McGregor wrinkled up her brow. "I've been told the people in the States take care of that. All I need to do is send them a picture and the relevant information on myself."

"Aren't you limited on how long you can stay?"

"I'm not sure," Mary said. "Right now my plan is to come back and register at Trinity for the fall semester."

"What classes will you be taking during your time with the internship?" Zack asked.

She paused, putting her finger to her chin, then she laughed. "Well, you know what, they didn't talk about classes. I understand the group tours government facilities during the day, then go to parties most every night. I can hardly wait."

"What is this program called?"

"The Irish internship."

"How many students have gone over so far?" Zack asked.

"About fifteen of my girlfriends... , but there could be more."

Zack had to ask, "Any men?"

Mary thought for a moment. "You know, that's kinda funny. No blokes have been accepted into the program that I know of."

———

They left McGregor's apartment and stopped at a pub on the outskirts of Dublin for a Smithwicks and a sandwich. After they ordered Zack asked, "Don't you think it's funny that they only accept women into this internship program?"

Shelia put her beer down on the wooden table. "Well, now that you mention it, yeah, it does seem different. Most of these programs tilt toward you blokes. We poor females get whatever is leftover."

Between the music and the conversations at other tables, the noise had picked up so Zack leaned forward to hear her. "Do you know any girls who have been interns and returned to Ireland? I'd like to talk to someone who's been through the program."

"Let me think. I could ring up a few of my girlfriends on my mobile. See if we can stop by and catch up with one of them."

After a few calls, she put her phone on the table. "That's funny. Their mobiles have been disconnected. I wonder what happened?"

Zack pondered that as they ate their sandwiches. He listened to the musicians, a flute, a banjo and a guitar. The fiddler set a fast pace and the others kept the beat. He found himself tapping his foot again. But what to do about Shelia's friends? Were they all right? Something... .

Shelia finished her sandwich and hummed to the music. "Wish we didn't have all these black clouds hanging over our heads. I enjoy spending time with you."

Zack enjoyed her too. Maybe too much. "You know, not being able to reach your friends sounds more and more suspicious to me. Why don't I drive and you can keep calling. See if you can find out when they'll return."

Shelia stood and punched him on the shoulder. "Remember to drive on the opposite side of the road."

Zack laughed. "You mean the wrong side of the road, don't you?"

"Sorry, the right side of the road. No pileups authorized."

———

The night surrounded them, their headlights cutting through the fog and darkness. Mountains rose in the distance off to Zack's left. The rolling hills reminded him of Minnesota, a few hills then miles of nothing but grassland. Sheep grazed in many of the fields.

The moon came out from behind a cloud, bathing the landscape in its glow. Gnarled branches on the trees they passed twisted into strange shapes as they spread out from the limbs. For a moment he thought back to his youth, images of his father floating into his mind, then he forced himself back to the present. Someday he'd find the truth.

Shelia kept calling friends on her mobile while Zack drove, but without success. It took them about two hours before the road curved to the right and they made a slow descent into Roscommon, the town where they were to meet their contact.

Zack tensed up, planning ahead. "How about if I drive by the house?"

"No way, Zack. In Ireland, when you say ten o'clock in the morning, you sure don't arrive at three o'clock. Good way to get yourself shot by these blokes."

Zack sure as hell wasn't going to wait until ten, but he could wait awhile. "Let's see if we can get a few hours of sleep before our meeting."

The hotel was located on N5, just off the N61, a mile north of Roscommon. Shelia went inside and rang a bell to wake the manager. Zack kept watch outside.

In a few minutes, Shelia came back outside, waving a key. "The manager told me we could park in the rear."

When Zack entered the lobby, he peeked into the restaurant. Empty. Not surprising for this time of night. He noticed the stained glass windows and natural wood walls. "Nice place."

"It's a very historic old town. I love it."

When they got up to the room, Zack pulled out his laptop. He powered it up and sent an e-mail to Garcia asking her to check out the internship. "What was the name of the school again?"

"Mary said it's not a specific college, but simply called the Irish internship."

Zack hoped that Garcia would come up with something, but he had a feeling that she wouldn't find a damn thing.

Shelia unbuttoned her shirt. "I'm going to take a shower." She stood there in her bra and slacks. Reaching back she took off the bra. "Gonna be lonely in that shower all by myself."

He found himself at instant attention. Setting aside his laptop, Zack walked over to put his arms around her, loving the touch of the soft, smooth skin of her back. "I can't think of anything else I'd rather do right now." Unless, he thought, find Blake.

Shelia pushed her slacks down, the baby-blue panties following. She tossed her clothes on the chair in a heap.

Zack set a record in stripping off his clothes. "You are one beautiful woman."

She came over and leaned against him, kissing his mouth. "You're not so bad yourself, soldier. Come on, let's get wet."

They soaped each other up and down, then made love. She felt soft, warm, feminine.

Toweling each other off, they barely tripped to the bed before making love again.

"That was wonderful." Shelia leaned back on the pillow and stretched. "You are some lover. You know, an Irish bloke's idea of foreplay is to whisper in his girl's ear, 'All right deary, spread 'em.'"

Zack had to laugh. He kissed her on the lips, then on the forehead and held her, listening to the wind blowing against the window. Finally her breath assumed the quiet rhythm of sleep.

He lay there for a long time, thinking about Shelia. He was damaged goods from Afghanistan and had no right, but he had to admit to himself that he might be falling in love with her.

21

North of Washington, D.C., 10:00 p.m.

Rene Garcia blinked against the rushing wind as the Harley carried her south along Interstate 270 toward the Washington, D.C. beltway. Was Zack in danger? Could he trust Shelia? Something about her made Garcia uneasy. Something... .

By the time she arrived at the office and powered up her computer, the clock read ten-fifty. She leaned back in her chair, put her feet up on the desk, and thought about Henderson. She'd really enjoyed dinner and talking to him. Interesting and fun... great sense of humor. Maybe it would be worth seeing him again. Who knew what might come of it?

Garcia's fear of commitment drove her friends nuts. The five friends had graduated from the University of Texas the same year. It took effort, but they had managed to gather at least once each year. Garcia loved their reunions.

Her closest friend, Mary, a clinical psychologist at the University of California, tried on several occasions to analyze what had happened in Garcia's childhood to make her so uneasy with men. Mary emphasized the solution rested with Garcia to loosen up a little. Live it up once in awhile. Take a chance on a man.

Well, she'd done that once with a major in Europe and got burned. Guy turned out to be a jerk and ran around on her. Sadly, Garcia was the last one to find out.

With the sound of Mary's voice whispering in her ear, Garcia had agreed to meet Henderson again for dinner halfway between Gettysburg and Washington at the Cozy Inn sometime soon. Maybe the two of them would end up staying overnight and getting cozy. That made her laugh. She needed a good laugh. This case kept driving her nuts.

Back to work. She read the message from Zack about the Irish internship. He wanted her to check to see what the FBI might have on the group. It seemed kinda far fetched to Garcia, but maybe worth checking out. She made a note, then closed up her PC.

In the middle of her desk, her assistant had set the coroner's report on the shooter. It included his body measurements, cause of death, a fingerprint card, and blood type. Nothing remarkable. The FBI had pulled down a firm identification on him from Interpol. She'd provide that to Zack in the morning. Maybe it would help him out.

Shelia had been right. Indeed Irish, the guy had a long record in Ireland. He'd been active with the IRA during the 1990s, then involved in a number of gangs since then. But up until his attack on Zack, he had never been convicted of anything more serious than a few breaking and enterings. Why an assassination attempt and why now? And more importantly, why Zack?

She picked up Henderson's file again and glanced on the left side to look at his efficiency reports. He had always received top block ratings so he should have been up for promotion to major. Zack had written outstanding comments on Henderson.

But yet, he left the Army before being considered. Why? Henderson wasn't married and had no children so there wasn't anything calling him back to the U.S. He had two brothers, both of whom lived in Kansas not too far away from his parents.

What had driven him out of the Army? Smiling to herself, she thought that might be a good subject for pillow talk. She felt a quick warm burn down low. Felt good.

On the right side of his file were a number of letters from special services officers in both Afghanistan and Iraq. Apparently Cliff and Zack had put together a combo that played at a variety of events to entertain the troops. She didn't realize Zack played the guitar. Lots of rave reviews.

Did Zack do something to make Henderson resign his commission and leave the Army? If so, would that be enough to make him pull some sort of crap? But to kidnap Blake? Nah, that didn't make sense. But assuming it did, how did all of that relate to the assassination attempt on Zack?

She needed to find out a little more about what Henderson had done as an interrogator. Tomorrow she'd check with her FBI counterpart. Maybe he could help.

Garcia gathered up her papers and called General Hightower. No answer. She glanced at her watch. Well hell, it was was after eleven o'clock. No wonder. Guy had gone home. Where she should be taking care of her cat. Poor Harold would jump all over her when she got home, squealing at Garcia for not feeding him sooner. She smiled. Loved that cat. Her buddy.

She left the General a message. Told him she met with Henderson earlier in the day. How he impressed her. Couldn't tell the General how impressed. She added a footnote that she was still working on sorting out any relationship between Blake's disappearance and the shooting in the Pentagon City mall.

Finally she mentioned her appointment with the FBI and she would head over to the Hoover building first thing in the morning to meet with their Mafia experts. She'd report back to him on what she found.

Garcia shut off the light and pulled the door shut behind her. On her way down the hall she wondered if she'd made a mistake. Should she have put something in her note to Hightower about Henderson's sudden resignation from the Army? No, not yet. Once she planted that information in Hightower's mind, he'd never forget it. Guy had a memory that astounded her.

22

Roscommon, Thursday, 6:45 a.m.

Zack and Shelia followed the directions McHugh had given them and fifteen minutes later pulled up in front of a boxy one-story house. Zack double-checked the address. "Do you have a screwdriver in the car? I may need to bust a hasp on the back door."

She reached for the door handle. "Sure. It's in the trunk."

"You wait here. Let me check everything out. I'll be back in a few minutes."

He pushed open the car door and stood on the sidewalk, checking up and down the street. All quiet. Opening the trunk, he pulled out a screwdriver, then walked around the side of the house by the attached garage, keeping an eye out for anyone who might be watching. So far, no one in sight.

He peeked through the back window of the house but didn't see anyone inside so he jiggled the door knob. Locked. He figured that might be the case. Pulling the screwdriver out of his pocket, he jimmied the lock. Listened again for any voices or footsteps. Still all quiet.

He opened the door and let himself in. The floor creaked when he entered. Zack stood and waited, listening. Still no footsteps. Thankfully, no dog.

Darkness permeated the kitchen and it smelled of moldy wallpaper. The sink was stacked high with dirty dishes, and the counters looked as if they hadn't been cleaned in months. He checked through a few of the notes on a table under the phone and pulled open several drawers in the cupboard. Nothing of interest.

He crouched down, then crept into the living room. Empty beer bottles lined the coffee table. A dinner plate, half full of some kind of rotting food sat next to a chair. A stack of gun magazines lay on an end table next to a frayed couch.

Zack pulled out his M-9 and tracked his way down the hallway toward the two bedrooms. Loud snoring sounded from the room on the left. He stopped and poked his head into the bedroom on the right. Empty. He checked the closet and under the bed to make sure. All clear.

Moving across the hallway, he stood in the doorway of the other bedroom. The snoring emanated from a huge man who lay on the bed, arms splayed out across the chest of a woman. She had scraggly brown hair and the sheet had been partially kicked off her, revealing her bony chest. Looked like the guy got all of the food.

Zack walked over and knocked the man's foot with his pistol. "Hey, buddy, time to wake up. You know, rise and shine."

The man kept snoring. Zack smelled stale beer. The woman jumped up and screamed. She reached down and pulled the sheet up to cover her naked body.

Zack put his finger to his lips. "Stop screaming. I won't hurt you. Just reach over and wake Sleeping Beauty."

Eyes wide, her mouth opened to scream again.

Zack put his finger to his lips. "Just wake him. I won't hurt you if you cooperate."

She pushed on his arm. "Michael, wake up."

He waved his arm and shook his head. Mumbled, "Goddamn, let me sleep."

"Hey, wake up, buddy," Zack called. "We need to talk."

The man raised himself onto his elbows and looked at Zack, bloodshot eyes trying to focus. "Who the fuck are you?"

Zack pushed some dirty clothes onto the floor and sat on the one chair in the room. "Terry sent me. You're supposed to have directions for me."

Bleary eyes squinted out at Zack, his fiery red hair sticking out in all directions. "What?"

"Terry sent me."

"Fuck, you're not supposed to be here until ten o'clock."

Zack kept the gun trained on the big man in case he got any ideas about a charge across the room. "I want to pick up the directions now."

The man threw back the sheet and pushed up. The bushy red beard matched his hair, and his fat gut overflowed his boxer shorts. He reached for his pants lying on the floor.

"Wait a minute. Sit your ass back down and give me those pants. That's it, nice and easy." Zack pulled the pants out of the man's hands, and as he thought, a .22 caliber pistol had been shoved in the back pocket. Zack slipped it in his jacket. "Don't think you'll need this. What the hell, we're all friends here. What's your name?"

"Michael."

"Well, Michael, get your clothes on so I won't have to look at your fat belly, and get me those directions."

Michael almost fell over when he put one leg in the pants. "Ain't got 'em." He flopped down on the bed and pulled on the pants.

Zack glared at him. "What do you mean you don't have them?" The big tub was screwing him around. Zack didn't like it at all.

"I ain't got them. Your contact is supposed to be here in an hour. He's got the damn things. The boss is pretty careful who knows his schedule."

"Don't try and pull that crap on me." Zack cocked the M-9 for emphasis. "Get me the damn directions."

Michael pulled on his glasses, small round glasses that looked out of place on his bearded face. "Wait a minute, man. It won't do any good to lean on me because I don't know. My partner's bringing them." He shrugged his large shoulders. "Boss don't trust me with paperwork and that sort of stuff."

Zack figured he'd get some sort of run around. "When do you expect him?"

Michael lifted his watch off the bedside table. "Should be here in thirty, maybe forty-five minutes."

"Hey, jackass," the woman called, "do you mind if I put some clothes on?"

Zack walked over to the closet and pulled a bathrobe out for her, taking a minute to check the pockets. All the time, he kept his gun trained on the man. "Here ya go."

She pulled on the robe, trying to keep the sheet in front of her.

"All right, we're going out in the living room and wait for your friend. If he's not here in an hour, I'm gonna shoot you in the right knee."

Michael's eyes got wide.

"Then if he's not here in another half hour, I'm going to shoot you in the left knee. Maybe by that time, I'll be convinced that you're telling me the truth. If not, I'm gonna put a bullet through your forehead."

"Goddamn, you're fucking insane."

"And don't you forget it. Now, move your ass."

Zack settled the two on a couch in the living room, then he opened the front door and waved to Shelia. When she stepped out of the car he called, "Why don't you park down the street and come inside. Looks as if we're going to be here for a while."

A few minutes later, Shelia pushed open the door and stepped inside. She gasped at the couple sitting on the couch, then glanced at Zack, his gun pointed at the man. "Guess we've had a change of plans."

Zack shared what Michael had told him. "He says the guy with the directions will be here in about a half hour."

"Let me see if I can find something to eat in this pit." Shelia glanced at the woman. "Not much of a housekeeper, huh?"

"Fuck you, bitch." The woman sneered. "You try keeping house with this animal running around messing things up as fast as I straighten them."

The man pushed his hair out of his face. "Hey, bring us a couple of beers while we wait?"

Shelia walked over and stood about two feet in front of him, glaring down at the monster. "Why don't you shut your fat trap or

I'll tell my friend to kick the shit out of you." She turned to walk into the kitchen, calling over her shoulder. "I'm not a fucking 'hey' and don't you forget that."

Zack had to smile. "Remember your right knee, asshole. You've only got one of those, and once it's gone, it's gone forever. So be nice to my friend."

In a few minutes, Shelia returned with a couple of sandwiches. "Wasn't much in the kitchen but I did find enough for a couple of sandwiches. Sorry, no clean plates to put them on, but it's food. At least I think it's food."

"Hey," Michael called, "what about us?"

"You can fix yourself a sandwich when you have your beer." Zack took a bite and motioned toward Shelia. "Why don't you keep an eye out front?"

She moved over to the window. "Window's so dirty it's hard to see through it."

"If the contact doesn't get here in a couple of minutes," Zack said, "we can get a bucket of water for Michael and start him on the windows."

"Fuck you, asshole."

"One more comment like that and the right knee gets it. I hate a clown with bad manners."

"Wait a minute," Shelia called, "a guy just pulled up to the curb."

Keeping the gun trained on Michael, Zack moved toward the window. "Let me know when he starts up the walk."

"Here he comes."

Zack motioned the woman toward the door with his gun hand and slipped behind her. "Open the door when he knocks. If you try and tip him off in any way, I'll shoot and it won't be in the knee."

She whimpered. "Don't hurt me."

"You have nothing to fear from me if you cooperate. We'll be out of your house in a few minutes."

A knock on the door. The woman opened it.

A deep voice said, "I wanta see Michael."

She motioned for him to enter. Michael sat on the couch, watching.

"I brought the pistol," the man said, then he laughed. "We can polish them off like the boss said, then dump the bodies in the river."

Zack kicked the door shut, causing the guy to jump. "That's what I figured, you bastards. I knew this was a trap. I ought to shoot your ass right now."

"Wait a minute," the man said. "I was only kidding."

"Yeah, like I believe that," Zack replied. "All right, up against the wall and spread 'em."

Zack frisked him and found the Glock. He lifted it, then spun the man around. "Sit your ass over in that chair. Don't make me shoot."

The man sat, hands in the air, voice quivering. "All right, all right, I'm sitting."

"Now, you've got about one minute to tell me what I want to know or I'll shoot you in the nuts. Do I make myself clear?"

"Wait a minute, buddy, I'll tell you everything I know."

"I'm not your buddy," Zack said, "and you're damn right, you'll tell me what I want to know. Who are we supposed to see in Galway?"

"Tuohy O'Toole."

"And where the hell will he be?"

"I don't know."

Zack fired a shot, hitting the wall next to the man's left leg. The noise echoed throughout the house, making everyone jump.

"Goddamn," the man said.

"You're right," Zack said. "Goddamn."

"O'Toole will kill me if I tell you where he is."

"Yeah, but I'll kill you if you don't." Zack tapped his foot. "And I'm here, and I'm waiting."

The man swallowed and glanced over at Michael.

"Tell the crazy bastard what he wants to know," Michael said. "Otherwise, he'll kill both of us."

Zack kept the gun pointed at the man's leg. "I hate to wait.

You've got another thirty seconds. Remember, you pricks were going to kill me. I've got nothing to lose. So tell me why you're gunning for me and where I can find O'Toole."

The man stared at Zack, watching, like he was preparing to wait it out.

Zack fired again, creasing the man's pants.

A wet spot appeared on the front of his pants. "You've pissed off someone really bad and they've put out a contract on your ass with Tuohy."

"How much?"

"Twenty-five thousand dollars."

"How do I get the contract canceled?"

"You don't. Once it's out there, it can only be pulled back by the man who put it out or O'Toole needs to call it off."

"Who put the contract out on me?"

"I don't know."

Zack fired again, causing a flesh wound in his leg.

"Goddamn."

"No more crap. Tell me how to find O'Toole. I'm tired of waiting."

The man stammered out directions.

Shelia stood. "I know where that is."

Zack backed toward the door. "Let's get some rope and tie up our new friends."

Shelia hurried into the kitchen. She returned with a roll of duct tape. "I found this. It'll work just as well."

Zack had to laugh. "Duct tape to the rescue. Just wrap it around their arms and legs."

Shelia tied the three of them up, wrapping the tape tight. "I'll go out and get the car."

"Now to finish up."

"Wait a minute," the man said. "I told you what you wanted to know. You can't kill me."

"Don't believe that for a minute. You seemed to be looking forward to killing me."

"That was only business. I got nothing against you personally."

"Yeah, right. You're lucky. I don't feel like killing you now. But so help me if I see you again while I'm in Ireland, you're dead meat. Understand?"

The three nodded.

Zack let himself out. He hurried down the sidewalk to the curb where Shelia waited with the motor running.

When Zack got in, she floored the gas pedal and the car squealed away from the curb.

He tucked the gun back in the holster. "What a bunch. Glad we got out of there in one piece."

Shelia glanced over at him. Smiled. "Welcome to Ireland."

23

Washington, D.C. Thursday, 10:00 a.m.

Garcia found a parking spot in one of the lots off Ninth Street for her Harley and hurried across Pennsylvania Avenue into the front door of the Hoover building. An armed guard checked her ID, then waved her through the metal detector. She took the elevator to the seventh floor and walked down the hallway to the office of Special Agent Albert Ferguson.

Ferguson reminded her of an economics professor she'd had back at the University of Texas. Short, with thick glasses and unkempt in a blazer with patches on the sleeves, he motioned for her to take a seat in one of his gun-metal gray chairs. Government issue all the way.

Garcia waited for him to sit behind his desk before she began. "Thanks for seeing me on such short notice. I'm working on Blake Lannigan's disappearance and I think you can help me."

Ferguson pulled a pen out of his pocket and made a note on the yellow pad sitting on the corner of his desk. "Your call sounded interesting. I hope I can assist."

Garcia summarized the events leading up to Blake's disappearance in Gettysburg. He wrinkled his brow when she mentioned Colonel Kelly hearing hoofbeats and shuffling feet.

"I know, I know," she said. "But you must realize that Colonel Zack Kelly is a stand-up guy. Not one to exaggerate. I'm convinced he heard what he heard."

Next, she walked Ferguson through the assassination attempt on Zack in front of the restaurant at the Pentagon City Mall.

"I heard about the shooting." Ferguson said. "I wish I'd known earlier the shooter might have been a member of the Irish Mafia."

"We didn't know ourselves right away. When we verified it, I wanted to make sure you realized the potential tie to Ireland."

Ferguson made another note. "I appreciate that. But you know, I can't for the life of me figure out why this shooter should be after one of our Army officers."

"Nor can we."

He ran his fingers through his short dark hair, now streaked with a tinge of gray. "I should share with you that we've noticed a noticeable increase in the pattern of their activities here on the East Coast in the past few months."

Now we're getting somewhere. "What can you tell me about them?"

"How about some coffee first?"

Garcia stretched. "Oh, man, I thought you'd never ask."

She followed him three doors down the hall to the coffee room. Ferguson poured each of them a cup, then he dropped three scoops of sugar into his. Garcia liked hers straight.

When they returned to his office he said, "Let me give you a little background first."

Garcia took out her tape recorder. "Do you mind? I like to study background material."

"Certainly, but I ask that you not make any of this information public without notifying me before hand."

Garcia took a sip of coffee. "Fair enough."

Ferguson leaned back in his chair, causing it to squeak. "When the potato famine hit Ireland in the mid-1800s, America became the dream destination for those poor people. As they arrived, the Irish immigrants settled in a few of our major cities. Unfortunately, they were victims of terrible discrimination, especially because most of them were Catholic. Street gangs formed into packs to protect themselves and their communities, and that's how the Irish Mafia first got its start."

"Kinda the same story of other immigrant groups."

Ferguson sipped his coffee, watching her over the rim of the cup. "I suspect you understand discrimination."

Garcia didn't say anything.

"The Irish and the Italians battled right into the late 1970s. Then things started to change. The Irish became better educated and started doing well in business. The election of President Kennedy was a real turning point for the Irish. They took pride in his election, and it enhanced their respectability around the country."

"Is that it?" Garcia asked.

"Almost. Things have stayed quiet with the Irish gangs until about a year ago. Now there seems to be something going on with a possible white slavery and weapons trade. We're not exactly sure what, but we're getting tips from informants that weapons are being exported to Ireland to stir up trouble. Maybe through leftover segments from the IRA."

"Do you think what happened to Zack Kelly could be tied to that?"

"I don't know," Ferguson replied, "but I'd sure like to find out."

"Have you heard of something called the Irish internship?"

Ferguson squinted at her. "Where did you hear about that?"

Garcia told him about the e-mail from Zack. "Zack is trying to gather information on the group from the Ireland side. He wants me to find out what I can over here."

"I've heard the name, but I don't know much more than that." He paused. "As you find out more, please let me know."

Garcia moved to the door, then stopped and turned. "Ah, do you have anyone here who's been through the interrogator school at Quantico, or knows about the military's interrogation process for Taliban prisoners?"

"Why do you ask?"

"Might be a factor in Blake Lannigan's disappearance."

Ferguson motioned her back in. "I attended a short course at Quantico a couple of years ago. Maybe I can help you."

She sat down and took out her tape recorder again. "What can you tell me?"

"For many years, the CIA has been interested in the use of drugs and harassment to either destroy memory or bring out memory. In the late '60s, a Russian double agent provided us the names of drugs developed by their scientists to affect human memory."

"Okay, now that's interesting. What else?"

"Humans have two types of memory, active and long-term. Agents involved in brainwashing can use one drug to destroy any new memories that come into our active memory. As far as I know, there is no drug that can affect long-term memory. They can use another drug to suppress memories that are in the active portion of memory to prevent other spy agencies from finding out that information. It's fascinating but confusing because there is another drug that can cancel out the suppression drug."

"Wait a minute," Garcia said. "You mean we can suppress or destroy this active memory?"

Ferguson nodded. "And subjects brainwashed with these drugs never seem to notice any loss in time."

Garcia looked at all the certificates on his wall as she thought about all this. Maybe she was on to something. "You mentioned brainwashing."

"Right. Edward Hunter, a journalist coined the term in 1951 because of all that was going on with our POWs returning from the Korean War. The combination of drugs with brutality and humiliation often led to admission of guilt or even betrayal of friends."

Garcia looked at her watch and stood. "I'm sorry that I have to get going now, but I'd love to hear more."

"Come back anytime and we'll discuss it some more. I can ask one of our agents who knows a lot more than I do about brainwashing to go into more detail with you."

"Great. I'll set up an appointment."

"Remember, much of this is still classified."

As Garcia walked across the street toward her Harley, she thought about Henderson and wondered.

A black Lincoln Continental pulled up to the dock, not more than thirty feet from where the double-decker paddle-boat stood moored. A block of a man got out of the front seat, looked around, then reached back to open the door.

In a moment, a slender man slipped out. Not at all what Zack had expected. The sun had tanned the man's skin and left streaks of yellow in his hair. Zack wondered where he got the sun because he didn't figure they ever got that much in Ireland. Maybe a tanning salon?

Another block of muscle rolled out of the driver's side and followed the other two.

The slender man walked up to Zack. He had a long straight nose and a pinched face that didn't seem to have ever smiled. "Are you Kelly?"

Zack nodded. "And you must be O'Toole."

"You've done enough to find me so let's board and get this over with."

They walked onto the boat. O'Toole headed to the rear, leaned on the railing and looked over the side. "Beautiful isn't it, Kelly? It's the largest lake in Ireland. One of the most scenic in all of Europe. I really like it here."

Zack realized that he and Shelia, along with O'Toole and his two bodyguards, were the only passengers on the boat. He reached back and touched the M-9 tucked into the holster on his belt and waited for O'Toole to say more.

The boat moved slowly out into the lake. "Don't even think about it, Kelly. If you try anything, you'll be dead before you can pull that weapon out. Terry has given you a free pass on this ride but only for a short period of time, so let's get to business. What do you want from me?"

Zack explained about Blake's disappearance and the assassination attempt on his life. "Shelia saw a tattoo on the shooter's wrist that tipped her off he was a member of the Irish Mafia. I'm trying to figure out why someone wants me dead. I've never had any dealing with the Irish Mafia before."

"All I can tell you, Kelly, is that you pissed someone off. Someone wants you dead."

"Who?" Zack asked.

"I don't know and even if I did, I wouldn't tell you."

"Didn't the contract come through you?"

"I'm not going to answer that question."

Zack faced O'Toole and looked directly into those dark-brown eyes. "What's it going to take to get that contract canceled?"

"That could be a problem. Before the man died, it would have been much easier. But now, you've got a number of brothers who want revenge for the killing of one of their own."

"Wait a goddamn minute, that guy would have killed me."

He pulled out a cigarette. One of the blocks hurried over to light it. O'Toole blew out some smoke. "Aye, but to these lads, that doesn't matter. You're dealing with former IRA members. Grudges can last a long time."

Zack was starting to get pissed off. He needed to take a deep breath. "Who can stop this? I don't want to kill anyone else, and I sure as hell don't want someone gunning for me."

O'Toole watched an Osprey swoop down and sweep up a fish in its talons. "Probably the only thing you can do is talk to God and hope to hell he hears you."

"Can you at least tell me if the contract started here in Ireland or back in the States?"

"Think about it Kelly. No one in Ireland had heard of you before a week ago. I understand they needed to do some research to find out who you were."

"Why is the Irish Mafia involved?"

O'Toole waited, blew out more smoke, obviously not going to answer that question.

Zack decided to try one more. "What can you tell me about the Irish internship?"

O'Toole swung around to stare at Zack. "How did you hear about that?"

"A friend."

"You know more than I thought you did."

"Well?"

"I can tell you this much," O'Toole said. "If you find the answer to one of those two questions, you'll jackknife right into the answer of the other. And, you're playing loose with a lot of people's money and political influence. In other words, be careful, Kelly. You're swimming with the sharks."

Zack figured the two were connected. Now he knew for sure. But how? He needed to talk to the families of the girls who were involved.

O'Toole motioned to the pilot of the boat and they turned back toward shore in silence.

24

Georgetown, 8:20 p.m.

Garcia parked her Harley along the cobblestone street a block down from the Lannigans' house and walked up the sidewalk. She'd known they had money, but the size of the mansion always astonished her. A three-story, it sported towers on all four corners, and a stone wall about five feet high surrounded it. This place must have cost a bundle. She crossed the street and stood watching from behind a towering oak tree.

Twenty-five minutes later, the gate opened and someone drove out in a Jaguar, then the gate closed. When the Jag passed under the street light, Garcia assured herself that both Lannigans were in the car. Probably out for the evening. Great.

She waited another thirty minutes until it was dark, then went back to her bike. Taking a flashlight, a camera, and a pair of gloves out of her saddle bags, she walked across the street. Stopping at the gate, she peeked in. No apparent cameras or sensors. So far she hadn't heard any dogs. Fifteen feet down the sidewalk, she spotted a low point in the wall.

She thought about Quinn, then she thought about Sean Lannigan. In her gut she knew he had something to hide, and she needed to find out what. Nothing else made any sense.

Deciding to go for it, she scaled the wall and dropped down on the other side, hoping the Lannigans didn't have guard dogs prowling the grounds. Don't argue with a bunch of sharp teeth.

Thankfully, no dogs appeared, at least none that ripped out at her right away. She jogged over and checked the front window. A dim light burned inside, but she didn't see anyone in the room.

During her military police advance course, she'd taken an elective in burglary. She'd never used that skill before but there was always a first time for everything.

She crept around to the back of the house, knelt and looked around for a moment, then slipped up to the kitchen door. Pulling the picks out of her jacket pocket, she took out the Y-shaped tension bar and the rake. She wiggled it. No luck. But the next time the pins moved and she was in.

Blake had told Garcia once that her parents didn't normally set the alarm if they were just going out for the evening. Garcia hoped to hell that Blake was right. If not... .

The hinge squeaked as she pushed the door open. If she got caught in here, it would be her job and probably her commission. Breaking and entering, and in the national security advisor's sister's house. But here she stood, ready to move forward.

She did a quick tour of the bottom floor, her nerves stretched taut. Everything inside her gut told her to turn around and get the hell out of there. But then something pushed her on. Blake. Her friend needed help.

She stepped into Sean Lannigan's study, sat down at the desk, and surveyed the room. Where would he put special things, things he didn't want anyone else to find?

The computer had been left on. She opened it, then pulled a flash drive out of her pocket. Slipping it into the computer, she started downloading data. There were dozens of numbers and lists of people. Probably most were business associates or members of the legal community. Lannigan could have her ass if she got caught. And of course, her own father would say he'd told her so. Okay, enough. Quit thinking about that and focus.

She pulled on the top drawer of the desk. Locked. Garcia took a few minutes to snap pictures of the papers on the desk. She'd analyze them later. A six-drawer file cabinet stood against the wall behind the desk. When she pulled on the top drawer, it opened. Great.

She began pulling open drawers and paging through files. In the bottom drawer of the cabinet, she found a file marked "Ireland." Spreading the contents on the desk, she snapped more pictures.

Wiping perspiration from her forehead, she glanced at her watch. She'd been in the house forty-seven minutes. Getting risky to stay any longer, but she wouldn't get back again so she needed to make this count.

The next drawer up in the cabinet contained phone bills. She snapped pictures of the bills, figuring she could compare these numbers to the address book in his computer and determine who Lannigan called most often. Particularly any calls to Ireland. Maybe that would give her a lead.

Deciding she had spent enough time in the den, Garcia hurried upstairs to the master bedroom. She flashed her light around in circles as she moved to make sure she didn't trip over something.

She sorted through drawers carefully so Mrs. Lannigan wouldn't know she'd been there. In one of the drawers she found a stack of porno tapes. Checking the titles, she noticed they were mostly bondage tapes. Uh-oh, that type of guy. She replaced them in the drawer, careful to make sure she put them back in the same order she'd found them in. Order might be important.

A door slammed downstairs. Garcia froze. She'd forgotten to keep checking out the front window and Lannigan had come home. Damn, what to do?

Footsteps sounded on the stairs. She heard two sets of voices. Must be Mrs. Lannigan. Where to hide? Laughter sounded, then loud voices.

Garcia glanced toward the closet. They'd check in there. Under the bed. Quick.

She slipped under the bed and pulled down the dust ruffle as she heard voices in the hall. The light in the bedroom flashed on. Loud voices and more laugher. Slurred talk from Lannigan. Must have had a few drinks. If they looked under the bed, she was toast.

A woman's voice and laughter. Didn't sound like Holly Lannigan. Uh-oh, Lannigan's got himself a honey on the side. Wonder how Holly Lannigan would like that?

She had a tiny slot of light and saw a woman's legs next to the bed. That voice. She knew it. Yes, she sure as hell knew it. Quinn. Darcy Quinn here with Sean Lannigan in his bedroom.

A skirt dropped to the floor next to the legs. More laughter.

Lannigan's voice, "Come on, honey, let's take a shower."

Quinn's voice, "Yeah, but I'd have to get naked first."

"Better hurry or I'll rip that outfit off you."

"Go ahead, stud. I don't care. I've got more of them."

Ripping material. Clothes fell to the floor. Garcia thought she might be in luck if they went in to take a shower first.

Groans and moans. God, she felt like a Peeping Tom. And on the national security advisor. Oh, man. She held her breath as her career flashed before her eyes.

More laughter, then both sets of the feet turned toward the bathroom. Garcia heard water running in the shower. The bathroom door slammed shut.

Garcia waited a minute. Peeked out. Hopefully they weren't coming right back out. She pushed out from underneath the bed. Maneuvered past the piles of clothes on the floor and jumped up.

She made a break for the door, ran out into the hallway, and took the stairs two at a time. When she hit the first floor, she ran toward the front door. Prayed there wasn't any alarm set yet, although they wouldn't hear it with the shower running. Garcia unlocked the front door, opened it and slipped out, pulling the door shut behind her with a little too much of a bang. Oh, well, they were busy and wouldn't notice.

Taking a minute to get oriented so she didn't trip, fall, and bust something, she ran toward the front gate. Spotting the low point in the wall again, she vaulted to the top. A dog barked. Damn thing must have been crated inside. A pit bull ran toward her, barking and showing a row of sharp white teeth.

Garcia dropped to the sidewalk on the other side her heart beating fast. The dog kept barking and jumping at the wall. Damn, that was close. Too close.

Garcia looked up and down the sidewalk. Empty. Lucky. Get moving. She hurried back to the Harley, hoping against hope that she hadn't left any calling cards.

Who could she tell that the national security advisor was having an affair with her brother-in-law? Anyone? Hell no, she couldn't tell anyone. Not a freaking soul. But worse yet, was Quinn in on something with Lannigan? How could she unravel this mystery when she couldn't confide in her boss? What a mess. Damn.

25

Galway, Ireland, 6:00 p.m.

As Zack and Shelia traveled toward Galway, something made Zack think about his father again. Had his dad been a hero, or had he been in the pocket of some slime-ball like O'Toole? That thought made him shudder. He'd never really admitted that possibility. Now, he knew he'd have to face up to it. Had to know the answer. Settle it once and for all.

Shelia glanced at Zack, her hands on the steering wheel. "What's the matter?"

"Thinking about my family." He didn't want to say anymore than that. Not now.

"Oh, Zack... ," Shelia reached over and put her hand on his arm. "Families can be tough to handle. I've been through plenty of those judgmental times myself."

"I know you have," Zack replied. "But enough of that. We need to focus on O'Toole and finding out all we can about the Irish internship."

"Maybe a Smithwick will help."

He had to laugh. "You never know until you try a tall cool one."

Zack watched the grazing goat herds as Shelia drove the curvy roads. After about three hours, they pulled into the outskirts of Galway, a young vibrant city on the west coast of Ireland. He'd kept watch in the mirror behind them as she drove and hadn't spotted anyone following them. If there were, they were pretty damn good.

Mary McGregor's house stood on the outskirts of town. Shelia had called ahead. Mary's father happened to be home and invited them to stop by.

The aging, red-brick two-story house stood in a row of identical houses in the midst of a development. Shelia pulled into the driveway and shut off the engine. "You'll enjoy the McGregors. I've known them for years."

As they walked up the front walk, they passed a tiny walled garden with plants popping up through the soil. When they reached the front door, a bearded man who looked as if his belly had held a lot of beer, threw open the screen. He wrapped Shelia up in his beefy arms. Everything about this man seemed huge. "Welcome, Shelia. I haven't seen you for way too long, little lass."

Shelia introduced Zack and they entered the house. The rooms were small, but spotless and decorated with wooden furniture. Mathew McGregor had prepared a pot of tea and offered a plate of cookies. The cookies tasted good.

After some small talk, Shelia told McGregor they'd seen Mary in Dublin. "I understand she'll be traveling to the States for an internship. That's wonderful for her."

McGregor bit his lip, then took a sip of tea. "I hope so."

"Why do you say that?" Zack asked.

"Just a feeling." McGregor looked down at his feet for a moment, then back up at Shelia. "This internship doesn't seem very well organized to me. I tried to check it out on the Internet without much success."

Shelia laughed. "You and the Internet? I didn't think the two of you ever got along."

"Well, that's true enough, but I'm making progress in that direction. And I wanted to make sure everything is just right for my Mary."

"I understand there are a number of students in the program," Zack said.

"Aye, that's true, but all of them are girls. I know that two of Mary's friends who are male and top students applied but weren't accepted. Now, why is that? Why only girls?"

Zack had the same question, although he was beginning to have a glimmer of an answer and he didn't like it. "What school in the States is sponsoring it?"

"That's another strange thing. It's not even sponsored by a college, but by some office in the federal judicial system. I told Mary she should ensure she'd get credit for her time, but how can she if there isn't any university involved?" He looked at Shelia. "How can she? Do you understand?"

Shelia took a sip of tea, seeming to pause before answering. "All I know is Mary seemed pretty excited about it when we saw her. I told her I'd love to be involved, too. She's going to see if she can get me a bit of information and an application."

"All she can see is an opportunity to go to the States," McGregor said. "She can't see past that."

"How long will she be gone?" Zack asked.

"That's the other thing. It seems to have a very flexible schedule. No official start date and no official end date. Just come when you can." His gaze searched Zack's face. "Does any of that seem right to you? Does it now?"

Zack stayed silent. He didn't want to share what he was thinking.

They spent another thirty minutes talking to McGregor, then Shelia looked at her watch. "I'm sorry, but we'd better go. Please tell your wife that I'm so sorry we missed her."

"She'll be upset. She would really love seeing you again. Things have changed so much since you and Mary used to run around the house playing and goofing off."

Shelia laughed, that musical laugh of hers. "We did, didn't we?"

They bid their farewells and waved to McGregor who stood in the doorway, light behind him, waving back.

As they walked down the front walk Zack asked, "What do you think?"

"To be honest, I have absolutely no idea what's going on. We're chasing shadows and all you'll probably do is risk getting yourself killed by kicking over rocks here." She reached over and took his hand. "And I wouldn't care much for that. Not a bit."

"Good to hear."

Shelia squeezed his fingers. "O'Toole is right. The Irish can carry grudges for a long time. What do you think we should do next?"

"By now Garcia and the police should have information on the shooter. With that, we could look up his family."

"Well now, you think they'll talk to you? They aren't going to be reasonable. You Americans have no understanding of the depth of family pride in Ireland. We've been crapped on by the British for so long that we tend to stick together. Outsiders can go to hell."

"Is there someplace we can go to get something to eat and maybe a beer or two while we think this through. You know, try and come up with some alternatives?"

"Let's drop our stuff at my parents' house, then drive back into town. We can head down to Eyre Square, which is the real hub of the city. Maybe after a beer or two one of us will come up with a brilliant idea. If not, we can go back to my parents' house and see what develops."

"Hopefully we won't be interrupted by someone with a gun and a hard-on for me."

It was Shelia's turn to laugh. "Let's hope you are the only one with the hard-on."

"If we're in the center of town, we should be safe, don't you think?"

"You have such faith."

They dropped off their bags and Zack checked out the building. Both the front and back doors had flimsy locks, and the windows could be easily forced. The house had no alarm system, but he could block the doors with a chair. He'd have to watch every step of the way.

Thirty minutes later, they arrived in Eyre Square and walked along the main drag. Normally not a shopper, Zack enjoyed looking into store windows. Clothes, shoes, musical instruments. The town vibrated with the vitality of youth moving around the city. A delightful place after all they'd been through. Zack still found himself checking out people who walked by. No one seemed to notice them or care what they were doing.

"About seventy-percent of the city is under twenty-five," Shelia said, "so it's an an exciting place to live in and to visit."

After about an hour of window shopping, they stopped at a pub with traditional Irish music and decided on a couple of pints. They both ordered Irish stew, Zack only now realizing how long it had been since he'd last eaten. The cookies were wearing thin.

"Do the spirits give you any leads on what we should be doing?" Zack asked.

Shelia leaned back and appeared to go into a trance, humming to herself. She opened her eyes, leaned toward him, and whispered, "The spirits told me you'd better watch your ass."

"You're really something, wee lass. Let's head back to your parents' house. Who knows what will happen."

Shelia leaned closer. "I think I have a pretty good idea. At least I hope so."

26

Arlington, Va, 11:00 p.m.

"Fifteen two, fifteen four, fifteen six, and a pair is eight." Zack's Aunt Mary raised her hands in the air with a loud whoop. "That's two games out of three, Theodore. Do you want to try and make it three out of five? I'm game if you are."

T.J. Wilson had to laugh. "Nope. You're the undisputed cribbage champ. I know when I've been trounced. But you'd better watch out, tomorrow night I'll make a comeback."

"Don't worry, I'll practice up and be ready for you." She stood and stretched. "Now, if you don't mind, I'm heading up to bed. I need to work out the cramps in my legs from all my sitting here and focusing on this game."

"Sounds good to me. You sleep tight. I think I'll watch a little TV first, then stretch out on the couch and doze off."

"Thanks so much for staying with us," Mary replied. "I don't know about Laura, but I certainly feel better having you around to keep an eye on us with all this stuff going on with Zack."

"Do you feel good enough to maybe let me win a cribbage game or two?"

"Don't be silly. Cribbage is an institution. You don't mess with an institution, and you sure don't let someone else win. At least I don't."

"Got it." Wilson pointed a finger at her, then walked over and turned on the TV. "I guess Laura is already asleep. I'll keep the volume low. See you in the morning."

Aunt Mary started up the stairs. "I'll make you some chocolate chip pancakes."

"My mouth is watering already." Wilson waited until Mary was upstairs before he stepped out onto the front porch. He stood there for a few minutes before he walked down the stairs and around to the back of the house. He needed to double check to make sure that everything stayed secure.

When he reached the back corner of the brick house, he saw a shadow. Pushing up against the wall he paused, then heard giggling. Waiting a few more minutes, he heard voices. They sounded soft and low enough so he couldn't tell what they were saying, but he sure as hell knew at least one of the voices. Miss Laura Kelly. Now what was she up to? Wilson was pretty sure he knew.

He stayed in the shadows as the two figures ran out of the backyard and down the street to a car. Wilson hurried around to the front door and locked it before getting into his own truck. The boy had parked his car three houses down the street. Wilson waited until the two drove off, then he started the truck and followed at a leisurely pace. Be kinda interesting to see where they went.

It took about ten minutes for them to reach a house and stop in front. Loud music blared from the windows and a number of kids were gathered on the front lawn laughing and dancing. Wouldn't be long before the cops got here. That's all Zack needed now. Bailing his daughter out of jail.

He waited a few minutes, then walked up the sidewalk toward the front door. Couldn't believe that someone hadn't called the cops before this. Standing by a tree, he waited, then walked to the screen door and pushed it open. Plenty of noise with kids dancing, making out, and drinking beer.

He walked through the crowd like a black Moses parting an ocean of white chippy faces. Most of the kids looked at him as if he were an alien from outer space, then they went back to whatever they were doing. He couldn't blame them. He'd done the same things years ago. Couldn't believe how many years that had been and how fast it had gone.

He pushed his way through the crowd until he reached the kitchen. Laura stood with her back to Wilson, drinking a beer.

He walked up behind her and tapped her on the shoulder. "Hey, Laura, how ya doing?"

She spilled part of the beer down the front of her shirt as she turned. "What...what are you doing here?"

"I guess I could ask you the same thing. Last time I checked, your aunt said you were tucked all warm and toasty in your bed. Something about school tomorrow."

"Oh, fuck, you're not going to tell on me, are you?"

He leaned against the fridge and crossed his arms over his chest. "Well, I guess that depends."

Laura's face seemed very pale. "On what?"

"On whether or not you leave with me now or try and stay longer."

Laura looked at her companion, a dark-haired young man in a sport shirt and a pair of jeans. Nice looking teen in fairly presentable clothes for a seventeen-year, maybe eighteen-year-old guy. "I'm sorry, but I guess I'd better leave." She set her beer on the kitchen table and weaved through the crowd, the boy following her, probably trying to figure out what was going on.

Wilson reached out to shake the young man's hand. "My name is Major Wilson, but my friends call me T.J.. What's yours?"

His hand disappeared in TJ's big mitt. "Ah, Matthew Johnson."

When they got outside, Wilson led them down the front steps and they stopped at the main sidewalk. "Well now, Laura and Matthew, what are we going to do about all this?"

Laura watched him, seeming to hold her breath. "You're not going to rat me out, are you?"

"Not a good idea for you two to stay here because it won't be long until the police raid the party. But if you were willing to go out and get a burger and a Coke, then make it home by one o'clock, I guess that would be okay. I assume you'd be able to fall out at first call for school in the morning, and fall out bright and cheerful."

Laura's face lit up. "Thanks. Oh, man, you're cool."

"See ya." Wilson turned and walked back to his truck, watching to make sure they did leave. After they drove off, he got back in his truck and drove slowly down the street, remembering the number of parties that had been raided in the District when he was seventeen. Didn't much care for that to happen to Laura and her boyfriend. He'd check to make sure Laura was home by one. Pretty sure she would be.

Yep, it was fun to be young, but could be painful too. He turned left onto Arlington Boulevard, heading back to Zack's. What was it that Laura had said? Nice to be cool in the eyes of that young woman. Not bad work for an evening. Not bad at all.

27

Galway, Ireland, Friday, 3:30 a.m.

The slender, curly-haired man climbed out of the car about halfway down the block from Shelia's parents' house. He strolled along the sidewalk, checking left then right for any people on the street. All quiet. Not surprising at this time of night. He needed to break into the house, do the job, and leave before the Garda arrived.

When he reached the yard next to his target, he stood behind a tree and studied the layout of the grounds. The house did not have a garage and it appeared only one door in the back and one in the front. A screened porch stood on the south side of the house and a light burned in one of the first-floor windows. He'd been told the parents were out of town and would not pose a problem.

The American had to be eliminated. Profits were coming in. Money would continue to flow. And this clown could ruin everything. If his partner had done it right the first time, this wouldn't be necessary. Now, it was up to him to finish the job.

A dog barked in the yard behind the house but other than that, everything seemed quiet. A fence ringed the yard and the gate in the center hung by only one hinge. He crept along the northern edge of the lot, staying in the shadows from the trees. Branches swayed as a gust of wind blew in from the water. He opened the gate and in about ten steps reached the back door.

Bending down, he looked around once more. Still all quiet. He placed his pick in the keyhole. In a matter of seconds, the mechanism snapped and the lock gave way.

The barking dog outside woke Zack who had slept in his clothes. He jerked up, instantly alert. Listened. Thought he heard a noise downstairs. Waited. Another noise? Yes. Someone had come inside through the back door.

He sat up. Reached over to shake Shelia and wake her.

She stirred, put her head back down. He touched her shoulder again. She looked up at him. He put his fingers to his lips.

She sat up, whispered, "What is it?"

"Someone's downstairs." Zack picked his M-9 off the bedside table and rolled out of bed. He crouched on the floor for a moment, staying low. "Call the police while I check it out."

She kissed his cheek. "Be careful, Zack."

He patted her arm. "Don't worry, I'm not interested in dying tonight."

Time to focus. Who waited downstairs? What sort of weapon did he have? Probably another professional?

Zack crept into the darkened hallway. Over the sound of the wind, he heard the scrape of boots on the tiled floor in the kitchen.

The house had two entrances. To be safe, Zack had put a chair to block the front door so the intruder must have come in through the back and had to be in the kitchen. Zack stayed low, creeping down the hallway. He looked over the banister but could see nothing in the darkness.

He reached the top of the stairs. Waited for the intruder to make his next move. Zack would only get one chance. He needed to make it count.

Another noise. The intruder must be moving through the kitchen and into the dining room.

Zack raised his pistol. Tense. Ready.

The intruder moved across the kitchen floor, careful not to bump into anything. He could hear the floorboards creak above him. Damn.

Target's alert and moving. Too bad. This would make it more difficult, but no need for a room-to-room search. Make it quick and get the hell out.

He raised his Glock and inched forward, his breathing slow and easy. Two more steps took him from the kitchen into the dining room. He pushed back against the wall, breathing controlled. Target at the top of the stairs.

He fired three shots upstairs, then ran and hit the steps two at a time. Bastard had killed his partner. He'd pay. Pay right now.

The bullets splintered the floor, ending up embedded in the wall. Zack dove back against the wall. He stayed near the top of the stairs. Fired three shots. Bad angle. One shot hit the wall, the others hit part way down the stairs. Heard footsteps on the stairs. Saw a figure at the landing outlined in the moonlight. Take him alive. "Drop the gun. Do it. Now."

The man dropped into a crouch, sliding down the stairs, his body bouncing against the wall.

Zack pulled himself around the corner at the top of the stairs. Fired three shots. Thought he heard a moan.

Footsteps sounded in the hallway. Zack flattened his body at the top of the stairs and fired three more shots.

The front door banged open. Zack fired again. Heard another moan. More running steps.

Zack slipped down the stairs and peeked around the front door frame. Saw the stranger running east down the street. Zack followed, afraid to shoot, afraid he might hit someone else.

Police sirens in the background. Three more shots from the stranger. Zack dropped down into a crouch. Rose and ran along the sidewalk. A car door slammed. Motor started. He took aim and fired at the car, shattering the rear window.

The car roared off, rear end swaying and tires squealing. Zack watched the car disappear around the corner as a police car came up the street from the opposite direction.

He turned and started back toward the house. Shouldn't have let the guy get away. Damn it all to hell.

———————

The police car pulled up to the curb and stopped, blue lights on the roof twirling. Two Garda officers jumped out. The closest officer had his gun drawn. He pointed it at Zack and yelled, "Drop the gun. Do it now."

Zack set his gun on the sidewalk and raised his hands. "My friend is the one who called you. Someone broke into the house and tried to kill us."

"What was the name of the person who called us?" the officer yelled.

"Shelia O'Donnell."

The officer stepped forward, his gun still aimed at Zack. "Are you all right?"

"Could you put that gun down before it goes off?"

The officer holstered his weapon as Shelia ran out of the front door and right into Zack's arms. Zack hugged her. "He's gone."

"Oh, Zack... ."

"I know, I know." He turned to the officers. "Let's go inside."

The two Garda followed him up the sidewalk as another police vehicle cruised down the street, siren blaring. By now, a crowd had started to form on the sidewalk and in the street.

A slightly chunky man in a dark brown suit got out of the second police vehicle and hurried up the sidewalk toward Zack. "Are you Kelly?"

"Yes, sir. Colonel Zack Kelly."

He introduced himself as Inspector Rourke. "I received a call last night from Detective Sergeant Powell in Dublin that you were planning on coming here today and might have a problem."

When they were seated on the couch in the living room, Zack summarized for the inspector what had happened.

"So you think someone in the Irish Mafia has put out a contract on you?" Rourke asked.

"That's right. O'Toole seemed aware of the contract, but wouldn't say anymore about it."

"Aye, that O'Toole is a nasty lad." Rourke made a note. "He had a leadership position in the IRA and has been in and out of jail since *The Troubles*. Don't think he'll ever be a productive citizen. I'm surprised you were able to meet with him and come out without a couple of bullet holes in your chest."

"That thought had crossed my mind but I tried to erase it."

Shelia started to shake. "I never erased it. We're both lucky to come out of this alive. I want to get out of here now. Tonight. I won't stay here another minute."

Rourke stood. "I agree with Ms. O'Donnell. You'd be better off leaving Ireland as soon as you possibly can."

"Can we leave Galway now?" Zack asked.

"I'm going to ask you to make a statement, then you'll be free to go. We'll put out an alert on O'Toole and bring him in, but he'll have an iron-clad alibi as to where he was tonight."

"Somewhere out there is a car with a shattered rear window."

Rourke made another note. "Did you happen to get the make of the car or a license number?"

Zack shook his head.

"We'll put out an alert, but by now the car's in a garage somewhere. And by this time tomorrow, it'll be in a lake or the window will be replaced. That's the way it is. Things never change here."

28

Westport, Ireland, Friday, 6:30 a.m.

When they arrived in Westport, Zack and Shelia found a coffee shop with wifi. After they ordered, Zack powered up his laptop. "I'm going to give Garcia the names of the women we believe to be part of the internship. Ask her to check them out and see when they entered the States and whether or not they're still in country. As far as I can tell, the first woman entered in March. Is that right?"

Shelia nodded. "How long can they stay in the country on a student visa?"

"Good question," Zack replied. "Garcia can find out from our State Department contact. Otherwise, it may work to Google it."

After he listed the names, he summarized the discussions they'd had earlier with Mary McGregor's father. Zack closed out the e-mail by providing their plans for the rest of the day and their proposed return time to the States.

Zack glanced over at Shelia. Her eyes kept closing. "Looks to me like you need another cup of coffee."

"True enough, but I'll pick up the pace after I finish my coffee and wolf down this roll."

"What do you think about getting a flight out tonight?"

"Not a bit too soon for me," Shelia replied. "I can't believe all that's happened to us in just a couple of days."

The waitress brought the pot over and filled their cups again. The caffeine hit the spot. Zack felt as if he might live.

"How well do you know Katie O'Shay's parents?" he asked.

She shook her head. "They're staying at the hotel here in Westport until their new house is ready. I called and talked to Katie's mother. Told her who I was, and that we'd like to talk with her."

Zack was having trouble sitting still. Too much to do. "What say we go."

"Fine with me, Mr. Colonel."

He loved her smile. "Looks like your humor is back."

"Coffee is a wonderful thing for the body and soul. Let's get it on, Mate, and move out."

Shelia found a place to park up the block from the Wyatt Hotel and they walked over. A five-story yellow building, it faced onto the Octagon in the center of town. No one seemed particularly interested in their arrival. Zack double-checked to make sure. Take no chances.

At the desk, they were directed upstairs. The hotel had long, curving hallways with dark blue carpets set off by freshly painted white walls.

Zack checked again to make sure no one followed them. "Nice-looking place. Looks new."

Shelia knocked and a tall woman opened the door. She had bright red hair and flashed a friendly smile. "You must be Colonel Kelly and Ms. O'Donnell." She motioned for them to enter.

The apartment had two bedrooms, but was bigger than that implied. It was decorated in bright colors. An Oriental carpet covered a portion of the wood floor. Sunshine shone through the sheer curtains covering the two windows in the living room.

"Please take a seat and for heaven's sake, call me Maggie."

Zack sat next to Shelia on the three-person beige couch. "We appreciate your time."

Maggie stepped over and picked up a plate of sweet rolls off the counter. "Would you like some rolls and perhaps a spot of tea?"

"Wonderful," Shelia replied.

After they were served, Maggie asked, "Now, how may I help you?"

Shelia took the lead. "I attended Trinity College with Katie and understand she's in the United States on an internship for pre-law students. Having just finished my fourth year, I'm thinking of applying. What can you tell us about the internship? What do you hear from her?"

"Katie got so excited when she first heard about it."

"How did she find out about it?" Zack asked, chewing on his roll. It hit the spot.

"Well, that's a good question." Maggie fluffed up her hair while she paused, then patted it down. "I'm really not sure. Apparently some of her friends had been accepted and were leaving sometime after spring break. Katie wanted to go, too."

"Was she accepted right away?" Zack asked.

"I was surprised when she called three weeks later and told me she'd been accepted."

"I imagine it's pretty expensive," Shelia said. "That would be a problem for me."

"Surprisingly, not that expensive. Apparently the fees are paid for as well as the airfare and accommodations once she gets to the States."

"Sounds almost too good to be true," Zack said.

Maggie stood and poured them each more tea. "My exact thoughts. I told Katie I'm suspicious when things seem that good."

"How's she doing?" Shelia asked. "Is she enjoying it?"

Maggie frowned as she sat back down. "We really haven't heard much from her. I got a letter right after she arrived, then nothing until about a week ago when I got a short note. It said that everything was fine and I shouldn't worry." She paused. "Sounded a little strange."

Zack admired the contemporary abstract paintings on two of the walls. "Ah, strange?"

"Very curt. Katie doesn't write like that. Her thoughts are normally more flowing. I've always looked forward to her letters. Anyway, I was glad to hear from her even if it was short."

"Do you have a way to contact her?" Zack asked.

She paused. "No, and I wish I did. The letter was postmarked from Washington, D.C., but she said she would contact me and that I shouldn't worry."

Shelia put her teacup on the end table next to the couch and stood. "Thanks so much for your time, Maggie. I hate to run off so quickly, but we have a couple of other stops and must get to the airport for a flight out tonight. I feel much better about applying now."

"Let me know if you get accepted. And for heaven's sake, when you get to the States, tell Katie to write me. I'm so worried about her."

Shelia hugged Maggie. "I will. And don't worry so much."

"You'll learn, my dear, that as a mother, one of my principal duties is to worry."

———

Rene Garcia sat at her desk in the Pentagon, planning out her next move. She'd forwarded the list of names that Zack had e-mailed her to the State Department, emphasizing how important it was for them to get right back to her. Blake's assistant had agreed to provide the list to the immigration staff and promised to expedite a reply.

Frustration surrounded her, closed in on all sides. Her efforts to find Blake had gone nowhere. Nowhere, dammit. Her friend had disappeared. And here she sat without a clue.

She'd sorted through much of the material she'd found at the Lannigans'. No way could she ask anyone for help because she wasn't supposed to have any of it. Zack would understand and help if he were here, but that didn't help her now.

It took a long time to wade through all the phone bills. One important thing she'd found had been numerous overseas calls. She'd have to follow up and find out who each of these contacts were, then compare notes with Zack when he returned. Damn it, Zack, hurry up and get back here.

Now, how to handle what she'd found out about Darcy Quinn and Sean Lannigan. Could she trust General Hightower with the information? Hell no, what would he do with it? What Quinn did on her own time was her business. But, they were investigating Lannigan. What if she found out something about him and it involved Quinn? What the hell would she do then? Best not to think about that. At least not yet. Take it one step at a time.

While she waited, she thought about Cliff Henderson. She'd had to cancel an earlier dinner because of checking out Sean Lannigan. Now, she thought, maybe it would be fun to get together.

Her cell phone rang.

"Hey, Garcia, it's Mandy at the State Department." Mandy was Blake's administrative assistant and very upset about what had happened to her boss.

"That was fast," Garcia said. "What did you find out?"

"It's kinda weird."

"Uh-oh," Garcia replied, her cop nose twitching. "Weird? I'm not sure I'm ready for weird. I'm already up to my neck in weird."

Mandy chuckled. "Well, ready or not, here it comes. These women have all been admitted to the United States under some special program for a period of three months. But if I count right, two of them are right at the three-month mark and a couple seem to be over it."

"Do you have any idea where they're staying?"

"Just a minute." The sound of papers rustling. "It's an address in Georgetown." She read off the exact number and street.

Garcia leaned back, shocked. "Would you repeat that?"

"Sure." Mandy read the numbers again. "Anything else."

Garcia exhaled, not sure what to make of it. "Let me stew on this for awhile."

Mandy sighed. "Be careful. You might want to wait until General Hightower can get a team together to check it out."

"Oh, sure."

"Yeah, yeah. The trouble is that I know you. You never wait for anyone. In this case, something big is happening. I can feel it. Lots of political influence. You could get burned. At least bring General Hightower into the equation, okay?"

"Yeah, okay. And thanks."

"Oh," Mandy said. "What have you found out about Blake? I'm so worried about her."

"We're working on it but no big breaks yet. We'll find her, Mandy."

"Yeah, but I don't want it to be too late."

"Okay, thanks again." Garcia disconnected the phone. She sat back and thought about all Mandy had told her.

The address of the Irish internship turned out to be only two blocks from where Blake's parents lived. Blake's family were Irish. Blake was missing. Two blocks away was this amorphous Irish internship. Was that a coincidence? She reminded herself that she didn't believe in them. Time to drive over and check it out. Then she'd be ready to brief Zack when he returned in the morning.

As she stepped out into the hall, her cell rang again. "Colonel Garcia."

"Hey, it's Cliff Henderson."

Something deep inside of her tingled when she heard his voice. "Hi, Cliff. What can I do for you?" Did that sound as cardboard as she thought?

"I was just thinking about you."

Her heart skipped a beat. "You were?" She kicked herself for sounding like some fifteen-year-old wallflower.

"We didn't get a chance to have that second dinner the other night. I hoped we might be able to get together this week sometime."

She needed to check out that house, but she did want to have dinner with him. "How about tonight?"

"That's what I was thinking. Could you make six o'clock?"

Garcia couldn't help but smile. "Sure. Cozy Inn? Halfway for both of us."

"Great. Look forward to it."

"See you then."

Garcia disconnected her cell. She should check out the lead on the Irish internship. But she thought about what her friends kept telling her. Garcia, you gotta get a life, girl. She had to smile. Well, maybe this girl was about to get a life.

Hell, the two of them could check the lead out tomorrow when Zack got back. She'd stop by her condo, maybe pack a bag, take care of Harold, then head out. On her way down the hall, she tried not to think about Blake.

29

American Embassy, Dublin, Ireland, 2:00 p.m.

Shelia pulled up to the front gate at the American Embassy. The Marine guard stepped out and greeted them. He checked Zack's ID, then Shelia's.

"I called ahead," Zack said, "and made an appointment with Colonel Reilly. Also, Colonel Reilly loaned me a weapon. I'd like to turn it in along with two clips of ammunition."

"I'll be glad to take it," the guard said. "I do need to verify with Colonel Reilly that this is what she gave you." He ran his finger down a list. "Here you are. I'll call and let her know you're here."

"Tell her I expended ten rounds."

In a minute he waved them through. "You can park over there. I told her about the weapon and she said that was fine. She'll meet you in the lobby."

When the two walked up the steps and opened the front door, Colonel Reilly hurried down the tiled staircase toward them. She wore her field uniform. "Welcome back. Sergeant Powell should be here any minute."

Zack shook hands with her. "You must be headed out to the field today."

"Yep. I'm glad you called ahead because after we're done here, I'm off to review a training exercise. Please come up to my office."

When they entered, Reilly closed the door and motioned for them to take a seat. "How about a cup of good Irish coffee before you leave this beautiful country?"

"Wonderful," they said in unison.

As Reilly drew two cups, a knock sounded on the door. Sergeant Powell walked in. "Inspector Rourke called and told me about the attack in Galway. I'm glad I called ahead and warned the local Garda you might have a problem."

"Good thing Rourke knew who we were," Zack replied. "Made it easier for us to tell our story and make a hasty exit before anything else happened."

"Rourke only gave me a summary. Please fill in the details for me."

Zack took a sip of coffee and could feel the caffeine pulsating through his veins. He needed the hit. "I'm convinced what happened in Galway is somehow tied to the incidents in the States. There's too much that doesn't make sense about the Irish internship. O'Toole implied that what happened to me is tied to the internship."

Powell scratched his chin. "Well, now, that's interesting."

"Right. He said that if I solved one, the other would fall into place. Also, he told me to watch out for political pressure. I believe the only thing that saved our lives during the meeting with O'Toole had to be the pass we got from Terry McHugh. Without that, who knows what he'd done."

"Let me tell you what I know." Powell stared at Zack for a moment, rubbing his chin again, "The Irish internship began about a year ago. As far as I can tell, this could be the third group. I talked to the professor at Trinity College who's in charge of the program. He says it's pretty informal."

"Somehow they've managed to keep it under wraps," Shelia said. "I hadn't heard anything about it from my friends at Trinity, and I saw many of them at least a couple of times a week."

Powell walked over and look out the window for a minute. "From what the professor said, some administrator at the federal courthouse in Washington contacted him. The administrator asked if there were female interns who might be interested in spending the summer in D.C. and learning about the federal court system."

"Only females?" Zack asked.

Powell nodded. "When he asked why only females, the guy in D.C. said that housing was a problem. They didn't want to mix males and females."

Colonel Riley snorted, almost choking on her coffee. "What a bunch of crap. Kids get mixed up all the time at the college level. My daughter is at the University of Iowa and all of their dorms are coed. Scares the hell out of me, but that's the way it is. His answer sounds phony to me."

"I agree," Powell added. "But I couldn't say much."

Zack took another sip of coffee. "When we get back, I'll check it out and e-mail you what I find."

"That would be great," Powell said. "And we'll keep you advised from our end."

Shelia finished her coffee. "I'll give you the list of my friends who are there now and also friends who are still here at Trinity. Maybe you can follow up with them. We may have missed something important."

"I provided the list of names to Colonel Garcia in the Pentagon," Zack said. "She's checking it out with the immigration folks from our end. When I get the results, we can compare notes."

"Aye. That would be helpful."

Zack looked at his watch. "We'd better get going if we're to catch our plane." He reached out to shake Reilly's hand. "Thanks again for the weapon. It probably saved my life."

"I'm glad you had it." Reilly stood. "Good luck to both of you."

"And be careful," Powell cautioned. "I've learned from bitter experience when the Mafia is involved, things change fast."

30

Dulles Airport, Washington, D.C. Saturday, 6:15 a.m.

The Aer Lingus flight from Dublin To Washington lasted six hours. Zack typed a briefing for Darcy Quinn and General Hightower on his laptop. Shelia added the names of the women who had joined the internship. Hopefully Garcia would have more detailed information on them.

Zack closed his computer and turned to Shelia. "This damn Irish internship has consumed too much of our time the last three days, way too much. I hope that Garcia has developed some clues about what happened to Blake. She's been gone a week now. I still can't believe it."

"Do you think she disappeared on purpose?" Shelia asked.

"I hate to say it," Zack replied, "but that idea has popped into my mind. The problem is she's got a head full of classified materials. I'm sure the security guys are sweating bullets."

"I don't think she'd do that. It's just not Blake."

"I can't see it either. The other possibility I've been mulling around is that she found out about the Irish internship and someone had to get her out of the way. With the possible tie between her disappearance and my attack, that makes sense. I put that alternative in my briefing."

Shelia bit her lip. "Is there any chance she could be working for another government? Maybe Ireland?"

Zack rubbed his chin. "What would be her motivation to do that?"

"Damn, boy, she's Irish. Maybe someone twisted her arm. Blackmailed her."

"You Irish are supposed to be our friends," Zack replied. "Why would she spy for the Irish government against us?"

She folded her hands and put her head down. "Just thinking."

They lapsed into silence. Zack didn't know how to express his feelings. Finally, he reached over and took her hand. "You know, I've become pretty fond of you."

Shelia smiled, a teary haze covering her eyes. "Zack, I'm really falling for you. I don't know what to do about it."

Zack squeezed her hand. "As a good Irish friend of mine once said, don't over analyze it. Just go with the flow and see where it takes you."

That got a smile. "Guess I'm better at giving advice than taking it."

"Let's go with it, then we can pick it up once this is over. See where we are."

Shelia nodded.

Zack realized he might not be able to take his own advice. What if Shelia were in danger? He couldn't let that happen. "You know that my daughter, Laura, lives with me in Arlington."

Shelia nodded. "I'd heard that. What's she like?"

"A fun kid. Almost seventeen, but acts a whole lot older. At least sometimes."

That brought another smile. Zack loved her smile. It made her whole face come alive.

He kissed her cheek. "You are one beautiful woman."

She kissed him back. "You're quite a package yourself."

He told her about Laura, then about his ex-wife in jail on drug charges back in Minneapolis. The missing dad as he was growing up, the rumors about what had happened. The long separations from his family due to his job, finally the nastiness of the divorce. Things he hadn't ever told anyone else, not even Garcia.

"How are you dealing with the backlash from the war?" she asked.

Zack froze up for a moment, then decided to let her in a little. "I spent one tour in Iraq and three in Afghanistan. Each night we would respond to intelligence about Taliban leaders or fighters who were preparing to attack our soldiers."

"Must have been very stressful."

Zack nodded. "We'd head out, normally around midnight when we figured the targets were asleep. I'd deploy my guys around the area and then send in a small force. Sometimes it would be clean and we'd get the guy, other times it got pretty messy."

"And those are the faces that haunt you?"

Zack nodded.

"Are you getting help?"

"I'm lucky. Doc Hale has been great."

"Zack, I can see the faces. They surround you. Maybe between the two of us we can figure out what it's going to take to send them up to the light and get them away from you."

Zack looked away again. Now wasn't the time to start on that subject. He placed his arm around her and she leaned her head on his shoulder. Together the two of them drifted off into a quiet sleep until the flight attendant came through the cabin to announce their arrival at Dulles.

Zack and Shelia drove from the airport along the Dulles Expressway into the Pentagon for the seven o'clock meeting with General Hightower. Even with just a few hours sleep on the plane, Shelia still looked beautiful. Beautiful to Zack. Zack, on the other hand, felt that he looked like shit. He'd worn the same outfit for three days. Needed to get home and change.

When Zack opened the door to the conference room and escorted Shelia inside, Barton Morgan and T.J. Wilson looked up from their discussions. Blake's administrative assistant, Mandy Polk, typed on her laptop. She waved when they entered.

"Hey, stranger, welcome back," Wilson called. "I thought you were going to become a permanent resident of Ireland. Nice blazer by the way. Trying to look like a real person?"

"It'll be nice to get back in uniform," Zack replied. "I'll have to say that when those clowns weren't shooting at me, I enjoyed myself in Ireland, and would like to go back one day."

Shelia smiled. Wilson glanced at Zack, didn't say anything, but wiggled his eyebrows.

"Thanks for keeping an eye on Laura for me. I really appreciate it. Took that burden off my mind. Anything happen?"

"All quiet. She's a great kid. Little bit of a wild streak."

"No kidding. I had to bail her out of another fight at school last week."

"I really enjoyed getting to know your Aunt Mary. She's a pistol. We played cribbage every night." He laughed. "I have yet to beat her, but she told me she might take it a little easier on me next time. Who knows, maybe she'll even let me win a game."

"Don't believe that for a minute," Zack said. "She's one competitive lady."

General Hightower entered the room. Everyone stood. "Hey, Zack and Shelia, welcome back. Let's sit down and compare notes."

Zack looked around. "Where's Garcia?"

Hightower shook his head. "I don't know. She knew about the meeting."

Wilson pulled out his cell. "I'll give her a quick call."

"Well," Hightower said, "let's get started. Garcia can catch up later."

Zack summarized the trip, starting out with the briefing at the American Embassy, including the Garda, then the meeting with McHugh. He glanced at Wilson. "Did you get a hold of Garcia?"

"Only voicemail. She always answers unless she's stuck in a meeting. I'll feel better when she walks in that door."

An uneasy feeling crept over Zack as he refocused on his briefing. He took a few more minutes to summarize the meeting with O'Toole, then the shootout at Shelia's house.

"Was anyone hurt?" Hightower asked.

"I think I winged the guy, but I'll probably never know for sure."

"What did the police have to say?" Hightower asked.

"When we got to the Embassy," Zack continued, "I told Sergeant Powell the whole story. He's with the Special Branch of the Garda. That's like our FBI. He plans to follow up on everything from their end, and we'll stay in contact with him. Good guy."

"Great," General Hightower said. "We need a point of contact in Ireland."

Zack took a sip of coffee. "Now, let me tell you about the Irish internship."

He shared the background of what he knew, then talked about meeting with the parents of the two women in the internship. "The parents all seemed concerned because they hadn't heard much from their daughters."

Mandy pulled sheets of paper out of her briefcase and handed one to each attendee. "Garcia had me check out the ten names you gave her."

"What did you find out?" Hightower asked.

"As you can see, the interns have all applied for visas to enter the country. What's interesting is that they seemed to get special treatment. Must know someone important." She smiled. "Way above my pay grade."

"What do you mean?" Hightower asked.

"There's a standard waiting period to gain approval for a visa. The applications for these women flew through the process, and their visas are open ended. Doesn't appear to be an expiration date like normal. Very unusual."

"Do you have the location of where this internship is being held?" Zack asked.

She looked down at her laptop and read off the address. "I gave it to Colonel Garcia last night when I talked to her."

Zack leaned forward, suddenly on red alert. "Damn, I wonder if she went over there by herself?"

"Knowing Garcia," Wilson said, "I bet she did."

"Do you see any tie between the internship and Blake's disappearance?" Hightower asked.

"Yes, I do," Zack replied. "The best link I can come up with is that Blake's family is Irish, her father is a Federal judge on his way to the Supreme Court, the internship is sponsored by our Federal judiciary, and these Irish college girls are getting special treatment. Furthermore, when I talked to O'Toole, he implied that the shooting and the internship might be related."

Hightower paused, fingers pointing under his chin. "You can't believe that Sean Lannigan kidnapped his own daughter."

"No, I don't," Zack replied. "But what if some deal fell through and the Irish Mafia kidnapped her. I'm considering the possibility of them forcing these girls into prostitution. You know, a white slavery ring."

Hightower raised his eyebrows. "Sean Lannigan can't be involved in something like that, but I guess it's an angle we need to look at."

Wilson leaned forward. "Why would the Mafia shooter go after you if they're the ones who kidnapped her?"

"Great question," Zack replied. "But what if they thought I was getting too close to something important?"

The room got silent as they all considered that option.

"But you weren't," Wilson replied. "Hell, you didn't know anything."

Zack nodded. "Ah, but they didn't know that."

"All right," Hightower said, "here's what I think we should do. Garcia briefed the FBI agent working the Irish Mafia issue, and the FBI agent working Blake's disappearance. Zack, I want you to talk to both of them. Make sure they're coordinating. I wouldn't be surprised if you had to introduce them to one another. Let them know the angle we plan to look at. Tie them into that Garda sergeant."

Zack made notes on his pad, highlighting the action items. "Sergeant Powell."

"Right," Hightower replied. "We've got to shake this damn tree. Blake has been missing for a week. That's unacceptable. We've got all of these resources. Let's make use of them."

"What about Garcia?" Zack asked.

Hightower bit his lip. "I'll call and have the police check her condo. Maybe she's sick."

"I don't believe anything would keep her from this meeting unless she was in trouble. Let me go over to the address of the internship and see what I can find."

"I'll go along with Zack," Wilson said.

"What about me?" Shelia asked.

Hightower paused for a moment. "How about if you check to see if Ms. Quinn is at the White House and has time to meet with you. Update her on everything you found out in Ireland, then highlight for her what our plans are."

Shelia nodded "Will do."

"Be sure to tell her we're unable to find Garcia." Hightower pointed at Zack. "I don't want you going inside that house. Not yet. Not until we know more."

Wilson stood. "I'll keep a strong arm on Kelly so he doesn't get any of his far-out ideas."

Zack couldn't shake the thought. *What if Garcia's in trouble?*

31

Georgetown, 9:30 a.m.

After stopping at his house to drop off his stuff and change, Zack cut across the Potomac River on the Key Bridge. The month of June had erupted on Washington and the summer tourist season would stay in full bloom until fall. Traffic, what a pain in the butt.

T.J. Wilson looked up from the map in his lap and pointed to his left. "The house should be a block up that street, right off 31st."

A couple walking their cocker spaniel crossed the street in front of them. Zack waited for them to pass. A half block later, he tapped the brake and slowed his truck to a stop across the street from the house.

Ivy crept up the dark-red brick walls surrounding the mansion, partially hiding the towering brick house. A wrought iron gate stood at the front and blocked the driveway. There appeared to be some sort of security camera on the wall next to the gate. Could there be sensors? Zack wasn't sure, but he needed to find out.

From this angle he could see through to the circular driveway that looped past the front steps. The door was framed by round marble pillars. Zack whistled. "Whoever lives here has big bucks."

"No shit," Wilson replied. "Place must take up at least a quarter of the block. What do you think we ought a do?"

Zack gave the truck a little gas. "Let's stay across the street, heading toward the gate. That way, if someone of interest comes out we can follow them."

He turned the truck around and shut off the engine. "This looks good. We can see the house, but we're screened by that oak from anyone in the house looking out through the window. Not much else to do. Guess we wait."

Wilson leaned back. "Stakeouts are so goddamn boring. Should have stopped for coffee. That'd at least keep me awake."

"Big night?" Zack asked, then yawned.

"Not bad. Went dancing with the school teacher again. Man, that lady is one hell of a dancer. I could barely keep up with her."

"That's at least four dates." Zack smiled. "Getting serious?"

"Good question. I'll have to admit she's not bad."

A regular stream of traffic flowed up and down 31st Street, but Zack spotted no action at the house. He had an uneasy feeling. "If Garcia came here last night, her Harley should either be out on the street or in the compound."

Wilson opened the door of the truck. "Let me walk around a little and see if I can spot it. I need to get off my dead end and move around anyway."

Ten minutes later he sauntered back down the sidewalk, whistling a tune. When he climbed in, he said, "Nada. Didn't see Garcia's Harley or a military staff car. If she's here, either they got rid of the bike or it's tucked inside somewhere. Thing is, they're not going to leave it around outside for people like us to see."

Zack snapped his fingers, startling Wilson. "I've got it. I'll hurry up to the gate and ask for General Hightower. Tell them I'm late for an appointment to meet him for an important meeting. That'll work. Looks like the sort of a place where a General would hang out."

"I don't like it, Zack. Hightower told us to check it out but not go inside."

"I'm not going inside, I'm just asking for someone." He smiled. "Then I'll leave."

"You're so full of shit. I told Hightower I'd sit on you, but I've obviously failed."

"T.J., this is Garcia we're taking about. I can't just sit here on my hands while she might be in trouble." Zack opened the door, leaned back inside. "Besides, it's no problem for you. You tried to stop me and can testify to that fact at my court martial."

"Yeah, right. That'll be a big help when Hightower chews my ass."

Zack hurried up to the gate, looking at his watch. He glanced around but didn't see any buzzer or bell. There was a camera attached to the upper portion of the wall, so whoever ran security should see him. The guy would probably hot foot it outside to stop him.

He turned the handle and pushed on the gate. It creaked open, surprising Zack. What the hell, he thought, why not walk up to the door and see what happens.

Zack had just stepped through the gate when a Doberman, probably waist-high, tore around the corner of the house, barking, teeth bared, eyes fixed on Zack. Zack's heartbeat shot up to full tilt. Oh, shit. He stopped. Waited. The dog pulled up within about ten feet of Zack and stood still, growling.

The front door opened and a heavyset man in a black suit walked toward Zack. His blunt nose looked as if he'd been in one too many fights and lost them all. Reminded Zack of one of the soldiers in *The Godfather* movie.

The big man stopped about three feet in front of Zack. "Who the hell are you? You're not supposed to be in here."

"I've got an appointment with General Hightower." Zack looked at his watch. "Supposed to meet him here at ten o'clock, and I'm running a little late. Damn D.C. traffic. Hope he's not too pissed. Guy's never supposed to keep a general waiting."

That made the man stop for a moment. He didn't seem as if he were used to thinking much. "There's no Hightower here. Now turn around and leave."

Zack noticed a lump under the man's left arm. Clown was carrying. "Isn't this the Hightower house? I'm sure it's the address he gave me."

"No General Hightower here, buddy."

Zack watched the man. "I guess I've got the wrong house. I'd better check my directions."

"Yeah, you'd better. Good way to get your ass bit off by one of our dogs."

"Okay, sorry to have bothered you." Zack turned and looked around at what he could see of the compound. Three cars, two Mercedes and a Lexus stood parked in the driveway, but no Harley and no military staff car. He'd like to check around back for the Harley but wasn't sure how to do that.

Zack decided to push a little. "Are you sure? This is the address he gave me. He's really going to be pissed at me if I miss the meeting. You know how that can be."

"There is no General Hightower here. You'd better leave right now before the boss wonders what you're doing here."

"Oh," Zack replied. "Can I meet him? Maybe he knows the General."

The man smiled, lots of gold showing in his teeth. "Take it from me, buddy, you don't want to meet the boss. She'd kick your ass."

Zack figured he'd pushed as far as he could. "Okay, thanks for your time. See you."

He stepped out on the sidewalk and reached back to pull the gate shut. The man watched. The dog growled. With the gate between him and the dog, Zack relaxed.

When he got back to the truck, Wilson asked, "Well?"

"The guy looked like a hood to me. I know these hotshot places can have pretty unusual security, but this guy looked Mafia. Somehow, I think we're in the right place."

"What now?" Wilson asked.

"Let's drive around the block and check the back. Doubt we'll see much but I don't know what else to do and I hate to leave."

As Zack pulled out from the curb, his cell rang. "Kelly."

"This is General Hightower. I just received a call from Chief Munson. One of his police cars picked up Blake Lannigan about an hour ago walking along a road west of Gettysburg."

32

Gettysburg, 12:30 p.m.

Zack and Wilson rolled into Gettysburg exactly two hours and seven minutes after Zack had spoken to General Hightower. He pulled into the parking lot next to the borough building and slammed on the brakes. Zack opened the door. "Let's go."

When the two got inside, Zack hurried to the reception desk. "I need to see Chief Munson right away."

The officer looked up, a bored look on his face. "He's pretty busy. Is he expecting you?"

Zack almost pulled the man out of his chair. "He called General Hightower in the Pentagon a couple of hours ago. Munson said he'd be here and he damn well better be."

"All right, relax. I'll check." The officer dialed and talked on the phone. When he hung up he said, "He'll be right here. You can take a seat over there."

Zack stood next to the desk, tapping his foot. He wasn't going to sit around and wait for anyone. Munson needed to get his ass out here before Zack and Wilson beat down his damn door.

Munson came out of his office and walked down the hallway, hand extended. "Colonel Kelly, I guess you heard the good news about Ms. Lannigan."

Zack shook hands with him. "Great news. That's what we wanted to talk to you about." He pointed at Wilson. "This is Major Wilson. I don't think you met him before. Last weekend he was the one flying the chopper looking for Blake."

Munson shook hands with Wilson. "Nice to meet you, Major. Please come back to my office. We can talk there."

Munson's office looked to be the standard public servant setting. A gunmetal gray desk with two chairs in front, a round conference table with five chairs around it, and a couch with small tables at either end. He motioned for them to take a seat at the conference table. "Coffee?"

"That would be great," Zack replied. "Been a long morning for both of us."

After they were seated, Munson said, "I got the call about eight o'clock this morning. One of my patrols came across a woman walking along the Cashtown Road."

"Cashtown Road?" Now that's interesting Zack thought. Why Cashtown Road?

"That's right. He recognized Mr. Lannigan from the APB we'd put out and stopped behind where she was walking, apparently startling her. The officer radioed in the information, got out, and asked her if she was Blake Lannigan."

Zack leaned forward, wanting to put a firecracker under Munson's butt. He motioned with his hand to hurry him up. "And?"

"She said she was."

Wilson's eyes widened. "Blake knew who she was?"

"That's right," Munson replied. "My officer told her that we'd been looking for her for the past week."

"Did she seem surprised by that?" Zack asked.

"Yes. She said she didn't remember what happened to her. Then, this morning she found herself walking along the road not sure why or where she was."

Zack swallowed before asking the next question. "Did she tell the officer what happened to her the night she disappeared?"

Munson walked over to his desk and picked up a sheet of paper. When he sat down again he scanned it, then said, "The report says that she remembers coming to Gettysburg with you. It seems the last thing she remembers is eating dinner at the restaurant on the square. Apparently she does remember discussing the Devil's Den and perhaps seeing a ghost, but has absolutely no memory of finishing dinner, or driving out to see Devil's Den."

This threw Zack off for a moment. He expected her to remember the details of what happened. He'd assumed she'd be able to fill in the blanks for him. Now she didn't remember any more than he did and that wasn't enough to sort this mess out.

Wilson followed up. "Did she say where she was coming from when the officer found her?"

"That's another funny thing. Ms. Lannigan said she found herself walking on the road. No memory of where she'd started from. None at all."

"What did she act like?" Zack asked. "Did it appear that she'd been drugged? You know, what was she like?"

"The officer said she seemed in perfect control of her faculties. Spoke clearly. Walked normally."

Zack couldn't believe it. "Except she has no idea where she's been for the past week."

Munson leaned back and took a sip of coffee. "Guess that's right."

"Did you talk with her?" Wilson asked.

He nodded. "They called me as soon as the officer radioed in his report. I drove right over. I'll have to say she seemed perfectly fine to me. The only strange thing was that memory gap."

Zack took another sip of coffee, trying to sort out what to ask next.

"There is another funny thing about this," Munson said.

"What's that?" Zack asked.

"She didn't have on the clothes you described her wearing when she disappeared. She had on a pair of jeans, a long-sleeved pink shirt, and a pair of black tennis shoes."

"What?" Zack exclaimed. "Where the hell did she get another set of clothing?"

"I asked her. She said she figured that's what she'd been wearing all along."

"Were they wrinkled?" Wilson asked. "Like she'd worn them for a week?"

Munson shook his head. "I didn't think of that. But since you mentioned it, the outfit seemed fresh. You know, neat and pressed."

Zack studied the certificates on Munson's wall. Where the hell did she get the change of clothes? His mind spun. This was crazy. "Did you notify Agent Spitz?"

"Right away. He'll be interviewing her at Walter Reed after he's done here." Silence for a moment, then Munson said, "I know what you're thinking. I feel the same way. This is the craziest case I've ever tried to handle. I have absolutely no idea what to do next."

No doubt in Zack's mind that Spitz would assume that Zack had been behind this. "Well I'm going to figure this thing out if it's the last thing I do."

Munson leaned forward. "After I made sure who she was, I called General Hightower. He seemed as surprised as the rest of us that she had no memory of what happened. He asked if I would hold her long enough for him to dispatch a medical helicopter to pick her up."

"And did you?" Zack asked.

"Right. She didn't seem in a hurry to go anywhere."

Wilson crossed his legs. "Did she know General Hightower?"

"Yes. As a matter of fact she talked to him on the phone for a moment."

"What then?" Zack asked.

"The General said he planned to have her evaluated at Walter Reed. That made sense to me so I agreed and she was fine with that. I got her breakfast and the chopper picked her up about an hour ago." He looked at his watch. "She ought to be at Walter Reed by now."

Zack took another sip of coffee. Time to change the direction of the discussion. "Ah, when is the last time you saw Colonel Garcia?"

"Why do you ask?"

Zack didn't like Munson's tone. He sounded defensive. "I need to find out if she's been down here in the last day or so."

"I haven't seen her since around noon last Wednesday. To be honest, I got a little frustrated with her. She asked the mayor about me. Kinda questioned whether or not I was doing my job."

Time to push a little. He had to make something happen with Garcia missing. "Do you think there's more you could have done to find Blake?"

Munson's face reddened. "Listen, Kelly, I don't appreciate your tone. I've been straight up with you and all the other military guys. Our department did everything we could. Handled it as a special case and all the time having the FBI crawling all over us. So knock it off."

"I understand your department is under severe budget constraints."

"That's right. Who isn't?"

"Having a front-page case like this would certainly add to the visibility of the department. Maybe bring in a few more resources."

Munson stood and walked toward the door. "I've had about enough of you, Kelly. It's time for you two to get the hell out of my office."

Zack faced him. "I'm going to find out what happened to Blake. Somebody did something to her, and I'm going to find out who."

———

By the time Zack and Wilson reached the Visitor's Center, it was almost four. "I hope to hell he's still here."

Wilson looked at his watch. "Hell, he should be. These guys don't have those kind of great hours on a Saturday, do they?"

"Maybe that's why he left the military."

Wilson glanced at Zack. "Did he skate on time?"

"Nah, only kidding." Zack thought about that for a moment. Henderson had worked hard and handled the interrogations of captured Taliban suspects effectively. Tough as hell when he needed to be and knew how to work with captives, too.

Zack and Wilson walked up the winding cement walk to the front door. People flooded in and out, laughing, shouting. Kids ran around, pushing one another and goofing off.

Zack spotted Henderson at the dining area behind the Starbucks. Henderson waved them over. "Grab yourself a cup and pull up a chair."

When they got to the table, Zack said, "Guess you heard that one of Munson's patrols found Blake Lannigan walking along Cashtown Road."

"Yeah. I drove out to the site right away, but didn't see anything unusual other than a bunch of cops running around in circles. I understand they found her wandering along the road. Good thing a police officer spotted her and put it together. How's she doing?"

"I'm not sure. She should be at Walter Reed by now. I'll try and visit her later today." Zack took a sip of coffee. "Have you seen Rene Garcia recently?"

"Not for a couple of days. After talking to the mayor, she dropped by to question me. Nice lady. Thorough as hell."

"She is that," Zack said. "Like the proverbial dog on a bone. Doesn't let anything go until she gets all the facts."

Henderson tried to hide a smile. "I enjoyed talking to her, even invited her out to dinner."

"When was that?" Zack asked.

"Let's see." He rubbed his chin. "Must have been Wednesday evening."

Wilson smiled. "Sounds to me like you two might have hit it off."

"Well, she's pretty, smart, and fun. I enjoyed her company and hope to see her again." He squinted at Zack. "Why do you ask?"

Zack took another sip of coffee trying to determine how much to share with Henderson. Finally he decided to come clean. "She seems to be missing."

Henderson frowned. "What do you mean, missing?"

"No one's seen her since she talked to one of our task force members Friday afternoon."

Henderson almost spilled his coffee. "What?"

"Yeah. What?"

"That's terrible. Did the staffer have any idea where she might have been going after he talked to her? Any leads?"

Zack shook his head. "Not a clue. They were discussing another case we're working. I suspect she may have gone over to visit that site. No one's heard a damn thing from her after that. I have to tell you, I'm worried as hell."

"Maybe you should go check that place out."

"I did. Couldn't find a damn thing."

"What can I do to help?" Henderson asked.

"I'll let you know if I can think of anything." Zack paused. "Do you have any idea what might have happened to Blake here? Anything. No matter how small it may seen."

"Damn thing is too weird. What say we drive out and look at where the officer found her. Maybe we'll spot something the cops missed."

Zack tossed his cup in the trash. "Let's go, time's wasting. We can take two vehicles."

When the three arrived at the site, police officers and people in civilian clothes stood around, snapping pictures, measuring, taking samples. Police cars. Sheriff's vehicles. Long ribbons of yellow, crime-scene tape. A couple of white vans and a number of guys walking around with FBI stenciled on the back of their blue jackets.

"Why all the activity?" Wilson asked.

Henderson shook his head. "I can't imagine they'll find anything, but one of the local cops told me they were hoping to come up with a lead. They've been interviewing people who live in the area. We should be able to get an update now." He walked up to one of the FBI guys and shook hands, then motioned Zack over. "This is Agent Henley Spitz. Henley, Zack Kelly from the Pentagon."

"Yeah," Zack said. "We met at the press conference."

"What are you doing here, Kelly?" Spitz asked.

"I heard that Blake reappeared. Wanted to see if I could find out what happened to her."

"You're still on my short list. This case reeks."

Guy pissed Zack off, but he had to play nice and pump Henley for information. "I'm so glad you're still thinking of me. Have you come up with anything yet?"

Spitz looked at his crew, probably debating what he could tell Zack. "Why do you want to know?"

"You know damn well we want to find out what happened to her. Now, what can you tell me?"

Spitz stared at Zack for a moment. "Some evidence, but not much. The police officer who picked her up thought maybe her car had broken down. But then he recognized her."

"Did she seem drugged?"

Spitz squinted at him. "Why would you ask that?"

Zack stood on shaky ground here. Spitz still thought he was involved so he needed to be careful. "Seemed like a possibility. That's all."

"Can't answer the question. The lab at Walter Reed is running a full tox panel on her. We should have their report soon. I'll maybe double check those results with our FBI lab."

"What do you think?" Zack asked.

"One of the strangest cases I've ever worked. No leads, no nothing, then all of a sudden there she is. Walking down the damn road like nothing happened."

"I might have another wrinkle for you," Zack said. "Do you remember Colonel Rene Garcia?"

Spitz leaned back, put his hand to his chin. "Garcia. Yeah, I met her the first day I was down here. Small lady, Army MP. Seemed really sharp."

"Garcia and I work together on the national security advisor's special task force in the Pentagon. Ah, now she seems to be missing."

"What the hell... ?"

"It's unlike her to disappear without letting someone know where she is." Zack gave Spitz his cell phone number. "Call me if you come up with anything. Anything at all."

"You sound like you're really concerned."

"I am. This isn't like her."

Spitz pulled out his notebook. "I understand you've been out of the country."

"Yeah. Tied to the other case we're working."

"That's the one where you beat the hell out of the shooter?"

Zack swallowed his frustration. "You cops are all the same. The guy was trying to kill me. I defended myself. Wouldn't you have done that?"

"Yeah, but I wouldn't have killed the guy."

"Bullshit, Spitz, you have no idea what you'd have done."

"Maybe not, Kelly, but here's what I think. Blake Lannigan comes down to see Gettysburg with you and she disappears. You have some sort of goofy story about hoofbeats, and you can't remember all that happened. Then you go off to Ireland. When you return, all of a sudden Lannigan shows up. Not a minute before you get back in country. Then you tell me that as soon as she reappears, this Colonel Garcia disappears."

Zack could see where this was going. "Why don't you back off and do your job? Find out what happened to Blake rather than chasing your tail after me."

"I'm watching you because I believe you're involved." He pointed at Zack. "You're not going to get away with it."

Zack turned on his heel. "Go to hell, Spitz." He stormed off, head pounding. *Bastard.*

Wilson caught up with Zack and took him arm. "Hey, wait a minute. I got a call from Hightower. He wants us back as soon as we can make it. We need to brief Quinn at seven-thirty."

Zack glanced at his watch, then waved good-bye to Henderson. "Looks like I've got time to see Blake first."

33

Walter Reed Army Medical Center, Saturday, 6:00 p.m.

Zack flashed his military ID to the security guard outside of Blake Lannigan's room. When he pushed the door open, Blake lay asleep in the middle of her bed. A tube dripped liquid into her arm, and a monitor tracked her heartbeats, which seemed regular. She looked great to Zack, but what did he know? Now with Garcia missing, could the two cases be related?

Blake must have sensed his presence because she opened her eyes. A smile lit her face and she pushed herself up on one elbow. "Zack, am I ever glad you came by."

He leaned over and kissed her on the cheek. "I'm so happy to see you. How are you doing?"

Her eyes seemed a little glazed. "Well, I'm not sure. My memory is all screwed up. I was hoping you could tell me some of what we did. That might help a few things come back to me."

Zack reached over and pulled up a chair next to her bed, then took her hand. "Well, let's see, where to start? First, do you remember dinner at that restaurant on the square in Gettysburg?"

She placed a finger on her chin. "Let me think a minute." Her eyes lit up. "Oh, yeah, it was a fun place. Great atmosphere and a funny waiter. I had the fish dinner. It was yummy. And those two margaritas. Boy, were they ever good." Another big smile.

Zack nodded, trying to be encouraging. "Yeah, that's right. That's good, very good. I had a steak and a couple of beers. How about after that? Any memories? Anything at all?"

"I remember we met that friend of yours, Cliff somebody."

"That's right, Cliff Henderson. Great memory." Zack had forgotten Cliff had stopped by their table at the restaurant. "Keep it up. You're doing great."

She squinted and frowned, then shook her head. "Gosh, it's so frustrating."

Zack almost held his breath. She had to remember. Maybe what she remembered would trigger something in his mind. The two of them were the key to this whole mess. "It's all right, take your time. No rush."

She leaned back. Shut her eyes. Opening them, her whole face seemed to light up. "Wait a minute. I remember after we finished, we walked out of the restaurant and got in your truck. You started it and we drove down that main road. We talked about going out on the battlefield."

"That's right." Zack leaned forward. Hopeful. "What else?"

She shut her eyes again. "I don't know. Where did we go after that?"

She's got to pull those memories out. Try to stimulate her. "Let's go back a minute. We drove down the main drag. Lots of people out walking. Talking. The sky starting to get dark. You wanted to drive out to the battlefield and look around. Then... ."

She squeezed his hand. "Yes, yes, I remember now. We were going to walk out and see if we could maybe find some ghosts."

Zack started to laugh. Maybe this would work. "That's right again. We drove to the parking lot by Little Round Top, the site overlooking Devil's Den. It took us about ten minutes. Really dark outside by then, although the moon hung low in the sky. Does that ring a bell?"

"Devil's Den you say?" She stared at the wall, her face in a grimace. "I remember driving up a curving road next to a large field. Yes, yes, darkness starting to set in. Hard to see. I figured it might be a good time for me to see ghosts."

"That's right." Zack kept getting more hopeful. Maybe, just maybe, it would all come back. "We pulled into the parking lot and looked at the path that curved up to the top of Little Round Top. Maybe we'd go out to Devil's Den after that. Remember?"

She closed her eyes and gritted her teeth. When she opened her eyes they were filled with tears. "Oh, Zack, I don't remember that. It's so frustrating."

He took her hand again, trying to hide the disappointment that gripped him. "I'm sure it is, Blake, but you keep trying. It'll come back."

The door burst open and Sean Lannigan stormed in. "I heard you were here, Kelly. What are you doing?" Glancing over at Blake, he must have seen the tears. "You're making my daughter cry. You goddamn animal. Get out of here."

"Wait a minute, Daddy, he's trying to help me remember what happened that Friday night. I'm crying because I'm frustrated I can't remember. I have come up with some things and want to remember more. All of it."

Lannigan faced Zack, both hands curled into fists. "If you don't get out of here this minute, I'll call for security to throw you out. Do you understand me?"

Zack stood his ground. "Mr. Lannigan, Blake is a grown woman. She can determine who she wants to talk to and who she doesn't."

"Don't argue with me. Get out. Now. Before you do any more damage."

The headache started again, a familiar throbbing. The webs seemed to stream toward his center. He was facing a Taliban leader. Someone he had killed. The face floated toward him. He stared, the pain almost overwhelming him. Locked in place. He couldn't seem to move.

Zack reached behind him but there was no M-9 tucked in his holster. Then his vision cleared and Lannigan rolled back into focus, staring at him.

"Well, are you going to get out or am I going to call security?"

"Don't Daddy... ."

Zack moved toward the door. "I'm not leaving because of you. I'm leaving because I don't want to upset Blake."

Zack turned back to Blake. "I'm glad you're doing better. I

want to help you remember. Maybe together we can sort this out." He whirled to face Lannigan. He wanted to say something more, but thought better of it. He pushed past Lannigan and opened the door.

Once out in the hallway, he leaned against the wall, head pounding, rubbing his eyes.

The security officer stepped over to him. "Are you all right?"

Zack nodded. No, he wasn't all right. Not one bit.

Zack drove to the Northwest gate of the White House and checked his watch. Seven-twenty. He passed through security and was met by a Secret Service agent who escorted him to the national security advisor's outer office. He entered and told Evelyn Brody that Quinn wanted to see him.

She nodded and dialed the intercom. Zack felt tired, pissed off, and not in any mood to brief his boss. But he pulled himself together and worked to organize his thoughts.

Darcy Quinn stepped out from her inner office and motioned for him to enter. "Come in, Zack. Tell me what you know. I don't have much time as I have another appointment at eight."

"Do you mind if I pour a quick cup?" he asked. "Get you some?"

"Please."

He walked over to the pot and poured each of them a cup, then sat down in the armchair across from her desk.

"Okay," she said, "let's hear what you found out in Gettysburg."

Zack spent about twenty minutes summarizing everything that had happened since their last meeting. After finishing, he added, "I stopped by Walter Reed on my way back."

"You saw Blake?" Quinn asked. "Walter Reed isn't exactly on the way from Gettysburg to the White House."

"I've been concerned about Blake and needed to see how she was doing. You know, try to determine what she remembered about that Friday night? I figured I could maybe help her by adding details. Maybe we could help each other remember what happened."

"And did you?"

"A number of things came back to her from my prompting. She knew everything up until we drove to Little Round Top to look out over Devil's Den. Then her memory failed. Kinda like turning off a switch."

Quinn took a sip and watched him over the lid of her cup. It always drove him crazy when she did that. Zack figured Lannigan had called Quinn to piss about him. He could tell by her reaction that the bastard had. Well, bring it on.

"Zack, Sean Lannigan called me after you left Blake at the hospital."

Zack dug his fingernails into his palm This was her show, but he wasn't going to make it any easier for her.

"He was upset that you were there." She rubbed her hands together. "Particularly after he told you not to see her any more."

Zack sat there a moment waiting to see if she had anything else to say. When she stayed silent, he said, "Ma'am, Blake is an adult. She was delighted that I stopped by to talk to her. It gave her a chance to try and piece together what happened to her."

Quinn looked ready to say something so he held up his hand. "Please let me finish. She's very frustrated about not being able to remember and I am, too. It may be that between the two of us we can help each other."

"I understand that."

Time to let out all of his frustrations. "Frankly, I didn't appreciate what he said to me at Gettysburg a few days ago. As a parent myself, I share his concerns and understand where he's coming from. But when he unloaded on me again at Walter Reed, I told him my frustrations. I suspect that's what he shared with you. I'm trying to help his daughter and he isn't making it any easier. As a matter of fact, Blake agreed with me and not with her father. She wanted me to stay."

"Zack, I don't want to debate the point with you. Sean has asked me to ensure that you leave Blake alone. I'm asking you to do so. She's in a fragile condition. He believes that your bothering her won't help speed her recovery."

"I won't visit her again unless I believe it's critical to our investigation. Something happened to Blake. Something very strange. Now, Garcia is missing. I believe the two events may be related. If they are, I might have to talk to Blake again if I think it will help find Garcia. I hope you can support me on that."

Quinn narrowed her gaze. "I have a great deal of respect for you, Zack, but I'm asking you to leave Blake alone. If you feel the need to see her again, come to me first. If I believe it's necessary to our investigation, I'll talk to Sean or get someone else to see her."

Zack stood at attention. His head pounded, and he couldn't believe she was doing this to him. "Yes, Ma'am. Is that all?"

She watched him, her fingers forming a steeple in front of her, pointing at her chin. "Yes."

34

Georgetown, 10:15 p.m.

Zack sat in his truck a block down from the house in Georgetown, fuming about his meeting with Darcy Quinn. He should go home and see Laura, but something held him here. He'd missed something about Garcia. What?

Over the next two hours, six cars pulled into the compound, then later drove out. Expensive cars – Cadillacs, Mercedes, BMW's. Five contained one man and one of them two men. A parking lot for the Washington elite. What were they doing here? Plotting against the government? Attending a meeting? Not likely, not this late on a Saturday. Maybe a social event, but they came and went at staggered intervals.

He got out of the truck and walked across the street, looking left and right. Watching for what he wasn't sure. When he passed the gate, he glanced inside and spotted a security camera trained on the gate. By staying off to the side and in the shadows, he shouldn't show up on the camera.

The gate opened and a Mercedes drove out. As it passed, Zack thought he recognized Holly Lannigan. Was that her? If so, what the hell was Sean Lannigan's wife doing here at this time of night?

———

Zack pulled into his driveway and shut off the engine. Sat for a moment, then climbed out and walked across the pavement. A light shone in the living room. Probably nothing more than Laura watching television.

He slipped around to the back of the house and peeked in the kitchen window just in case. Nothing out of the ordinary. He unlocked the back door and went inside. Heard only the television.

He crept through the kitchen, into the dining room, and stood in the entryway to the living room. An old Humphrey Bogart movie flickered across the TV screen. Laura sprawled across her favorite overstuffed chair. Zack stood there and looked at her. A beautiful young woman. So vulnerable, yet so full of her own thing. Zack's heart swelled with love for his daughter.

Laura must have sensed Zack's presence because her eyes popped open. She jumped when she saw her dad, then settled down and smiled. "You scared the crap out of me."

"I'm sorry, didn't mean to do that. When I got home, I saw the light on in the living room and figured I'd better check to make sure you were okay."

"I'm fine but where have you been?"

"It's this case I'm working. Things have been crazy."

"I heard on the news that the police found Blake Lannigan walking along a road outside of Gettysburg. A cool lady. Doesn't take any crap off anyone." She laughed. "A perfect role model for me, don't you think?"

"She is that. I like her a lot."

"What happened to her?"

"I still don't know. That's what makes it so weird."

"Doesn't she remember anything at all?"

"That's the crazy part. She has no memory of where she's been for almost a week. I talked with her at Walter Reed. We compared memories, but she still can't come up with what happened to her that night, or the next week for that matter."

Laura bit her lip. Zack knew that sign. She had something on her mind that she wanted to talk about. "I saw pictures on the news of that man who tried to shoot you. It showed you going after him and knocking the gun out of his hand. It made me so scared for you, Dad."

Zack tried to figure out where Laura was going with this.

"After you knocked the gun away, it showed you beating on him as three or four people tried to pull you off. Colonel Gàrcia grabbed at you and started yelling, but you kept hitting the man."

Laura looked at the television for a moment then back at her father. Her gaze seemed to penetrate inside Zack. "It scared me, Dad. It seemed almost like you were out of control."

"The guy tried to kill me. He had a gun in his hand."

"I know, I know. You had to defend yourself, but then you kept kicking him and hitting him."

Zack walked over and hugged her. "I'm sorry it scared you."

She leaned back and looked up at her dad, tears streaking her cheek. "I keep thinking what if you get mad at me again? Would you lose control?"

"Thanks for seeing me so early on a Sunday morning, Gordy."

Hale took his normal position in the lawn chair on the back porch and put his feet up on the footstool. "What's up? You sounded pretty desperate on the phone."

"Laura threw me a curveball last night." Zack told him about their conversation. "I told her that I reacted by beating up the guy because I had to defend myself from a killer. Make sure he couldn't come back at me again."

Hale watched him. Waited. He was good at waiting. Listening.

Zack looked away, feigning a sudden interest in a cardinal sitting on the bird feeder hanging from the stately oak next to the porch. He glanced back at Hale. Had to drop his gaze. Goddamn it, Gordy, he thought, say something. Help me understand this.

Hale looked out at the lawn, silent.

The frustration built in Zack's gut. It threatened to blow out the top of his head and spatter all over the porch. "Goddamn, I hate it when you do that."

"Do what?"

"Just sit there. You're supposed to help me."

"Why did what your daughter said bother you? Seems to me

it's a perfectly logical thing for her to talk about. Actually, for her to be concerned about. She saw you lose control. Has it happened with her? Could it happen to her?"

Zack sat there, fighting back the tears. He couldn't cry. Not here. Not now.

Hale put his hand on Zack's arm. "Why are you here? What do you want from me?"

It all came flying out of Zack in a burst. "She's afraid of me. My own daughter's afraid of me."

"But that's not really what's bothering you, is it?"

"Hell, yes. I'm mad that my own daughter is afraid of me."

"Zack, look at me." His gaze bore into Zack. "Are you angry because she's afraid of you, or are you worried that she may have cause to be afraid of you? Maybe there's something there."

Zack leaned back in his chair. Looked at the bird feeder again. Then his gaze fixed back on Hale. "In the past week, I've done things in the heat of action that I have no memory of. No memory at all. None."

Hale nodded. "Now we're getting somewhere."

"What if I get in another argument with my daughter?"

Hale looked down at his big hands, picking at a nail. "Why is that a problem?"

"Could I hurt her? Goddamn, Gordy, could I hurt her?"

"I don't know." He waited, then said, "Could you?"

Zack didn't want to answer that question. It had boiled in his gut ever since Laura had come out to stay with him. He had moments of blacking out. Moments he couldn't remember. God, what if he hurt Laura thinking she was some Taliban puke. What if he did that?

Hale leaned over and put his hand on Zack's hand, the huge paw dwarfing Zack's. "Let me tell you a story. My father served as an Infantry officer in Vietnam. A brand-new second lieutenant right out of OCS. He got into all kinds of really bad shit during the Tet Offensive when the North Vietnamese came across that border. Acted like a tidal wave sweeping everything in its path."

Zack didn't know about Hale's dad—only that Hale had been in the Rangers, maybe four or five years ahead of Zack.

"'Course, I didn't know anything about that. Just a little pup. I don't think my mother realized anything was wrong. No one talked about PTSD in those days."

Zack waited. His turn to wait for Gordy.

"One morning he took a nap on the couch in our living room. I was probably three, maybe three and a half. I wanted to play with him so I tottered across the living room and patted his cheek. Wanted him to wake up like right away. He was a big guy, I mean a really big guy."

"That's where you get your size."

"My dad came off the couch with a war yell, his arm caught me and threw me across the room. I slammed against the wall and slid down to the floor. Knocked me out. Out cold. I don't remember a thing until I woke up in the hospital ER with a broken arm. The docs were afraid of a concussion but thankfully that didn't happen. But it could have. Zack, he could have killed me that morning and he knew it. My mom knew it, too."

Zack stared at him.

"War is a son-of-a-bitch, Zack. Every time I watch the State of the Union speech, it makes me want to puke. Those big-gun assholes applaud some war hero with no concept of what it means to be a war hero. The nightmares, the flashbacks, the possible horror of doing something you could never fix. Soldiers have to live with that. It's my job to help them live with it. Help them reenter society and become useful citizens. Lots of them never do and there's not a damn thing I can do about it. All I can do is try. Every soldier has to figure it out for himself. Decide where he or she fits back into society or even if they do."

Hale stood and walked around the porch looking off at the trees, then he came back to the chair and sat down again next to Zack. "The only way I can guarantee something awful doesn't happen to your daughter is to tell Social Services to remove her from your home and put her in foster care."

"Oh, shit, don't do that."

"Did you hear what I said, Zack? I can't guarantee that you won't harm you daughter in some damn flashback. If you do, then it will weigh on me for the rest of my life that I could have protected her and didn't."

Hale put his hand on Zack's shoulder. "But I'm not going to do that because we're going to work like hell to glue you back together. Now, remember, don't take too long to get back to see me. We need to keep working on this. Don't make me sorry about my decision. Then I'll have to live with it, too."

35

Arlington, VA, Sunday, 10:30 a.m.

When Zack got back to the house, Laura sat in the front room, struggling with her advanced algebra, and waiting for Zack in her jogging clothes.

Zack changed into a T-shirt, shorts, and jogging shoes, then he drove them to the Pentagon.

This four-mile run was a favorite of Zack's. Laura liked it too. Stretching for a few minutes first, they jogged across the Memorial Bridge, then up to the Lincoln Memorial. Zack enjoyed the sun and the light breeze on his bare chest. Helped the aches from his fight with the shooter disappear.

"I'd like to spend some time at the Smithsonian," Laura called to him. "The Air and Space Museum would be fun. Haven't been there in quite awhile."

Zack stayed determined the two of them would enjoy this day. "Sure. Let's come back this afternoon."

Her face lit up in a big grin. "Thanks, Dad, that would be great."

They circled the Washington Monument, jogged back along the mall and across the Memorial Bridge, then down George Washington Parkway to the Pentagon parking lot.

Once they got back home, they each cleaned up. Zack decided to put on a sport coat, a pair of khaki's and his cordovan loafers. Might as well look like a cool dude for his daughter.

When Laura came downstairs, looking great in a blue blouse and a pair of black slacks, Zack asked, "What say we go over to Fort Myer and fill ourselves up on their buffet?"

Laura headed toward the door. "Cool. I'm starved and ready for that buffet. Maybe there'll be some cute guys at the club. Isn't that where all those Old Guard soldiers hang?"

Zack had to laugh. "Uh-oh. Maybe Fort Myer isn't such a good idea."

"Dad ..."

"Just kidding."

On their way into the club, Zack slipped on a tie and Laura helped him straighten it.

"Okay, thanks," he said. "I'm glad I don't have to wear one very often. Hate ties."

They had to wait about twenty minutes for a table. As they were eating, Laura stopped chewing for a moment and asked, "Where did you go this morning?"

Zack almost choked on his omelet. He didn't know what to tell her. That her father had a problem with flashbacks and found himself back in Afghanistan every time he got mad? That he sometimes lost control and didn't know what he was doing?

Zack decided to come clean, at least a little clean. "I'm seeing a therapist."

"A therapist?"

"Sometimes I get flashbacks from when I was in Afghanistan. I, I ah, I need help in working through those flashbacks."

"Flashbacks? You mean like you're back in Afghanistan?"

Zack took a bite of roll and chewed slowly to consider his response. "Yeah, something like that. It's pretty common among a lot of my peers."

"Are you going to be okay?"

"Oh, yeah, I'm going to be fine. It's just that I need to talk through some of the stuff I saw and how it affected me."

"I'd be glad to listen if you want me to. Can you tell me any of this?"

Zack thought about that. Much of what he'd done stayed classified, but he could maybe tell Laura in general terms some of the stuff. "The Rangers were given missions based on the best intelligence we could get on where enemy fighters were or where they were hiding their equipment or bombs. Then we'd go after them."

"Were you scared?"

"Sometimes, sure. We always moved at night when the bad guys were asleep so we could sneak up on them before they knew we were there. Our night vision goggles gave us a leg up. We called it 'owning the night.'"

"Did you ever shoot anybody?" Laura asked.

Zack finished chewing his omelet. What was he to say to that? Then he thought, she deserved to know the truth. "Yes, sometimes I had to shoot people."

Her eyes got wide. "Did you ever kill anybody?"

Zack nodded. "When we arrived and I deployed my troops, sometimes the bad guys knew we were there and started shooting. My job was to coordinate the activities of my soldiers, but once in awhile I ended up exchanging fire with the people inside."

Laura took a bite of bacon and chewed, looking out the window.

A waitress brought coffee to Zack and filled his cup. Zack figured Laura was debating the next question. He was afraid he knew what it was.

Laura looked at her dad, her gaze strong and direct. "I read in the paper that sometimes our soldiers ended up killing civilians. Did any of your soldiers ever do that?"

What would she think of him? Zack would always see the little girl who came running out of the building before the bomb went off. She was probably only four or five years old. The bomb exploded by her, and he saw her flying through the air. Saw this in his dreams. *Oh, God, what to say.*

"Dad?"

"Once in awhile we made mistakes. We were told there were only enemy in these places and went we got there, sometimes we found families. That's why I have these awful flashbacks. I can see some of the people my soldiers killed. They haunt my dreams, and I don't know how to stop it."

Laura sat and chewed some more. "I know you wouldn't hurt anyone like that on purpose. I'll try to help you in anyway I can."

Zack reached over and touched his daughter's arm. "Thanks, honey. You know I love you."

"I love you, too, Dad. We'll get through this together."

They walked to Zack's truck hand-in-hand and he drove into Washington. Tourists filled all the available parking places. Zack finally found a spot a block off the Mall down Ninth Street.

They hiked the three blocks to the Air and Space Museum and spent a delightful two hours touring the museum. This was one of Zack's favorite spots, and he loved to watch Laura's excitement at everything she saw.

On the way home, Laura said, "I'm sorry if I've been a pain in the butt to you. But I was getting bored, and I didn't know all that you were going through."

"It's more my fault," Zack said. "I've been so busy. I'll try to do better."

Laura smiled. "Yeah, there's that, too."

36

The Pentagon, Arlington, VA, Monday, 8:00 a.m.

Zack sat at his desk, reflecting back to the fun he'd had with Laura on Sunday and vowing to do more with her in the future. He started sorting through the mountain of papers that had accumulated since he'd been on the road. God, he hated paperwork.

He double checked e-mails, voicemails, messages, but found nothing recent from Garcia. Her last e-mail, dated Friday afternoon, provided him a summary of what she'd uncovered so far. She did say that she had a lead to check out but didn't say what. Was it that damn house?

His cell rang. "Colonel Kelly."

"It's Shelia. Oh, Zack, I just got a call from Katie's mother. Remember, Katie is here on the internship."

Zack had to think for a moment. "Oh, you mean Maggie O'Shay. How is she?"

"She told me that Katie called her, whispering on the phone. Said she needed help. Then the phone disconnected. Mrs. O'Shay sounded frantic. She didn't know what to do so she called me."

Zack stood and grabbed his hat. "Where are you now?"

"I'm at my hotel."

"Stay put. I'm on my way."

"Okay. I'll be waiting for you outside. Hurry, Zack."

Twelve minutes later, Zack pulled up in front of the Pentagon City Marriott. Apparently Sean Lannigan had agreed to pick up the tab for her visit. One nice thing the clown had done.

Shelia stood outside the front door, looking stunning in a pair of black slacks and a short-sleeve white shirt. When she saw him, she ran toward the truck and hopped in. "Oh, Zack, I'm so worried about Katie. I wish you could have heard her mother. She sounded desperate."

Zack pulled out of the driveway and turned left. "Tell me exactly what she said. But first, have you had anything to eat? We can pick up something for you, then drive over to that house. See what we can uncover."

"Okay, that sounds good. I'm starved." She took a deep breath. "Her call caught me off guard. She was so upset that I found it hard to understand her. I had to make her repeat everything so I think I've got it all straight."

"Okay, take another deep breath." He waited. "Now, when did O'Shay call?"

"Maybe five minutes before I called you."

"And her daughter had just contacted her before that?"

"Right. Maggie said it was strange that Katie whispered. She had trouble understanding what Katie said. But it was something like, 'Help me. I need help.' Katie's voice sounded slurred to her mother."

"Like she'd been drugged?" Zack asked.

"Exactly."

"What else? Did Katie say where she was?"

"Her mother asked her, but she didn't know for sure. They must be keeping them inside."

"Them? Are there more than just Katie at this place?"

Shelia thought for a moment. "I don't know for sure. During the call, Maggie implied a number of the girls were there together. I don't think she's positive about that."

Zack cut across the Key Bridge into Georgetown. He stopped for two coffees and a sandwich for Shelia. He parked the truck a block down the street from the house.

Leaning in toward him, Shelia whispered, "I believe the key to this whole mess is the Irish internship. That seems to be in the middle of everything."

Zack nodded. "I'm more and more convinced that all this is tied together."

"And you think Colonel Garcia may have gone over to the internship building and run afoul of some shady characters."

"That's what I'm worried about. If Garcia could be with us she would."

"Okay, hear me out. My idea is for me to walk over and bang on the gate of that building and pop in to see them. Why don't we make, as you Yanks call it, a frontal assault?"

Zack shook his head. "I can't let you do that. It's way too dangerous."

She leaned back, her brown eyes darkening. "Now you wait a minute, good colonel. It's important for you blokes to realize you don't *let* me do anything. We can do things together and you can back me up, but you sure as hell don't let me do anything or stop me from doing what I think is right."

Zack raised his hands in mock surrender. "Oops, sorry, bad choice of words."

"Aye, my good friend, it is that. And I'm hoping you won't let it happen again."

"You can bet on it." Zack told her about his visit to the house the other day. "I talked to this big moose at the gate with lots of gold in his teeth, didn't get anywhere with him."

"Aye, but you're not me." She wiggled her eyebrows. "I seem to have a way with men."

Zack had to laugh. "You do that. No question about it."

"And once I get inside, I'm hoping I can get a sense of the building, determine what's been going on in there, and maybe find Katie. It's too important. We can't wait."

Zack thought about that for a moment. Her instincts had proven to be useful on more than one occasion. "Maybe you can uncover evidence we can take to the FBI."

"So, the thing is, Mister Colonel, we can do this together or I can go in on my own."

Zack toasted her coffee cup with his. "Together it is."

Zack and Shelia drove back to the Pentagon. He hurried inside and requisitioned a portable microphone set for Shelia to pin to the inside pocket of her jacket and a tiny earbud. Then they'd swung by her hotel so she could pick up a red jacket.

Zack pulled up in front of the mansion and shut off the engine. An uneasy feeling churned in his gut. First Blake, then Garcia. He sure as hell didn't want to lose Shelia, too.

She tugged on her jacket. "How do I look? Does the mic or earbud show?"

Zack looked her over and shook his head. "You look great as always."

"Here's the deal," Shelia said. "I'll go up to the gate. You wait here."

"Now, if you get in trouble," Zack said, "just say *Quinn* and I'll come running."

"I'll remember that." Shelia got out of the truck, then leaned back in through the window. "You worry too much. I'll be fine and back in a flash, hopefully with useful information."

"Be careful."

Shelia walked across the street, swinging her rear end for his benefit. "Have I got your attention, mate?" she whispered over the microphone.

Zack had to smile. Yes, she had his attention.

When Shelia arrived at the gate, she looked around then rang the bell. Soon the bruiser who had chased Zack off came outside and leaned against the inside portion of the gate.

Shelia told him she was from Ireland and here on vacation. She knew that a group of her friends were staying there, and she wanted to stop by to say hello.

Zack had to admit, it made a great cover story.

Zack watched through binoculars. The guy looked confused. Be careful, Shelia, that guy may be dumb, but he's dangerous.

"You'll have to wait here while I check with my boss on what to do." He walked inside.

Zack heard a whisper over the microphone, "What do you think?"

"Good job," Zack replied. "Keep it up."

"Usually that's my line."

When the big guy came outside again, he opened the gate and motioned her inside. "I'll take you to meet the lady who coordinates the program."

Zack couldn't visually follow Shelia after the door closed. He was glad they had the microphone so he could track her. Hopefully they wouldn't search her and find it.

A woman named Melody introduced herself. Shelia repeated what she had said at the door.

Zack heard the woman say, "I'm sorry but your friends are involved in a program for the next day. When they return, I'll be glad to tell them you stopped by."

"Where are they now?" Shelia asked. "Maybe I could see them there."

"I'm sorry but they're out of town," Melody replied. "In the middle of a private activity."

"Doing what?"

"I'm sorry, but I'm not at liberty to say."

"Why the secrecy?"

"We'd prefer they not be disturbed. It might impair their learning experience."

"I hope to apply myself in the future," Shelia said. "It'd be great to hear about the program and what they're learning."

Careful, Shelia, Zack thought, don't push too hard.

"The program is full at this time," Melody said. "We may be opening another session in the fall. Give me your name. I'll put it in our file."

"Don't they get any free time? Maybe I can catch up with them then."

The woman's voice seemed to harden. "Like I said, when they return, I'll tell them you were here. I'm sure one of them will call you."

"But you don't even know which of the interns is my friend."

Slow down, Zack thought, don't piss the woman off any more than she already is.

The woman's voice returned to normal. "Of course, give me the names of your friends. I'll make sure they get the message."

There was silence while Zack figured that Shelia was writing the names on a notepad.

The woman must have looked at the list. "Wait a minute. Katie O'Shay is here. She's been sick and didn't go on the trip. Would you like to talk with her?"

Zack heard lightness in Shelia's voice. "That would be wonderful. Katie's one of my best friends."

Now we're getting somewhere, Zack thought.

Zack heard footsteps as the woman walked out of the room.

"Keep your fingers crossed," Shelia said. "We should learn if it's the real deal now or not."

"Be careful," Zack said. "You still need to get out of there in one piece."

"If I don't get out in one piece, lad, which piece would you prefer makes it out."

Zack had to smile. "The whole package, lassie, the whole package. It's such grade-A material."

"Oh, thank you, Colonel. Oops, here they come."

Zack heard footsteps, then Shelia said, "Hi, Katie, how are you doing?"

"Shelia, is that you?" O'Shay's voice seemed hesitant, almost like she was drugged. "Is that really you?"

"You bet it's me. I wanted to see how you were doing. What do you think of the internship? Maybe I can apply and get in for the fall."

Katie talked in a flat tone. "I like it. We learn a lot of things."

Melody's voice joined in. "The girls have spent time visiting the Supreme Court, the attorney general's office, and are now participating with various elements of the federal court system."

"I think of all the fun we had growing up in Dublin," Shelia said.

"And now here you are, learning about American law in Washington, D.C."

Katie's voice sounded hesitant again, confused. "Oh, yes, growing up in Dublin gave us the chance to see the big city and learn so much in school. Are you still living in County Wicklow?"

"Aye," Shelia replied, "I hope to be back there soon."

The woman's voice broke in. "I hate to cut this short, but I think Katie's got to get back to bed. She's had a terrible virus, and I don't want her to get worse."

Zack heard the women rise and after a minute Katie and Melody left the room.

"She's all messed up, Zack."

"Don't say anything until you're out of there."

Zack heard footsteps, then Shelia said, "Thank you for your time. I hope to hear from my friends soon. Do you think it will be in the next two or three days that they'll be back?"

"I can't say for sure, but you may want to check back by the end of the week. Will you still be here in Washington by then or will you be back in Ireland?"

"I'll still be here."

"Give me your number and I'll call you."

Shelia provided her cell phone number and the woman wrote it down.

Zack held his breath until Shelia appeared in the doorway. He trained his binoculars on the woman in the doorway. She resembled Sean Lannigan. She could be his sister. Or maybe the woman in the car the other night.

He exhaled when Shelia opened the gate. She let herself out and waved back at the woman. The woman returned the wave. Shelia walked up the sidewalk.

Starting the truck, Zack pulled out from the curb. He looked in the rearview mirror. A Ford Taurus parked about a block behind him, pulled out at the same time. Zack turned right at the next intersection and the Taurus drove straight ahead past the intersection. Zack could see two men sitting in the car. The one in the passenger's side turned to watch him.

He pulled to the curb and waited for Shelia. When Shelia climbed in the truck she said, "Let's get out of here."

Zack put his hand on her arm. "Get down. I think there's someone in that car watching us." He crept down the street, keeping his gaze on the mirror.

When he turned left at the next intersection, the Taurus moved past them along the other side of the street. It turned right up the street Zack had just left.

He kept watch in the outside mirror. Thought he saw the man in the passenger side look back at him. The Taurus disappeared in the direction of the house. Zack continued up the street until they reached Wisconsin Avenue.

As Zack turned onto Wisconsin, he put his hand on her knee. "Okay, you can get up. The car's gone.

She sat up and pulled the microphone out from inside her coat, but didn't say anything.

"That woman looked an awful lot like Sean Lannigan," Zack said.

"I thought so, too. He has a sister but I don't know her."

"I know where there's a coffee shop," Zack said. "We can get a cup of coffee and talk over what we found out. Then I want to e-mail Garcia's contact at the FBI."

Shelia looked over at Zack, hands shaking. "Stop the damn truck and hold me. I'm about to shake into a million pieces."

37

Georgetown, D.C., Monday, 12:30 p.m.

Starbucks burst at the seams with Georgetown University students laughing and calling to one another. Shelia and Zack found a table in the back corner where they could talk.

Zack patted her shoulder. "Why don't you sit here, decompress, and keep an eye on the table. I'll get your coffee. Maybe even throw in a cookie on the side."

She looked up, her gaze searching his. "Oh, Zack, I'm still shaking."

"You did a great job." He leaned down and kissed her on the cheek. "Gutsy lady."

The sparkle returned to her eyes. "That's a good lad. Little bit on the blarney side, but still a good lad. All right, off ya go. Make sure you bring back that cookie."

When he returned with their coffees and her cookie, Zack sat and took a sip. "How are you doing now?"

Her lips were pressed together, and her hands still trembled. "I'm getting it together, sort of. Thinking back, it was pretty scary to be in there with that woman."

"You were terrific. What did you think about her?"

"Place is a phony." Shelia broke off a piece of cookie and chewed it slowly. "Something is definitely wrong in there. I could feel the negative energy flowing through the place. It surrounded me. Weighed me down. Dark energy. Dark."

She took another bite of cookie. "Katie has always been a dynamic sort. Today, she looked as if she were hooked on drugs. Deadened in all of her responses."

The espresso machine whirred in the background. Zack leaned forward to hear her.

"I talked to Katie about our growing up in Dublin and some of the things we did together. All the fun we had as kids."

"Right, I heard that."

"Zack, we grew up in Galway. The two of us never made it to Dublin until we met again at Trinity."

"That's right, I forgot. And the woman wouldn't have caught that. Pretty slick."

"Katie picked up on it because she asked me if I still lived in the Wicklow Mountains. She knows I'm in Dublin now, not County Wicklow."

"That settles it. We need to do something to get her out of there and we need to do it right now." Zack pulled out his cell phone. "Garcia sent me the name and e-mail of her contact in the FBI. Let me check. See if we can meet with him right away."

"And not a moment too soon."

"I bet they've got Garcia tied up somewhere in that house. Oh, man, I hope she's okay."

He sent the e-mail using Garcia's name and explaining who he was and what he wanted. He added his cell number to the message and asked that the agent contact Zack right away.

The two sat talking, watching students hustle one another, enjoying the normalcy for a few minutes. The caffeine surged through his body. Felt good. His cell rang. "Kelly."

"Colonel Kelly, this is Special Agent Albert Ferguson."

"Agent Ferguson, you got my message. The two of us were at the site of what is called the Irish internship. I'd like to talk to you about what we found."

"I know. We saw you."

"Oh, those were your guys in the Taurus."

"I'm on the seventh floor of the Hoover Building. When can you be here?"

Zack looked at his watch. He covered his ear because someone had fired up the damn espresso machine again. "Thirty minutes."

"See you then. I'll tell the guard at the door to expect you."

"I'll have Ms. Shelia O'Donnell with me."

"I suspected you would."

———————

Thirty-five minutes later, Zack and Shelia stood in the lobby of the Hoover Building, waiting for Agent Ferguson to come down and meet them.

"Colonel Kelly?"

Zack turned. A short man with thick glasses and wearing a sport coat with patches on the elbows, stood behind Zack. "Agent Ferguson?"

"In the flesh. Welcome to the Hoover Building."

Zack extended his hand, then motioned toward Shelia. "This is Ms. Shelia O'Donnell. Shelia and I have been working on this case since the day after Blake Lannigan's kidnapping in Gettysburg."

"Hello, Ms. O'Donnell. Colonel Garcia updated me on your background and how you were helping Colonel Kelly in Ireland." He pointed toward the elevator. "Let's go up to my office."

As they walked, Zack said, "You probably know that Colonel Garcia is missing?"

Ferguson jerked back. "No. Are you sure? I haven't talked with her for the last couple of days, but I figured she was busy. As a matter of fact, I've got a call in to her for some information."

When they arrived at Ferguson's office, he offered them coffee. His office had the normal gunmetal gray furniture, with a conference table next to the window. He motioned toward the table.

"Wow, a window," Zack said. "You must be somebody."

"No, just lucky." Ferguson sat, knitted his fingers together and said, "Now, tell me what you found out."

Zack updated him on the trip to Ireland and their interaction with Shelia's friends who attended the Irish internship.

Shelia explained about her visit to the internship building that morning. "My friend, Katie O'Shay is a very active person. Today she looked to me as if she were drugged. The woman I met told me that all of my other friends and the rest of the interns were somewhere else, but she wouldn't tell me where."

Ferguson took a sip of coffee and drummed his fingers on the table. "I'm going to have to trust you both, because what you're about to hear is sensitive material." He stood and walked over to the four-drawer file cabinet. Pulling out a file, he came back to the table and sat down. Most of what he did stayed slow and deliberate. Zack wanted to wind him up to get him moving. Maybe drop a firecracker down the back of his shorts.

Clearing his throat, Ferguson said, "As far as we can tell, eleven women from Ireland have entered the United States over the past two months under the guise of this internship program. We're not sure yet about past history."

"Is it legitimate?" Zack asked.

Ferguson pulled on his goatee. "Well now, that's a good question. We can find no professors involved in the program. It appears the women have attended four federal court sessions and watched a Supreme Court hearing. But other than that, we can't figure out what sort of education they're getting."

"Do you have any idea where they are now?" Shelia asked.

"At least ten of them are at the house."

Shelia's eyes widened. "Wait a minute, why didn't that woman let me see them?"

Ferguson pulled on his goatee again. "Another good question."

"Who is she?" Zack asked.

"She's the younger sister of Sean Lannigan who's... ."

"The father of Blake Lannigan," Zack finished his sentence.

"That's correct." Ferguson organized some papers and closed the folder. "It appears that Mr. Lannigan is helping to arrange the young women's visits."

Zack leaned forward, tiring of this guy's laissez-faire approach to this case. Something big had to be going on and this guy fiddled while the internship burned. "Agent Ferguson, you don't seem particularly concerned, but we need to do something. And we need to do it right away before anyone is hurt."

Ferguson walked over to the cabinet and returned the file. "My best estimate is that the young women there now have been brought into this county to serve as prostitutes for some of the richest and biggest names in D.C. And this may be the second or even the third group of young women. It appears the Irish Mafia has been getting hundreds of thousands of dollars from this program as well as a great deal of political influence with some very important people here in D.C."

Zack sat back, suspicions confirmed. He hadn't mentioned it to Shelia but the idea had been perking in the back of his mind. "That explains what Tuohy O'Toole talked about. He said the issues were interconnected. Find out who's after me, and it would trace to Blake's disappearance and the internship."

Shelia eyes started to tear up. "Do you mean my friends are being held against their will and forced to sell themselves?"

Ferguson held up his hand. "Wait a minute. I don't know if they're being forced to do anything. My guess is they are being used as escorts for big shots and are attending some pretty high-level parties. We believe drugs may be involved. Some of the girls may be involved voluntarily, then if they try to leave, they're forced to stay. How willing some of them are to participate with these big shots is anyone's guess."

Zack jumped up. "Goddamn, we've got to get them out of there."

"I agree," Ferguson said. "With the information Ms. O'Donnell has given me and the information from the Garda in Ireland, I should be able to obtain a warrant to raid the place tonight."

Finally some action, Zack thought. "We need to contact Sergeant Powell in Dublin. He's with the Special Branch of the Garda and is coordinating things from their side."

Ferguson smiled. "I don't believe we need to involve Sergeant Powell. We have a representative from the Garda who has been working this case undercover for the past year and arrived in D.C. this morning." He walked over, opened the door, and called down the hall. In a moment, Terry McHugh stepped into the room, his ever-present watch cap hanging from his right hand.

"Terry, Terry, is that you? Is that really you?" Shelia ran over and gave him a hug. "Terry... ."

"Aye, lass, it's me."

Zack moved over to shake hands. "You've been working this case undercover?"

"That I have, although when this is over no doubt my cover will be blown wide open. But I figured if my five-year undercover stint had to end, it best end with nailing the bastards who are tricking these young girls into white slavery. They're real pigs, and I mean to bring them down."

"Okay," Ferguson said, "let's sit down and get back to business. We've got a lot to plan and not much time to do it."

McHugh took Shelia's arm and moved her toward the conference room table. "We need to be incredibly careful so none of these young ladies get hurt."

Ferguson stirred some cream into a fresh cup of coffee. "I suspect we'll nail a bunch of hot shots when we hit the house tonight, so we need to plan what to do with them."

"What time do you think we should conduct the raid?" Zack asked. "Do you have any idea if Garcia could be in there or not?"

"I'm sorry, Colonel, I can't answer the first part of your question yet, and unfortunately I don't know about Colonel Garcia. As I said, I was trying to reach her to share this information before you told me she'd gone missing." He glanced down at his papers. "I'll call you as soon as I have a time."

"I want to go along," Shelia said. "These are my friends."

Ferguson thought for a moment, then said, "You won't be able to go in with the initial SWAT team, but you can accompany me later. You'll be helpful in identifying your friends and figuring out who's there and who's missing."

"I need to stay here and work with Agent Ferguson," McHugh said. "Maybe after this is over we can get together and have a pint or two for old times' sake."

Zack stood. "After this is over, we'll have a whole bunch of pints." He glanced at Ferguson. "We'll be waiting for your call."

Ferguson shook his hand. "I'll have to trust that you won't say anything to anyone."

Zack nodded. "You have my word."

"Good. I'll see you out."

38

Zack unlocked the front door to his house and stepped inside. He called for Laura but she wasn't home yet. Then he remembered on Monday she had soccer practice and normally didn't get home until six, hungrier than a bear.

He put on water to boil for pasta, then walked into the music room and picked up his guitar. He hadn't been playing regularly, hell—he hadn't been playing at all. Time to take a few minutes to relax, maybe sharpen up a few of his skills again.

Back in Afghanistan, when they'd been in garrison, a group of guys had formed a band to entertain the troops. With a little practice, they'd gotten pretty good. Zack played the guitar, Cliff Henderson and Michael Sullivan jammed on the fiddle, then one of the guys played rhythm on drums and another on bass. They had a ball playing folk and country music.

Zack played a couple of songs, trying to get his timing back. He was halfway through Red River Valley when Laura pushed open the front door.

"Hey, Pops, sounds pretty good. When are you going to do some George Strait?"

"Give me a break. I'm having enough trouble doing a little Zack Kelly."

She laughed. "What's for dinner?"

"Pasta and a big salad." He checked to see that the water was boiling so he dropped in the pasta. "Let me put a little garlic bread in the oven."

Laura put her finger to his chin. "Gee, let me think for a minute.

Guess that means we'd better put red wine on the table tonight rather than white. Why don't I go ahead and open it? That way it'll be ready when we are."

Zack set his guitar back in its case. Vowed to practice more. Yeah, right. When would he have the time. "Wait a minute, what do you know about wine? You're only a little kid."

She started to protest, then must have spotted her dad's smile. "Almost seventeen, Dad, not a little one anymore."

"I know," Zack said, "believe me I know. And I think about that every day."

Zack mixed up a salad to serve along with the pasta. He poured a glass of red wine for himself and a quarter of a glass for Laura. Might as well get used to it, Kelly.

Laura came downstairs after a quick shower and spotted the wine. "Hey, pasta looks great and oh, my, what's in that glass?"

Zack raised his glass. "To my darling daughter who's not so little anymore, and is growing into quite a young lady."

Laura toasted with her dad, took a sip, then made a huge sigh. "Note to self. My dad's not such a bad guy after all. I think he's gonna make it. Needs some work, but he's going to make it."

They talked about her day and soccer practice.

"What about you?" Laura asked. "Have you been able to find Colonel Garcia yet?"

"Nothing new on Garcia and I'm really worried. Shelia and I were at the FBI today and we're going with them on a bust tonight. I'm hoping that we can find Garcia. If not... ." Zack didn't want to think about that.

Laura took a bite of pasta. Chewed and swallowed. "I did some research on the Internet last night. Guess flashbacks and headaches are a big deal for lots of soldiers coming back from Iraq and Afghanistan."

"That's the tough part. We lost great people over there." Zack looked out the window for a moment. He always felt it personally whenever one of his soldiers got hit.

Laura walked around the table, putting her arms around her

dad's shoulders. "I'm sorry, I shouldn't have brought it up. I don't want to bring the bad stuff back to you."

"You're helping me a lot more than you know."

His cell rang. "Kelly."

"Agent Ferguson here. We've set things for nine o'clock tonight. Meet me here at the Hoover Building at eight."

Zack and Shelia squeezed together in the back of a FBI surveillance van camouflaged as a laundry truck and listened to a multitude of voices spilling out from the radio.

The FBI SWAT team had parked a half block down the street from the building housing the supposed internship. The team took about twenty minutes to encircle the area and close off possible escape routes. The satellite pictures on the television screen showed the house from various angles. Seven cars stood parked in the lot. So far, everything looked quiet in the house.

Shelia leaned into Zack, touching his hand. "Oh, Zack, I'm so worried for my friends. Things feel dark to me. Negative energy. What if… ."

"Don't even think about it," Zack replied. "The team will get to the girls in time." He glanced back toward the screen, not wanting to admit he worried for them, too.

Terry McHugh sat on the other side of Shelia. He whispered something into her ear, bringing a hint of a smile. The guy had really faked him out and Zack was glad. He liked McHugh.

Agent Joe Shepard, the SWAT Team commander, leaned over to listen to the radio. A short, slender man, his quick jerky actions telegraphed the adrenalin which must have been pumping through his veins. He listened again, then said to Ferguson, "The house is surrounded. Awaiting your orders."

Ferguson glanced at his watch and made a note on his pad. He keyed the microphone. "Nine twenty-six. Let's do this thing."

Shepard pushed open the back door of the van and jumped out, Ferguson and McHugh right behind him.

"Wait here," Ferguson whispered to Zack. "I'll let you know when it's safe to come in."

The TV showed teams of men in black uniforms and masks, each with an AK-47 machine gun, moving across the street toward the front gate. Simultaneously, teams moved in from the back of the house and the north side. A fourth group of SWAT team members waited on the south side in case someone tried to slip away in that direction.

Zack waited, the frustration simmering to a boil. What if they didn't find Garcia? What the hell would he do then?

Shelia squeezed his arm. "I sense that things will turn bad. The negative energy I'm feeling from this building is like a dark cloud spreading over my head. I don't like it."

Zack put his arm on her shoulder. "I hope you're wrong." But he worried she wasn't. She'd proven to be sharp on her feelings. It didn't bode well for the future when she turned dark.

He turned back to the screen in time to see the SWAT Team use a battering ram to smash through the iron gate, then use the same battering ram to break down the front door. The team members wore microphones. Shouts and screams sounded through the speakers inside the van. Some single shots, then one machine gun cut loose. Oh no, Zack thought, don't let any of those girls be caught in a crossfire.

More shouts. A scream of pain. Another male voice yelling.

Zack's gaze flipped between the screen and his watch. Shelia's fingernails dug into his arm, murmurs falling from her lips like rain. He did his best to keep track of time.

In fourteen minutes, Ferguson's voice came over the system, calling an "all clear."

Zack couldn't sit still any longer. Garcia's life was at stake. He pushed open the back door of the truck and pulled out his pistol. Glancing at Shelia he said, "Let's go. Stay behind me."

They ducked down and ran across the street, through the gate and up the porch stairs. Zack estimated the foyer to be at least fourteen by twenty feet. In the center, a circular chandelier with four tiers of lights glittered from the ceiling. A wall-to-wall Persian rug covered most of the floor. Damn johns needed elegance to get it up with the young girls.

To his left through an arched entryway stood the living room. Overstuffed chairs, end tables with Tiffany lamps, and couches each with coffee tables in front of them, were arrayed around the room. Zack checked to make sure no one hid behind them. In the center of one of the rugs lay the moose who had chased Zack away two days before. A SWAT Team member kept his AK- 47 trained on the man and one of his buddies.

Yells and curses swirled around Zack. Shouts from upstairs, an angry scream from a woman, but so far no more gunshots.

Ferguson walked into the room. Zack pulled him aside. "What did you find?"

"These two guys here are the muscle in the house. Team took 'em down fast. There's a woman upstairs in one of the rooms who appears to be in charge. She's not happy with us. Not happy at all."

"What about the girls?" Shelia asked.

"Three of them are in rooms by themselves, lying in bed, not responsive, apparently zoned out on something. Our doctor is checking them now."

Shelia headed for the stairs.

"Wait, let me finish," Ferguson called. "Three more are in rooms with guys who appear old enough to be their fathers. One of the men tried to jump out a window onto the back porch but we grabbed him. My guy said he recognizes him. Thinks he's a big deal federal judge."

"Bastard," Zack murmured.

"Yeah," Ferguson responded.

"That's it?" Zack asked. "What about Garcia?"

"So far it appears those are the only women. I distributed pictures of Colonel Garcia to all of the team members. No one has spotted her yet, but we're not done. There's still the basement and four outbuildings."

"What about the others?" Shelia asked. "There should be another half dozen here."

"I'm not sure yet of any more. Most of the rooms look occupied, you know, clothes in closets, unmade beds. I'm guessing a number of the women are out on the town with their johns."

"Okay if we look around?" Zack asked.

"Just stay out of the way of the team."

Zack hurried across the entry hallway into the dining room, Shelia right behind him. The table, centered under another tiered chandelier, could easily seat twenty guests. Zack checked under the table to make sure the team hadn't missed anyone.

He pushed open an oak door to his left and entered a modern, state-of-the-art kitchen. An enormous butcher-block workstation ran down the center of the room with rows of pots and pans and cooking utensils hanging above it on stainless-steel hangers. There was a refrigerator-freezer combination large enough to serve a battalion, two built-in stoves with microwaves over them, and all manner of pots and pans along the cabinets, shining and immaculate. It reminded Zack of the classroom at the community college where he'd taken French cooking classes.

Two FBI agents kept their guns trained on three Hispanic men and four Hispanic women, the cooking staff's screams and cries evoking instant sympathy. Zack doubted they were involved – just hired to do a job. Other agents searched through the kitchen and the adjoining store rooms.

Zack and Shelia headed back out to the central hallway. Ferguson stood at the base of the stairs. "I'm going upstairs to question the woman who appears to be in charge."

"You mean the madam?" Zack whispered under his breath.

"Yeah," Shelia replied. "The bitch madam."

"You're welcome to listen in to my questions, but I ask that you stand back and not say anything."

Shelia headed toward the stairs and started up, murmuring, "You mean I can't scratch her eyes out?"

39

Georgetown, VA Tuesday, 12:15 a.m.

Zack and Shelia followed Ferguson up the circular staircase. One of the SWAT Team members motioned them into the third door on the left.

Red drapes outlined frilly white curtains that covered the drawn window shades. Two large chest of drawers were pushed up against opposite walls. The closet appeared stocked with a complete assortment of women's clothes. Stylish clothes from what Zack could tell.

A king-size bed stood in the center of the room with a full-length mirror overhead. Two book cases lined the wall in the corner, housing an extensive collection of books. A red bedspread and red-silk throw pillows were strewn on the floor. Rumpled satin sheets outlined in blue and gold covered the bed. The sweet smell of marijuana, mingled with sex, permeated the room. This appeared to be the woman's own room.

Terry McHugh leaned over the woman sitting in what looked like a Chippendale captain's chair. The woman, who resembled Sean Lannigan, wore a white blouse open at the neck and black slacks. Barefoot, her long brown hair mussed, her hands cuffed, and her face twisted in obvious anger.

She glared up at McHugh. "What do you bastards think you're doing? Bursting into my house like this. I'll have your badges, and I'll personally shove them up your asses."

McHugh gave her a slight smile. "You're all through shoving things up men's asses."

Ferguson sat in a chair next to the woman and laid the warrant on her lap. "First of all I want to advise you of your rights." He read her a Miranda warning. "We believe you are running an escort service here which is a front for a house of prostitution. I warn you that whatever you say may be used against you in a court of law."

She leaned forward and tried to reach Shelia. "You bitch, I remember you. You call yourself Irish, but look how you treat your fellow Irish."

Shelia looked about ready to pull the woman's hair out. "Right back at you, bitch."

Terry McHugh moved around to stand between Shelia and the woman. "I've been following this case from Ireland for the past year. I'm not pleased to call you Irish."

The SWAT Team chief stuck his head into the room. "Agent Ferguson, can I see you a minute?"

Zack and Shelia followed Ferguson out into the hallway.

"I'm afraid it doesn't look good."

"I knew it." Shelia put her face in her hands. "The negative energy is strong in here."

"Upstairs in the attic, it looks like a house of horrors. There's equipment to torture people. Looked like blood stains on some pieces of the equipment. I've called for the lab guys to come in. We'll see what they find."

Zack started toward the attic stairs. Ferguson put a restraining hand on his arm. "You can't do that, Colonel Kelly. It's a crime scene."

"But Garcia... ." He stopped, knowing Ferguson was right.

"The team has completed an initial review," Ferguson replied. "We'll initiate a comprehensive room-by-room search checking for hidden passages or anyplace they could stash someone. We'll have to sort it out. Don't know anything for sure yet."

"How about the outbuildings?" Zack asked. "What about them?"

"A three-car garage, and a couple of sheds. We're going through them now."

"We can't let all the horny old bastards get away. When they see the SWAT guys here, they'll keep on going."

Ferguson smiled, his first of the operation. "No, they won't. We've got the license plate numbers and pictures of all the pricks who have been coming and going out of here for the past week. We're in the process of going house to house now to round them up."

Zack gave him a thumbs-up. "Mind if we look around up here."

"Let's see. We've moved the young women to a hospital for observation so it should be okay. Just be careful and try not to touch anything."

Zack and Shelia poked their heads into the other bedrooms on that floor. All elegant, all with king-size beds, and all with mirrors over the beds. The beds were made in two of the four rooms, the others mussed.

"Not very original," Shelia said.

"But remember, you need something special to inspire these senior citizens."

"What is it the Brits say? You know, keep a stiff upper something."

Zack had to laugh in spite of the tension. "I think it's a stiff upper lip."

"Don't think that would do these guys much good... ." Her face crumpled into tears.

Zack put his arm around her as they walked out into the hallway. "We'll find them. All of them."

Ferguson came over. "I suspect we'll locate more of the girls as the night goes on. They're either being forced to be escorts, or are voluntarily acting as escorts because they enjoy it. We'll bring them into a central processing point. I'm sure these distinguished citizens will be all lawyered up by the time they get there."

"Lawyers piled on top of lawyers," Zack said. "Should be quite a sight."

Ferguson cleaned his glasses, then pushed in a number on his cell. "I've already tipped off the *Washington Post* so they'll be at the station we've set up to process these guys. Before we're done, the president is going to have to appoint a whole bunch of new federal judges, and probably a group of senior studs in the attorney general's office and who knows where else."

Zack and Shelia hitched a ride with Ferguson and McHugh to the Old Post Office where the FBI had set up a processing point for all the men who had been rounded up in the raid.

Located three blocks up Pennsylvania Avenue from the Hoover Building, the local shops inside the building were closed at this time of night, but the noise level remained high. Agents in blue jackets with FBI stenciled on the back brought in gray-haired men, all yelling about this outrage. More men followed the agents, complaining about governmental abuse of their legal rights.

Throngs of reporters milled around outside the building, taking pictures and calling questions at the men as they were brought in. TV cameras captured it all on film and fed it to the networks. Zack had never seen so many guys ducking around, trying to cover their faces with coats, jackets, or anything else that might be available.

Shelia squealed with delight when Katie O'Shay arrived. O'Shay spotted Shelia and ran to her. The two hugged and cried. She still seemed wobbly on her feet, but her speech sounded clear and she was able to talk in complete sentences.

"Oh, Shelia," Katie said, "it was awful. At first, everyone seemed so nice. After those first two days of orientation, we were told that if we didn't want to be deported in disgrace back to Ireland, we'd need to act as escorts for these men. That seemed all right to most of us. We were treated to a few drinks and went to parties. I had fun, but before I knew it, this guy was ripping my clothes off back at the house. This big guy slapped me and told me to play along or he'd beat me until I did."

Ferguson stood next to Shelia listening to what Katie had to say. After she finished he said, "I need for you to come with me so that I can take your statement for the record. I'll have to ask you to identify the men who did these things to you."

"All right," Katie said. "Whatever you want. But first, I'd like to call my mum. They wouldn't let me make any calls, but I managed to get to my mobile and sneak out a call."

"That's what tipped us off for sure to where you were and the trouble you were in," Shelia said. "Up until that point, we only could guess where you might be. Your mother called me. Zack and I drove over to the house and that's when I saw you."

"Thank heavens you did," Katie said. "I was so doped up, I'm not sure how much longer I would have lasted without your help."

"Here Katie, I've got my mobile." Shelia pulled it out of her purse and pushed in a number. She handed it to Katie.

After a minute, Katie said, "Yes, mum, I'm out safe. Shelia and her friend brought in the FBI and they got us out of that awful place." Katie squinted and put her hand up to her ear. "Let me go someplace so I can hear you better. It's really noisy in here." She walked over to a corner and continued to talk into the phone, crying, laughing, smiling. After she finished, she gave the cell back to Shelia, then after hugging Shelia and Zack, she walked off with Agent Ferguson.

Zack asked Ferguson again about Garcia, but there was no sign of her. Melody Lannigan claimed she'd never seen anyone named Rene Garcia. After extensive questioning, Zack believed her. She said she saw a female Army lieutenant colonel from the window one evening when Garcia came to the front gate, but that was the only time.

Zack called General Hightower a little after two and updated him on everything that happened. Hightower agreed to brief Quinn. Questions in Zack's mind surfaced on Sean Lannigan's involvement and what that might mean for Quinn.

At three-fifteen, Ferguson brought an arrogant Sean Lannigan into the building for questioning. When Lannigan saw Zack, he yelled, "This is your fault, you bastard. I'll see to it that you're finished in the military. By the time I'm done with you, no one will want you. Do you hear me? No one."

Zack had about enough of him. "Listen here, Lannigan, you're nothing but scum and you're going down. And you know what? I'll be there to watch you go to jail."

Shelia moved between the two men. "Stop it, Zack. Let the FBI take care of him."

Lannigan turned to Shelia, his face red and screamed, "I thought you were my friend."

"I'm sorry for you, Sean, if all this is true. I thought you were a special guy. The father of one of my best friends. But if you let those old men prey on young girls, girls who thought they were getting an education, well you gave them a pretty sad education and you're going to pay for it."

By the end of the evening, Agent Ferguson, with Shelia's help, counted three girls still missing. Zack remembered the blood stains and shivered when he thought about what might have happened to them. Zack and Shelia watched and waited, hoping for the arrival of more young women and Garcia.

Finally about four-thirty in the morning, Zack dropped Shelia at her hotel with plans to meet the next day for an early lunch. Zack found himself stumped about Garcia.

40

Arlington, VA, 6:00 a.m.

The sound of Laura's alarm upstairs woke Zack from where he had fallen asleep on the couch in the living room. While she showered and dressed, Zack cooked her a three-egg omelet and one for himself as well. They sat together at the kitchen table, and he shared all the highlights from the night before.

Laura scooped up one last bite of omelet. "You'd better go back to bed, Dad. Your eyes look like they're going to hemorrhage before you can even leave the house."

Zack stretched and yawned. "Sleep does sound good."

On her way out the door Laura yelled back, "Love you, Dad." She waved as she boarded the bus. Zack came back inside, thought about going upstairs for a shower, then decided to lie down on the couch again.

He had just dozed off when his aunt came down the stairs. "I'm planning on going back home this morning. I've got some things I have to do." She walked over and gave Zack a kiss on the forehead. "Uh-oh, you don't look so good."

"Long night." He sat up, shook his head to clear it, then told her what happened. "You'll be able to read all the gory details in the *Washington Post*. I'm going into work later this morning but will be here tonight for Laura. Thanks again for hanging out with her."

His aunt sat in her favorite antique rocker that she'd bought as a house-warming present for Zack. "You're welcome, Zack. I do love that girl." She shook her head. "Oh, my, those poor young women. Brought over here to learn about our legal system, then pressed into prostitution."

"I agree." Zack pushed himself up to stand. "Guess I'd better take a shower, then hit the road. The Pentagon awaits, and I'm sure I'll need to provide a detailed briefing for Hightower and Quinn. Quinn is going to need to brief the president."

The doorbell rang. Zack walked over to the living room window and pushed aside the sheer curtains.

A uniformed officer sat in each of the two police cars parked in his driveway. Two unmarked car he figured might be the feds, idled in the street. "What the hell is this all about?" he murmured, as much to himself as to his aunt.

Mary hurried to the window, stood behind Zack, and looked over his shoulder. "My goodness, what in the world?"

He opened the door. FBI Agent Henley Spitz waited outside on the top step. Behind Spitz stood a group of four men, two in Arlington police uniforms, the other two in civilian clothes. Spitz was dressed in a dark blue blazer and a pair of gray slacks, normal fare for law enforcement.

"Agent Spitz, what's going on? " Zack asked. "And who's with you?"

Spitz handed Zack an official-looking sheet of paper.

Zack glanced at it. "A warrant? For what?"

Spitz seemed to be trying to hide a smile. "To search your house, Colonel Kelly. You'll need to step back and let us in."

Zack grabbed the paper and looked at it. "What's this all about?"

"Just let us in and I'll tell you. You probably don't want your neighbors seeing all of us hanging around on your front porch, and trust me, we're not going away."

"All right." Zack opened the door the rest of the way. The group trooped in, their shoes smearing dirt from the early morning mist all over the light green carpet in the living room.

"My Lord," Mary cried out. "Wipe your feet."

Zack pulled Spitz aside as the others spread out through the house. "What the hell do you think you're doing? You're tearing my house apart and scaring my aunt. My daughter just left on a school bus. You would have put her in a panic."

Spitz watched Zack, saying nothing.

"For your information," Zack said, "I just got back to the house at four-thirty this morning after helping your fellow FBI agents break up a huge escort service in D.C. This includes the girls who had been brought over from Ireland thinking they'd be in some sort of legal internship."

Spitz still didn't say anything.

"And I still don't know what happened to my friend and partner, Rene Garcia. Now, you've brought this herd of agents in to tear apart my house. You're really pushing me, Spitz. I demand to know what's going on."

"Okay," Spitz said, the smile creasing his face. "As I think you know, Blake Lannigan's father has put up a $100,000 reward for information leading to the return of his daughter and finding out who kidnapped her."

"I knew that." Zack didn't tell Spitz that he suspected Lannigan would be in jail before the internship mess got straightened out.

Spitz pulled a sheet of paper out of his blazer pocket. "We've received several tips in response to the reward."

"I'm sure," Zack replied. "How many?"

"Well, over five hundred. Most of these tips were pretty far-fetched, but one is of particular interest to me."

"And what was that?" Zack asked.

"That you had a flashback when Ms. Lannigan disappeared and couldn't remember what happened to her. The informant said you were acting strangely the last time he saw you and had confided in him that you had some of her clothes upstairs in your closet. Kinda like a prize you told him."

Zack's eyes widened. He tensed. Couldn't believe what he was hearing. The headaches started again. "You're tearing my house apart based on that?"

"Not only based on that tip. You know I've been concerned about you, Kelly. The way I heard you acted at the restaurant in Pentagon City. You killed that guy. And it wasn't necessary. You went wild and from what I understand, you had no knowledge of what you were doing. Actually I heard you seemed to be having a flashback to Afghanistan."

"He tried to kill me, for Christ's sake."

"I've told you before that I understand all that, but several witnesses said that you lost complete control and were yelling about the Taliban trying to bomb your men."

Zack stared at him. Remembered the flashbacks. The headaches.

"You've got a problem, Kelly. Even though I applaud your service, I believe we need to check to make sure you didn't do anything with Ms. Lannigan... ah, maybe something you couldn't remember, may not even remember you did."

"This is incredible."

"Just go along with it for now, Colonel. If we find nothing, we'll be out of your house in an hour."

Aunt Mary stomped out of the kitchen. "Look at this carpet. I can't believe you're doing this to Zack's house. I hope you're planning on cleaning up this mess."

Spitz shrugged. "I need to check you for weapons, Kelly."

Zack did as he was told and turned around, the headache creeping across his skull, thundering down his neck. He shook his head to stay clear. Don't overreact, he thought. Get these clowns out of here. Remember what Gordy Hale told you, don't overreact.

Spitz patted Zack down. When he finished he said, "Why don't you wait in the kitchen with your aunt. I'll go upstairs and check to see how the group is doing. Be back down in a few minutes."

Zack sat at the kitchen table, rubbing the back of his neck. Footsteps thumped around upstairs, and the voices of men and women sounded from the living room. No one had checked the kitchen yet. They'd be in here soon.

He tried to remember if he had anything here he shouldn't. Weapons? Couldn't come up with anything. He had trouble thinking with the headache crashing in on him.

Spitz walked into the kitchen, carrying a plastic bag, a frown on his face. "You remember, Kelly, that when the officer found Ms. Lannigan walking along the road in Gettysburg, she was wearing a different outfit than the one you described her wearing when she disappeared."

"Yes." Zack got a sinking feeling in his gut as to what might be in the bag.

"One of my men found these clothes in your bedroom closet. We'll double check with Ms. Lannigan's mother to make sure, but I have to ask you, Colonel, what is Blake Lannigan's outfit doing in your bedroom closet?"

Zack stared at the bag in disbelief. Tried to remember that night. He'd seen Blake at the hospital, but he sure hadn't taken any of her clothes. Where the hell did they come from?

His aunt stormed into the kitchen, looked at the bag. "I can't believe this. There must be some mistake. I've never seen these things before. One of your men must have planted the clothes there."

"No mistake. This is what we found upstairs in the master bedroom closet."

"Come on, Spitz," Zack said, "you know someone planted it there. If those clothes were for real, I wouldn't have left something like that in the house."

"Well now, we're getting somewhere. Where would you have planted it? In someone else's closet?"

Zack had to shut up and call for a lawyer. Don't say anything. Don't overreact.

"I'm aware that it's not very smart to leave things in your own house, but the fact still remains that you do have problems remembering things." Spitz handed the plastic bag to a female agent. "Maybe you did something with Ms. Lannigan and didn't remember it at the time. It came back to you later. You travel to the place where you left her, force her to change clothes, maybe even forced her to have sex with you. Then you bring the clothes back to your house for whatever reason."

"Spitz, that's a bunch of crap. You can't really believe that fairy-tale."

"I'm not saying that I do," Spitz replied, "but the fact still remains that we found Ms. Lannigan's clothes in your house, upstairs in your bedroom. Maybe you had her hidden upstairs for a couple of days. Maybe longer. Who knows what's going on in that mind of yours."

Zack's anger boiled over. "Get real. My daughter lives with me. I'm not going to bring some drugged-up woman into the house and put her upstairs."

"How do you know she might have been drugged?" Spitz asked.

"I have no idea what happened to Blake, but if I were to bring her here, either she came willingly or she'd need to be drugged. Otherwise she'd be yelling her head off. I know Blake. She's not going to go along with something like that willingly. Check Walter Reed. Was she drugged?"

"The lab there says they couldn't confirm drugs in her system." Spitz bit his lip, probably angry at himself for his slip of the tongue. "Whoever took her must have either known her or used something else to take her. You knew her well. What did you use?"

"You can't really believe that I kidnapped Blake Lannigan. We're friends. She was looking forward to seeing the battlefield. You can't possibly think of any realistic scenario where I'd do anything like what you're suggesting. And if I did, I certainly wouldn't leave her clothes where you could find them."

Spitz read Zack his rights. "Now just stay where you are. Don't make things any worse than they are right now."

Spitz stepped into the dining room and motioned for another agent to stand guard over Zack.

His aunt came into the kitchen. "Who would do something like this to you?"

"I don't know, but I plan to find out."

Mary walked over and dialed the phone. She talked to someone, then hung up and walked into the other room. "This is awful. So unfair. Awful."

The agent in the doorway didn't say anything, but nodded to her as she walked by.

Spitz came in once to check on Zack. "We'll be leaving for the

Hoover Building in about twenty minutes. You may want to get yourself a lawyer. Looks to me like you'll need one.

Zack waited. What should he do? What could he do? Probably not a damn thing.

Aunt Mary came into the kitchen every few minutes and looked out the window.

"I'm sorry about all this," Zack said. "It's a huge mistake, and I hate to put you and Laura through this."

"I know." She walked back into the living room murmuring, "This is so unfair."

Zack decided to use his one phone call to contact General Hightower and update him on what had happened. Hightower would realize this was a mistake and that Zack would get it straightened out. Right now, Zack stayed more of a liability to the general than an asset. Zack needed to turn that around and damn fast.

A loud moan sounded from the living room, then a thud. Zack jumped up. The mirror in the dining room which angled into the living room showed his aunt sprawled on the floor. "Mary, my God, what's wrong." He yelled at the agent. "Get help, you fool, get help. She has a bad heart."

The agent ran from his position in the doorway and knelt on the floor in the living room next to Zack's aunt while Zack reached for the phone to dial 911.

The back door burst open. T.J. Wilson slipped in and whispered, "Let's get you the hell out of here."

"But, Aunt Mary... "

"She's fine. Now, come on."

Zack followed him out the back door. They jumped the wooden fence that circled the back yard, then ran through the next yard to the street behind Zack's house where Wilson had parked his truck. They hopped in and Wilson fired it up.

Zack couldn't believe what he and his friend were doing. "Hey, T.J., we're in deep shit."

"No kidding, but we gotta figure out who's got it in for you. You can't do that from inside some dumbass federal pen. Besides, damn Spitz keeps this up, I'll call the brothers to put out a contract on him."

A calliope of thoughts cascaded through his brain, none of which Zack could believe. What the hell was he doing? He leaned over toward Wilson. "How did you know what was going on?"

"My cribbage partner called me," Wilson replied. "She said the feds were working some sort of frame on you and you needed help. So, here I am."

"Great to see you," Zack replied. "But you know our careers just got flushed down the toilet."

"Fuck 'em." Wilson turned onto Arlington Boulevard and floored the truck. It leaped forward and they sailed down the street. "Besides," he said, "who wants to make a below-the-zone promotion to lieutenant colonel anyway."

"Better take it easy on the speed friend, you've got an escaped criminal in your vehicle."

"Escaped criminal, my ass. A guy who's been screwed by the fucking feds." He tapped the brakes to slow the truck down. "What do you think we should do?"

"Head to Garcia's condo. Someone's got her, and she's got to be the key to this whole mess."

Wilson downshifted. "Guess we do need to be careful. Garcia lives in Old Town, doesn't she?"

"Yeah. I'll give you directions."

Wilson took the exit to Arlington Boulevard. "What do you hope to find?"

"Maybe we can get a lead where she might be. I know damn well that wherever she is will lead us to the person behind what's going on."

"Think it's Lannigan?"

"I don't honestly know. He's tied up in this white slavery mess, but I can't come up with any scenario where he'd kidnap his own daughter. If that's what we find, then he's even lower than I thought. And that's pretty damn low."

41

Old Town Alexandria, 10:15 a.m.

Wilson pulled into the alley and parked in a space behind Garcia's condo. Zack got out and peeked into the garage to check for her Harley. Empty. Where the hell was it?

The two cut through a hedge in the back, then tromped on a couple of tomato plants in Garcia's postage-stamp garden. In spite of the tension, Zack had to chuckle. "Garcia's gonna have my ass for crushing her plants."

"Fuck that," Wilson replied. "We find her, I'll buy her a whole crate of organic tomatoes."

Zack held up his hand and they stopped to scan the area, then walked up the narrow sidewalk between Garcia's condo and the adjoining building. Zack looked left then right before climbing the three steps to her back porch.

He glanced around one more time for any nosy neighbors, then pulled out a brick in the wall and grabbed a key to the back door. Wilson kept watch behind them.

Zack unlocked the door and pushed it open, then replaced the key. "We're in. You check the bedroom, I'll get the kitchen."

The counters were spotless, no food or trash anywhere. Zack would have expected no less. He saw a couple of vet appointments on the wall calendar, but nothing posted for the past Friday.

He moved onto the living room. Thick wall-to-wall carpet covered the floor, and a large-screen television stood in the corner nearest the window. A three-cushion couch was pushed up against the wall opposite the windows, and a square mahogany table separated two overstuffed chairs. A coffee table stood in front of the couch, magazines neatly stacked along one edge.

Wilson came out of the bedroom. "Damn, nothing out of place. No crap laying around. Everything dusted. I feel like I should take my shoes off."

"Probably looks exactly like your place."

Wilson snorted, "Yeah, right."

"You finish in here," Zack said. "I'm going into the den. We've got to find a lead to where she went Friday night before she disappeared."

As Zack stood at the door to the den, he thought he heard a noise from inside the room. What the... ? Sounded like something fell.

He ducked down and crept into the den, watching. Something brushed his leg. He jumped, almost fell backwards before catching his balance. Harold stared up at him. Goddamn, Garcia's cat. He'd forgotten all about him. Zack bent down and picked up the cat who meowed like mad. "Harold, you must be starved."

Zack walked back into the kitchen, Harold weaving between his legs. Sweeping aside the pantry curtain, Zack searched the shelves until he found what he wanted. "Hey, buddy, I wish you could talk, my friend. Maybe you could tell me where Garcia's gone. You probably know and I ain't got a clue. Oh, if you only could talk."

He pulled out two cans of cat food, opened them and scooped the contents into Harold's dish. Poor cat wolfed it down like a dog. Harold was Garcia's best buddy. She would never have left him unattended for more than a day. Zack dumped and refilled the litter box, then, remembering milk gave Harold diarrhea, he filled Harold's water dish.

Having taken care of poor Harold, Zack moved back into the den and sat down at the desk. He fingered the keyboard of the computer. Tried to remember Garcia's password. Couldn't.

He walked over to the three-drawer file cabinet against the wall and pulled open drawers. Nothing but receipts, tax returns, and paperwork on her stocks.

Zack sat down on the single bed next to the filing cabinet and thought, what am I looking for? Garcia was highly organized. Wrote down everything. Drove him crazy but he needed it now.

Back to the desk, he sat and looked around. Tried to visualize her sitting there last Friday. What would she do? Come on Garcia, help me figure out what's going on. He twisted back and forth in the chair a couple of times looking at the incredibly tidy room. He spotted her personal desk calendar almost hidden by the blotter on the desk. Snapped his fingers. Come on.

The calendar lay open to the Friday page. He looked at it. Saw her neat printing. Then it hit him. All so clear. How could he have been so stupid?

He jumped up and ran into the living room, startling Wilson. "Come on, I know where she is. Let's hope she's still okay. We gotta hurry... "

Two hours and fifteen minutes later, Wilson pulled into the parking lot in front of the Visitor's Center and shut off the engine. He leaned back in the seat. "What now?"

Zack stared at the door to the building. "We wait. We wait for the bastard, and we follow him. I hope we're not too late."

"I feel like a sitting duck here," Wilson said. "I'm sure by now the feds know who busted you out and what sort of a truck I own. They've probably got an APB out on us."

"I know, man, I know. We gotta get to him before the cops find us."

Wilson opened the door and stepped out. "Time to fix our sitting duck status."

"What are you going to do?" Zack asked.

"Practice a skill I finely honed as a teen in D.C. I'm already on the fed's shit list, so if we get caught now, a little more won't hurt."

He walked over to a Ford F-150 in the corner of the lot, looked around, then bent down and loosened the screws holding on the license plate. Brought the plate over and exchanged it for the one on his truck. Then he walked back and put his plate on the other truck. It took him no more than five minutes for the entire operation.

When Wilson got back in the truck Zack said, "Hey man, you're fast."

"Years of practice, my friend, years of practice."

"Won't the police spot the plate?"

"They'll check out the truck first. If it's the make and model they're looking for, then they'll check the plate. Poor bastard wasn't smart enough to buy a Chevy so the cops won't look at the plate number."

Zack had to laugh. "The voice of experience."

They sat waiting for another twenty minutes when Wilson called, "Get down, it's the fuzz."

A Gettysburg police car pulled into the lot and drove slowly up and down the lanes. The car came to a stop behind Wilson's truck for a moment, then moved on.

Zack held his breath but the police car kept moving, pulled out of the lot, and turned right onto Washington Street.

Wilson chuckled. "I rest my case."

"What happens when the guy who owns the truck comes out?"

"Nothing. How often do you check the plate on your truck. I suspect the guy won't check it for days, maybe weeks. By then, we'll be legal again. At least we'd better be or we'll need to head south of the border."

"Or be attending the long course at Fort Leavenworth."

"Come on," Wilson said, "let's have a little faith here."

"I believe, T.J., I believe. Hell, I gotta believe."

At four forty-two, Cliff Henderson strolled out of the Visitor's Center and climbed into his Jeep.

"There he is," Zack said. "Let him pull out first, then we follow him."

Wilson tapped his fingers on the steering wheel, and waited until Henderson pulled out of the parking lot, then turned right onto Washington Street. He started the truck, pulled out of the driveway and stayed about a block behind the vehicle as Henderson moved down Washington Street. Fortunately a number of vehicles filled the road so keeping two or three between them wasn't a problem.

At the square in the middle of town, the jeep turned left onto Buford Avenue which soon turned into Chambersburg Pike. They passed the Lutheran Theological Seminary on the left and followed the pike west out of Gettysburg. The road passed through rolling hills with trees lining either side.

They almost got too close when the stoplight changed at Herr Ridge Road. Zack ducked down in the seat. His heart pounded as he waited for the light to change. Their target shouldn't know Wilson's truck so they were probably all right. But Zack found himself covered with sweat because Garcia's life could depend on what they did. Don't screw it up.

"Damn, I didn't see that light," Wilson said. "There's only one vehicle between us. Think it'll be okay?"

"Hell," Zack replied, "it's gotta be."

The light changed and Wilson pulled out slowly, letting their target widen the space between the two vehicles.

In another mile, the jeep pulled off to the left and stopped in the parking lot of a PDQ Food Mart. The man got out, looked around him, and walked inside.

Wilson kept going another half block, then he pulled into a lot on the opposite side of the road and slipped in behind another vehicle.

"What do you think?" Wilson asked.

"Should be okay here," Zack said. "Uh-oh, what's this."

Two guys on motorcycles pulled into the parking lot, got off and looked around, then sauntered inside the store.

"Think it's a meeting?" Wilson asked. "Guys look pretty squirrelly."

"Don't think so. Those guys don't look like his sort, but who knows. Whatever's going on, we wait."

Fifteen minutes later, Henderson came back outside, carrying a brown paper bag. He climbed into the jeep and pulled back onto Route 30, still heading west. He passed them without looking in their direction.

Wilson waited a couple of more minutes, then pulled out of his parking place and followed, staying two blocks behind the jeep.

"Watch out," Zack called. "He's turning left onto old Route 30."

Fortunately another vehicle pulled into the left turn lane ahead of Wilson so he could wait, then turn left and follow. Zack ducked down in the seat again.

As they started up again, Zack said, "This is the way to the Cashtown Inn."

"Do you think he could be going there?" Wilson asked. "Maybe it's some sort of meeting place."

"We'll see."

They followed the vehicle west on old Route 30 for another mile or so, staying well behind it.

"Heads up," Wilson said. "He's got his left turn blinker on. Looks like he's gonna turn at that old church."

"Slow down and pull up over there." Zack watched the vehicle turn left. "Okay, now let's get closer to the turn and check it out."

When they reached the church, Zack squinted at the sign. "He turned left at the Flowers Lutheran Church and, no shit, onto Flowers Church Road. Let's drive past the turn and I'll check out a map to see what's up that road."

"Will do." Wilson edged the truck past the turn, Zack watched the vehicle they'd been following disappear around a bend in the road and over a slight hill.

"Okay, why don't you turn around," Zack said. "Let me look at the map again and see what it looks like up that road. We can't afford to lose him on these country roads."

Wilson made a U-turn and stopped on the side of the road.

"Map shows there aren't too many turns off this road so we should be able to find his place."

They made a right onto the gravel road, passing an old fieldstone wall bordering a cemetery on the left. The road curved to the right then down a gentle hill, farmland stretching out on both sides.

"Where did he turn off this road?" Wilson asked.

Zack looked down the first turn to their right. "Oak Tree Lane. Let's stay on the main road for a couple of miles, checking the various turnoffs. My bet is he turned up this first one."

"Yeah," Wilson replied. "I can still see some dust from a vehicle up there."

"If there's not a better turn, we'll come back here, park across the road over there, and walk up the road."

Wilson downshifted the truck to slow down. "Sounds like a plan."

42

Approximately nine miles west of Gettysburg, 8:14 p.m.

The sun had descended in a blaze of orange, the shadows lengthening as Wilson parked his truck on the west side of Flowers Church Road about a quarter-mile north of Oak Tree Lane.

The two got out and followed the main road to where the lane cut into the brush.

"Heads up," Zack whispered. "If you see lights, duck back into the trees."

They walked along the lane for maybe a third of a mile, seeing nothing on either side but trees. A gentle breeze rustled the leaves in the trees, and a great horned owl hooted twice in the distance. Zack thought he smelled smoke from a wood fire. Smelled good.

"Not much traffic," Zack said. "That's good for us. Hopefully we won't get surprised by another vehicle."

Zack stepped carefully, watching for holes or anything that might trip them up. He kept his flashlight off, but in his right hand in case he needed it. "Damn, I wish I'd brought my M-9."

"Not like you had a lot of time to plan."

"Well, that's true. Say, thanks again for bailing me out."

"No sweat. By the way, spooky, isn't it?" Wilson chuckled. "Want to hear a couple of ghost stories?"

"No, thanks," Zack replied. "I think I've had enough ghost stories for the week, thank you very much. Maybe for the rest of my life."

Zack spotted a light up ahead. "Wait." He ducked down and held out his hand. "Off the road. This must be his place."

They stayed along the edge of the lane and made their way to a clearing with three trailers in the center. A slight incline led up to where the trailers stood. Zack reached a rusting chain, held in place by a number of posts, that stretched across the gravel road.

He bent down and crept under the chain. "Wish I had a pair of binoculars."

Wilson pulled a square black case out of his jacket pocket. "Your wish is my command."

"Damn, T.J., you think of everything."

"Not quite everything. I should have brought my M-9 along. Left too fast."

One of the three trailers showed lights in the window, the other two stood dark. Zack pointed. "There's his vehicle. This is the right place."

"What now?" Wilson whispered.

Zack motioned to his right. "You go around that way, and I'll skirt along the other side. Shouldn't take too long to get to the far side of the clearing. Maybe we can see more from there."

"Makes sense," Wilson replied. "We don't want to barge in. particularly since neither one of us is armed."

"Two whistles will signify friendly."

"Got it." Wilson moved east through the brush. Zack picked his way along the west side of the clearing. He stopped every few minutes to scan the trailers. Still only one with lights.

It took Zack about twenty minutes to track around to the other side of the clearing, the multiflora roses cutting at his skin. He whistled twice and got two whistles in return. In a minute, he spotted Wilson emerging from the brush and moving toward him.

"See anything?" Zack asked.

"Nothing so far. All quiet."

"I don't like it. Too quiet. Not sure what he's doing."

"The only way we'll know for sure is to sneak up to that trailer and look inside."

Zack scanned all three trailers with his binoculars, settling on the one with lights. "You wait here. If the bastard catches me, he won't know you're here, too. If I'm not back in twenty minutes, call 911 for help."

"That's all I need is the cops. Hope those clowns believe we're the good guys. I'm sure by this time the feds have an APB out on us."

"Don't think about that. Wish me luck." Zack crouched and moved forward toward the trailer. He heard the great horned owl again. Other than that, all quiet.

When he reached the trailer, he straightened and peeked in the window. A television set glowed in the corner. Must be the living room. No one in the room. What to do? Maybe check out the other two trailers.

Zack crouched down again and moved across the clearing toward the second trailer. Still completely dark. Something rustled in the brush. The white tail of a deer disappeared toward the west. He held his breath and listened, then tried the door. Locked. Looked in the window. Couldn't see anything. Couldn't hear anything.

Crouching back down again, he moved across the clearing to the third trailer. Reminded him of a hunting camp. He pushed up on his toes and looked in the window. Dark. No noise from the inside.

He turned back toward the first trailer. Saw a light in the back room. Maybe a bedroom? Crouching down, he moved across the clearing. Reached up and looked in the window.

His heart jumped. Garcia sat on the bed, dressed in a white terrycloth robe, facing that fucking Cliff Henderson. The bastard was talking to her, but she didn't appear to be saying anything.

Henderson probably had an arsenal of weapons in there. Go back and get the police? No, they'd never believe him. Up to the two of them. Got to make it work. They'd only get one chance.

He moved back across the clearing toward Wilson, heart beating fast.

FBI Agents Henley Spitz and Albert Ferguson sat on one side of the conference table in Darcy Quinn's office, General Hightower on the other.

Quinn walked in and plunked down at the head of the table. Even tired, she still looked in charge, dressed in a tweed sport jacket and dark blue slacks. "All right, gentlemen, you asked for this meeting. What do you want from me?"

"Ms. Quinn," Ferguson said, "we're faced with somewhat of a sticky problem. As you must know, we raided the building last night that housed what is called the Irish internship."

"I'm aware of that. I understand you found a number of young women, and"—she frowned—"some not-so-young men."

"This must be particularly painful for you because we believe your brother-in-law and his sister were leaders in the internship."

Quinn kept a poker face. "I know that Sean's sister was arrested last night at the site of this internship. I have no knowledge Sean is involved in any of this."

"It will take a few days to sort this all out, but we believe Mr. Lannigan will prove to be involved." Ferguson folded and unfolded his hands. "In any event, we have statements from five of the girls that they were forced to have sex with older gentlemen."

Quinn cracked her first smile. "I'm not sure if any of these men can be called gentlemen. But go on, please continue."

"Four of the women are in George Washington Hospital Center, under treatment for drug abuse. We believe these women were fed drugs to gain their participation."

"What about the others?" Quinn asked. "Do you have a total count?"

"Four more of the women are in protective care in Social Services and three are still missing. We believe that's all who were involved this time. We're still trying to gain information on what we believe were two earlier groups of women."

"A total of eleven that you know of now?"

"Yes," Ferguson replied. "With the help of Ms. Shelia O'Donnell, we've been able to notify the parents of all but two of the girls. We're working on that now."

"Will the parents be able to come to the States?" General Hightower asked. "Help these young women through what must be a very traumatic event."

"It looks as if four or five sets of parents will be traveling here."

Ferguson got a pinched look on his face. "This, of course, concerns me for the safety of Mr. Lannigan. He's out on bail now, pending formal arraignment."

Quinn's eyes widened. "You have enough to charge him?"

"We believe so. Of course, that's in the hands of the attorney general. Because of the individuals involved, it will no doubt be quite messy for a long time."

Quinn nodded. "No doubt."

"Now," Ferguson continued, "let me turn it over to Agent Spitz. He'd like to discuss two members of your special task force who escaped earlier today."

Quinn turned toward the other man. "Agent Spitz?"

Beads of perspiration formed on Spitz's forehead. "Ms. Quinn, I realize how close you are to these two men."

"You have no idea of that so don't make assumptions you can't back up. I believe there have been enough of those for one day."

"I agree," Spitz replied. "As you may know, we received a tip from a confidential informant that Ms. Lannigan's clothes would be at the home of Colonel Kelly. We requested a warrant from a federal court to search his house. While there, we found clothes stuffed in a plastic bag in the upstairs closet at Kelly's house. Her mother later confirmed those clothes did belong to Blake Lannigan."

Quinn clucked her tongue. "My, my, isn't that a coincidence? Wraps things up very nicely for you, doesn't it? I'm surprised your source didn't put a ribbon around it and a bow on the top."

Spitz swallowed hard and looked down for a moment. "You may not agree with my actions, but I couldn't afford to ignore this information."

"And of course, it helped that Colonel Kelly was exhausted from working with Agent Ferguson to rescue the young Irish women from that house of horrors in Georgetown, bringing those behind the Irish internship to justice. . ."

Spitz held up his hand. "But... "

"Since he was up all night and hadn't slept for three days, including the time he's been searching for Colonel Garcia and trying to help Blake Lannigan, he was a sitting duck for you."

"Ma'am, I'm not here to argue the case with you. I believe we would have released Colonel Kelly, but what his aunt and Major Wilson did has changed things."

"I would agree," Quinn replied. "His aunt helped him get away as did Major Wilson. I can't condone those actions. But I'll have to admit, and wouldn't do so under oath, that I might have done the same thing myself. What you had in the way of evidence was incredibly weak."

Agent Ferguson leaned forward. "I think it's time to move on from this discussion to what we're going to do now."

"Agreed," Hightower said. "This isn't getting us anywhere."

"Thank you, General," Ferguson said. "Sir, do you have any idea where these two officers may have gone?"

"I think I know exactly where they went," Hightower replied. "Knowing Colonel Kelly like I do, he went after Colonel Garcia. We've been tied up in these other two messes and haven't given enough attention to that. I know how frustrated he was that Rene Garcia's still missing."

"Where do you think they'd go?" Spitz asked.

"Where would you go?" Hightower replied.

Spitz thought for a moment. "If we agree that these issues may be related, then I believe that Colonel Garcia may be somewhere in the Gettysburg area and that's probably where they headed."

Hightower nodded. "That would be my guess. But where? We had assumed that Garcia was in the building the FBI raided last night. But she wasn't, so it would seem that Gettysburg would be the next logical place. Whatever happened to Blake is probably exactly what happened to Garcia."

"I've got a warrant to search Colonel Garcia's house," Spitz said. "I'd like you to come along. You may spot something that I miss."

"Let's go," Hightower replied. "Time is of the essence."

Quinn stood. "Now I feel that we're headed in the right direction. These three officers are special to me so keep me in the loop. I'll authorize all means necessary to find them."

43

West of Gettysburg, 10:23 p.m.

Zack and Wilson met on the edge of the clearing. Zack leaned over and whispered, "She's in the trailer with Henderson."

"You sure?"

"Hell yes, I saw her."

Wilson moved toward the trailer. "Hot damn, let's go in that dump and blast her out of there. Beat the crap out of Henderson."

"Hold it. I'd feel better if we each had a weapon. He sure does."

Wilson thought for a moment. "Take too long to get one."

"Screw it. I'm going in that trailer. You wait out here for a few minutes, then come over and check things out. We'll have to adjust as we go."

"Just like in Afghanistan."

"Roger that." Zack ducked down and ran across the clearing, staying as low as he could. He crept around to the door of the trailer. Tried the handle. Not locked. Okay, he thought, here goes.

Pulling the door open, he stepped inside. Henderson sat in an overstuffed chair, a shotgun pointed at Zack. "Why, hello Zack, I wondered how long it would take you to quit screwing around out there and decide to come inside."

Zack moved toward the center of the small room. "It's over, Cliff. Let me take Garcia. If you don't hurt her, it'll go much easier on you."

"Don't bullshit me, Kelly, not this time. Not again. You won't do shit for me just like you didn't do shit for Michael Sullivan."

Zack squinted at Henderson. "What are you talking about?"

"You ordered Sullivan into that building, knowing it would be hot. Poor bastard got knifed and you didn't do a damn thing to stop it. Shouldn't have happened that way."

"Cliff, we were on a tactical operation. Sullivan was military and knew the risks. We all knew the risks."

"But, you always picked the gay guy for the really tough ones, didn't you? That way if he got killed, it didn't matter. That's what you thought, Kelly. Admit it. You're among friends."

Zack thought about the operation. Thought about Sullivan. He hadn't realized it before, but he should have. Sullivan and Henderson together at the bars, rooming together. Goddamn, it should have dawned on him, but it didn't.

"Cliff, I never gave a thought to Sullivan's sexual orientation. He was the best man for the operation. But, he haunts me. Haunts me every day. I've carried that one with me, just like all the others who didn't get back."

"You no-good lying son-of-a-bitch." Henderson waved the gun at Zack. "Admit it you bastard, you set him up, ended up glad when he got blown away. Another gay guy, but who gives a shit."

Zack searched the room. He didn't see anything that he could use as a weapon. Got to keep Henderson talking.

Henderson laughed. "And don't think Wilson is going to save your sorry ass."

Zack played deadpan. "What are you talking about?"

"I've been watching the two of you creep around out there. Took you long enough. I figured you'd be in here twenty minutes ago. But no, you had to check out every corner, each of the trailers. I almost fell asleep waiting for you."

The television turned out to be closed-circuit TV. Glancing over, Zack saw that the picture showed T.J. at the edge of the clearing.

"Yeah, it's night vision stuff. Cost me a bundle, but I knew sooner or later you'd be coming. All I needed to do was sit and wait. Figured you'd be smart enough to sort out what happened to Lannigan. But no, you always depended on the brains of your fucking team. Garcia's sharp. She figured it out while all you were doing was playing with that Irish cunt."

Henderson's nuts. Zack had to do something. Maybe slip toward the kitchen.

"Don't, Kelly, don't even think about it. We're going into the bedroom. You wanted to see your buddy, Garcia. Well, she's in there waiting for you."

"Wait, Cliff, why did you take Blake?"

"Isn't it self-explanatory? You left me the message you were bringing Blake Lannigan to Gettysburg for a tour. Wanted me to escort her around. I stopped at the restaurant and charged up your drinks. Dropped a Roofie into Lannigan's drink, and half a Roofie into yours."

Zack searched his mind. Remembered Cliff at the restaurant, his arm on the shoulder of the waiter. And a Roofie, what was a Roofie? Holy crap, the date-rape drug.

Henderson laughed. "Yeah, I can see your mind working. Flunitrazepam is a prescription drug under the name of Rohypnol. On the street we call 'em Roofies. The hot-shit date-rape drug. Some booze and a Roofie and that's all it takes. After you guys drank your drinks, all I needed to do was to follow you to the park, then rig up that recording of the hoofbeats. You wanted ghosts, I gave you ghosts. I had so damn much fun watching you get all stressed out and go into your fucked-up flashback mode."

He made it sound so simple, Zack thought. *But what he did to me and Blake. Not simple at all.*

Henderson laughed again. "Once I grabbed Lannigan and gave her a shot to get her asleep, everything else fell into place. From then on it was simple drugs and mind control. Just like I did all the time in Afghanistan."

Zack had to keep Henderson talking. Needed time to think. "Why Garcia?"

"When Garcia came down here, it was perfect. That's why I let Blake go. I knew you'd come after Garcia and wouldn't stop, no matter what. If only you'd done that for Michael we wouldn't be having this conversation."

"Cliff, you've got it wrong."

"Stow it, Kelly. I don't want to hear it. You got him killed, and he was the only person I ever loved. We were going to get out of the Army after that tour and head west. Someplace where nobody knew us. Get a fresh start. And you, you bastard, you got him killed."

"But... "

"All of our plans blew up when he got knifed. You stood there and watched. I promised Michael, promised myself I would get revenge. It took awhile but here it is, and I'm not going to let you slip away."

Henderson looked as if he might cry.

Zack had to keep him talking. "What about Blake's clothes?"

"Piece of cake. Learned the art at Quantico. Popped the lock on your back door and slipped inside. Dropped off the clothes and left." He stood, motioned with the shotgun. "You want to see your girlfriend, well go into the bedroom. I'll be right behind you. Don't do anything funny. You know how big a hole this baby can put in somebody. And don't think I won't do it. You'd be wrong."

Zack walked down the narrow corridor, past the tiny bathroom on the right, sweat on his forehead. He entered the master bedroom, sizing things up as he went. Henderson would pull that trigger in a heartbeat. What could he do?

As he'd seen her from the window, Garcia sat on the double bed, dressed in a white robe. A three-drawer chest and a wooden chair fleshed out the furnishings in the room.

Zack hurried over to her, knelt down on his right knee, and took her hand. "Garcia, thank God I found you. Are you all right?"

Garcia stared at him, her gaze unblinking. In a monotone she said, "Who are you?"

Zack stared back at her, disbelief funneling through his mind. "Garcia, it's me. Zack Kelly. What's wrong with you?"

"Nothing is wrong." Same monotone. "I'm very happy. I'm with the man I love."

"See, Kelly," Henderson said, "not everybody loves you. Garcia has already decided that I'm the man for her."

"Look, Cliff, it's not too late. Let's figure out where we go from here. We can work our way out of this."

"You're right, Kelly, we can. It's going to be easy. You busted in here. Garcia and I are having a quiet couple of days. You get all pissed off. Attack us. Garcia grabs the pistol. She has to shoot you. It's a plain case of self-defense."

"Cliff be real. Garcia's not going to shoot me."

Henderson smiled, a big smile. "Wanna bet? She's going to shoot you, then she's going to shoot Wilson. What the hell. She doesn't realize who he is. He bursts in. Scares her. She's been having a great time with me. Haven't you, Garcia?"

"Yes. I've been having a great time with Cliff. I always have a great time with Cliff."

Zack glanced over, saw the dazed look in Garcia's eyes. She's been drugged.

Cliff kept the shotgun trained on Zack. "Pick up the pistol, Garcia. It's next to you on the bed. Remember, it's time to shoot your enemy. He's been trying to attack you. Wants to attack me. Don't let him attack you or me."

Garcia reached down. Picked up the pistol. She turned and pointed it at Zack.

"Now, Garcia," Henderson said, "now shoot him before he hurts you."

Same monotone. "Yes, I must shoot him before he hurts me or hurts Cliff."

44

General Hightower sat at the desk in Rene Garcia's study, searching through the drawers, trying to figure out what he was looking for. Harold sat in Hightower's lap, licking his lips after the general fed him.

Agent Spitz came into the room. He laughed when he saw Harold. "Looks like you've got a good friend there."

"Yep, it's amazing what food will do for a hungry cat."

"I talked to Chief Munson in Gettysburg," Spitz said. "He's pulled in extra officers to search through the town. So far nothing on the two of them."

Hightower banged his fist on the desk in frustration. "I know there's something here. I can feel it. But where?" He glanced down at Harold. "Where is it, Harold? You know. Oh, if only you could talk."

Spitz had to chuckle again. "Don't think he'll be able to help you. Do you have any idea where she keeps her appointments? Maybe she had something planned for Friday, something that would give us a clue."

"That's what I've been looking for. Her appointment book is here, but the page for last Friday has been torn out. Goddamn, that's it." Hightower pulled a pencil out of a drawer and started rubbing the lead point over the next page, hoping something would come up. "Sometimes this works."

He could see her writing. "There's something here. I bet Zack found the page for Friday and tore it out. Maybe that gave him a lead."

He kept sketching, trying to make out the note.

"We can get the lab guys over here," Spitz said.

"That'll take too long. Wait a minute. Wait a damn minute, I've got something coming up. I can almost make it out." He read it. "Six o'clock. Dinner with Cliff Henderson. That's it. She went down to meet Henderson Friday night. That's where she is. That's where Zack is."

Spitz pulled out his cell. Pushed in a number. "Munson, this is Agent Spitz. We know where they are. Can you get me an address for Cliff Henderson? That's right, Cliff Henderson."

He waited a minute. Listened. "Yeah, the park ranger. We think that's where Colonel Garcia went and Kelly and Wilson followed her. We've got to round up the three of them and sort this out. Be careful, we believe Henderson may be behind the two disappearances."

He disconnected.

Hightower had his cell phone out. "Ms. Quinn, this is General Hightower."

"Yes, Aaron."

"I think Zack and Wilson are in Gettysburg. Can you set up a chopper for us at the Pentagon pad? Munson's trying to get an address for the park ranger, Cliff Henderson."

"I'll have it waiting for you."

"We'll be there in twenty minutes."

Hightower set down Harold and hurried toward the door, Spitz right behind him. "Hang in there, Harold, we'll get her back for you. Hell, for all of us."

Spitz shook his head. "I'm gonna feel like crap if I was wrong about Kelly."

———

Zack stared at the pistol, steady in Garcia's hand. Dead shot at this range.

A look of indifference covered her face. "I must shoot this man. Must shoot him before he hurts Cliff. This man is my enemy."

Zack's mind whirled. Slow down and focus. How could he stop her? "No, Garcia, wait. Henderson has you drugged. Don't do it. This is murder."

Henderson kept the shotgun trained on Zack. "He is your enemy, Garcia. You must kill your enemy. You must do it now."

"Yes, he is my enemy. Must kill my enemy."

Zack scanned the room. Nothing he could use as a weapon. If he moved, Henderson would blow him away with the shotgun. If he didn't, Garcia would kill him with the pistol. Laura. My God, he wouldn't get a chance to say good-bye. Tell her he loved her. Think. Think.

Garcia faced Zack. "Must kill my enemy."

Henderson started to laugh. "This is payback, Kelly, payback for getting one of the best guys who ever lived killed. I've been waiting a long time for this. I'm going to enjoy it."

Zack dove toward the door. Gotta knock down Henderson. Do it for Laura.

Two loud bangs. The noise reverberated in the trailer, his ears ringing. But, he didn't feel anything. No pain. No blood. Saw Henderson writhing on the floor, blood pouring from his right arm and leg. What the hell?

Looked up to see Garcia smiling at him. "Kinky bastard thought he could hypnotize me. Didn't know who he was dealing with. Well, fuck him. That one was for Blake."

———

Zack and Garcia sat at the kitchen table, surrounded by police officers. Garcia had managed to slip into the bathroom and change out of the white robe Henderson kept her in and put on her blouse and a pair of slacks.

An ambulance had arrived twenty minutes earlier. Orderlies were in the bedroom getting Henderson ready for transport under the watchful eye of a police officer. His angry voice reverberated throughout the trailer.

The door opened. Chief Munson climbed into the trailer. "I got the word that you were here and came out right away. Are you both all right?"

"Guess so," Zack replied. "I owe my life to Garcia's mind. Henderson thought he had her under his control, poor guy didn't realize that no one controls Rene Garcia."

"Henderson didn't know my mom had taught me how to meditate and how to block my mind if I didn't want to listen to something."

Munson rubbed his jaw. "I'll be darned."

"Yeah. I had to wait until I had proof before I could turn on him. When I knew Zack had heard everything and could confirm my story, it was time to act. Now, my next priority is to get somewhere and grab a shower. Maybe a nice, long bath to get the crud from this trailer off my skin."

"What happened?" Munson asked.

"Henderson kidnapped Blake to get at me in revenge for his lover's death," Zack said. "Michael Sullivan died during an operation in Afghanistan. Henderson apparently blamed me for Sullivan's death."

"No apparently," Garcia said. "That's all he could talk about."

"Anyway," Zack continued, "I called and left him a message Blake and I were planning to visit Gettysburg, hoping he could give us a tour."

Munson made a note.

"I'm sure he figured how crazy it would sound for me to try and explain her disappearance, then the hoofbeats and shuffling feet."

"Gotta admit that was the craziest story I ever heard in all my time as a police officer."

"He stopped by the restaurant and slipped some drugs in our drinks. You need to find out which waiter we had. I think he may have helped Henderson."

Munson made another note. "He really had it all planned out."

"When he met Garcia, he thought he could play some more games with my mind so he... ." Zack turned to Garcia. "Why don't you take it from there?"

Garcia leaned her elbows on the kitchen table. "Henderson turned on the charm and it almost worked. He can be a very pleasant guy so I met him for dinner Friday night at the Cozy Inn in Thurmont, halfway for both of us. We had a nice dinner, then he invited me to come to Gettysburg."

"Did you suspect anything at that time?" Munson asked.

"Something tingled in the back of my mind. Told me to be careful. Kind of a sixth sense kicked in. I spilled the drink he gave me. He'd probably doped it up."

Zack patted her hand. "Maybe a ghost at work."

Garcia laughed. "Yeah, maybe. Anyway, when we arrived at his place, we got to talking. I told him how busy it's been at the Pentagon. He asked me if I'd ever tried meditation to help reduce stress."

"Ah," Zack said, "the old meditation trick."

Garcia laughed again. "I remembered from his Pentagon file that he'd been trained in interrogation at the CIA facility. When he told me to relax and meditate, my BS meter went wild."

Munson's turn to laugh. "Your BS meter?"

"Yeah. Thank heavens for my mom. When he tried to brainwash me, I closed my mind, making him think he had me. Henderson was good, and I had to concentrate to prevent him from taking over my mind. Fortunately I didn't have any of the drug in my system, although I had to dump a couple of other drinks during the last three days."

Munson leaned back in his chair. "I don't know the best way to ask this... ."

"No, he didn't try anything when he thought I was under. Remember, the guy was gay so I held no real interest for him other than a tool to get at Zack. I did have to change out of my clothes in front of him but he didn't try to take advantage of this poor damsel in distress."

Zack laughed. "Damsel in distress my ass."

Garcia had to smile again. "Well, there is that."

The two orderlies wheeled Henderson out of the bedroom. Munson moved over toward the wall to make room for them.

Henderson looked up at Garcia. "You bitch, you played me."

Garcia glared down at him. "Right back at you. I told you I would get the bastard who kidnapped my friend, Blake. I guess you weren't listening."

Henderson tried to lurch up toward her, but he was tied to the litter with a strap and a police officer stood between him and Garcia.

"Just try something, and I'll flatten you some more." Garcia turned away. "Now get that jerk out of here."

The orderlies wheeled Henderson to the door and lifted him over the frame.

"Where's T.J.?" Garcia asked.

"He took the truck back to the visitor's center to pick up General Hightower and Agent Spitz," Zack replied. "Hope Spitz isn't too mad at me."

"I talked to him," Munson said. "He'll want to get statements from you and Wilson, but I don't believe there will be any problem with him or the FBI. You were the victim here, not the bad guy."

Garcia punched Zack's arm. "Tell Spitz to be careful or I'll get the pistol out again."

Zack laughed. A fun laugh. A long laugh. Something he hadn't been able to do since this all started. Now, he needed to get back to D.C. and check on Blake. He was still missing something.

45

Thurmont, MD, Wednesday, 3:15 a.m.

Zack and T.J. Wilson stopped in Thurmont to fill the gas tank and take a break before the two of them got sucked onto the Washington, D.C. beltway. They had to be ready to face the onslaught of the early-morning commuters trekking south on Highway 270 from north of D.C.

Zack hustled into McDonald's to fill his caffeine void and try to feel human again. Chief Munson had invited them to stay at his place but they'd declined. General Hightower wanted Zack back at the White House first thing in the morning to brief Quinn on the most recent turn of events.

Garcia pushed to ride back with them, but Hightower insisted she fly back on his chopper. He worried about any negative effects from her ordeal, and wanted her at Walter Reed for at least a day to get checked out. Munson had agreed to watch her Harley.

She looked tired and finally agreed. Zack figured she'd bust out of the hospital before the twenty-four hours elapsed, and he'd find her back at her desk in the Pentagon.

Wilson gassed up, then took another swig of coffee. "What say we get back on the road? Probably another hour and fifteen back into D.C."

Zack settled back. "You're in the driver's seat."

As they pulled onto Route 15 and turned south again, Zack's cell rang. "Kelly."

"Zack, it's Shelia."

Her voice made Zack smile. "Hey, lots of good news. We found Garcia and she's safe. Turned out that Cliff Henderson kidnapped both Blake and Garcia. So, things are finally starting to make sense. How are you doing?"

"Ah, not so good, Zack. I'm with Sean Lannigan. He, ah, wants you to come to his house."

"Now?"

"Yes, right away. He's very insistent, and I think pretty serious."

After a shout and some static, Lannigan's voice resounded on the phone. "What Shelia is saying, you fuck head, is that if you don't come to my place like I say, I'll shoot her. Got it? How is it they say...you don't want to lose a sweet piece of meat?"

Be careful, the clown sounds nuts. "Wait a minute, Lannigan, don't do to anything to her. I'm about an hour away from Washington. Be there as fast as I can."

"You got ninety minutes, you prick. If I don't see your face by then I'll kill her, and she's much too pretty to die. I suspect you've figured that one out."

"All right, all right, take it easy. I'll be there."

"And don't think about bringing any of your cop friends along. This is between you and me. If you come as I say, I'll let Shelia go. Then it'll be you and me. If you bring anyone along, I'll kill her."

Anything else Zack should say? Hell, no. "I'll be there as fast as possible. Don't hurt her. You want me. I'll take her place."

"Ninety minutes."

A click and the line went dead.

Wilson took another sip of coffee. "Who's that? Sounded serious."

"Shelia. I've got ninety minutes to get to Lannigan's house or he'll shoot her."

Wilson almost swerved off the road. "Are you serious?"

"Deadly serious. Ninety minutes, so step on it. I don't know what's going on with him."

Wilson gunned the engine and sped up. "How about if we call Spitz? Get him involved."

"No. Lannigan said if I called the cops he'd kill her. Sounded so screwed up that he might do it. This is between Lannigan and me."

"You got it." Wilson kicked it up to eighty. "Goddamn."

Zack had to develop a plan in a hurry. "Yeah, Goddamn."

———————

Seventy-four minutes later, Wilson pulled up in front of Lannigan's house. "What now?"

"He told me to come alone," Zack said. "I gotta do exactly what he says. Hopefully, I can talk him out of hurting Shelia."

"Yeah," Wilson replied, "but what about your ass? Sounds to me like you're walking into a trap you might not beat your way out of."

"It's between the two of us. Shelia's got nothing to do with it. When she comes out, call Hightower and the D.C. police. But don't call anyone until you see Shelia. I don't want her to get hurt by that asshole."

"Better watch your back. He hates your guts."

"No kidding. I've got to get him down from whatever perch he's on."

Wilson held out his hand. "Good luck, man."

"Thanks." Zack shook hands, then jumped out of the truck and hurried across the street. He pushed open the gate and walked up the steps to the front door. He looked in the window, but the living room stood dark. Putting his hand on the door handle, he jiggled it. Unlocked.

Zack pushed it open and stepped inside. All quiet.

No lights on the bottom floor. A light shined down from the second-floor hallway.

"Hey, Lannigan," Zack yelled, "I'm here and I'm coming up the stairs."

Lannigan's voice echoed in the dim light. "You'd better be alone you son-of-a-bitch. If you've got anyone with you, you know what I'll do. And her death will be on your conscience."

Zack started up the stairs, one step at a time. "I came alone." His mind swept ahead, but he couldn't come up with an angle. "I'm walking up the stairs. I did exactly what you told me."

When Zack reached the second floor, light shined from the

bedroom at the end of the hall. "All right," Zack yelled, "I'm at the top of the stairs and walking down the hallway."

"Come ahead, Kelly, we've been expecting you."

Zack crept toward the open doorway, heart pounding. Focus, damn it, focus. He pushed the door the rest of the way open and walked into the bedroom. Shelia sat on the bed, dressed in a sweater and slacks. Her hair looked mussed, but she didn't seem harmed.

Lannigan sat next to her, holding a Glock pointed at her head. He motioned for Zack to take a seat on a chair next to the bed. "Come in, Kelly. Sit on that chair over there."

Zack did as instructed. Glanced at Shelia. "Are you hurt?"

She shook her head.

"All right, Lannigan, I'm here just like you asked. What do you want?"

"What the hell do you think I want, wise guy? Before this week started, I'd been nominated for a position on the Supreme Court. Shoe-in for confirmation." His voice broke. "Finally made it all the way to the top from that hole in Boston where I grew up. Now, thanks to you, I'm about to face charges of facilitating prostitution."

How to handle this? Tough or easy? Try tough. "That wasn't me, Lannigan, that was you. No one forced you to set up that Irish internship. You pulled all this stuff down on your own head. It's time you took responsibility and quit trying to hurt others for what you did."

Lannigan jumped up, face red, eyes bulging and shouted, "Guys have been getting a little on the side for years. The girls had a chance to see the federal government at work. We'd have sent them home with a wealth of education. Then you step in and put your nose where it doesn't belong. Now it's all fucked up."

"No, Sean, it's you who's all fucked up." Darcy Quinn stood in the doorway, an M-9 pistol in her hand. "Checkmate, Sean."

Lannigan waved his pistol at her, trying to also watch Zack. "Darcy, get the hell out of here. This is between me and Kelly."

"No, it's not, Sean. Not any longer. I suspected what you were up to, but I couldn't believe it. I came over here to warn you, then I stood outside the door and heard what a slime-ball you really are."

Tears formed in her eyes. "I loved you and this is what you do. You cheated on Holly. I couldn't bring myself to tell her because I was the cause. Then you bring all those young women to the United States on the pretext of teaching them about our federal justice system. All they're taught is what a bunch of filthy old men you know."

"You hypocritical bitch. It's all right to fuck around with me, but no one else can. Is that it?"

Zack stood and glanced at Shelia. Her eyes got wide. He shook his head. Put his finger to his lips. Don't say anything.

"Sean, I won't let you hurt Shelia. She's done nothing but try and help us find your daughter. And all the while, you set up this white slavery mess."

"If you try and stop me, Darcy, I'll shoot Shelia right here and now."

"No, you won't," Quinn said. "It's over, Sean, put the gun down. No one is going to get hurt."

"You haven't got the guts. You're in love with me, and you haven't got the guts."

With Lannigan and Quinn in their face-off, Zack moved to his left, trying to spread Lannigan's range of vision. He moved slowly, step by step, away from Quinn and slightly closer to Lannigan.

Quinn brushed away another tear. "You're right, Sean. I've been in love with you ever since we were kids. You chose Holly, so I settled for second. But all that stops now. Put down the pistol and let's call the police."

"No way, Darcy." Lannigan cocked the gun. "I'm going to kill Kelly, then take Shelia. Now get out of my way before I shoot you, too."

Zack yelled, "Shelia, down." He dove at Lannigan's feet, aiming for one of his best open-field tackles. He hit Lannigan amid an explosion of gunshots.

Lannigan fell to one knee. Looked down at his stomach. Blood seeped down the front of his shirt. He pointed the pistol at Zack.

Zack shoved Lannigan's arm up. Two shots hit the ceiling.

Another shot. Pain radiated from Zack's left shoulder. He dropped to the floor and rolled to his right. Lunged up, grabbed

Lannigan and threw him against the wall. Looked for Shelia. Didn't see her.

Lannigan raised the weapon once more.

Zack knocked his arm, another series of explosions and shattered glass. The nerves in Zack's shoulder sent waves of pain to his brain. *Ignore it. Get Lannigan's gun. Protect Shelia.*

He punched a fist into Lannigan's chin. Another explosion. Pain seared up from his hip. Shit, bastard hit me again.

Zack slammed a right hook into Lannigan's face. Then another. Lannigan fell to the floor. The gun flew across the room.

Shelia slid out from the bed, ducked down, then ran to pick up the gun. She trained it on Lannigan but that wasn't necessary. Not any more. He was out cold on the floor.

What about Quinn? She'd fallen to the floor, blood gushing from her forehead. No, no, not her.

Zack reached for Shelia's hand. Heard footsteps on the stairs as he slipped into darkness.

46

Walter Reed Army Medical Center, 6:00 a.m.

The emergency room entrance at Walter Reed Army Medical Center was jumping with activity as the air ambulance dropped onto the heliport, stirring up clouds of sand and dust. The medical attendant continued to press compression bandage to Zack's shoulder as the crew chief slid the helicopter side door open.

Orderlies stood next to the pad, waiting for the all clear from the crew chief. Once they were cleared, they rushed forward to lift Zack off the chopper and place him on a mobile stretcher. They wheeled him into the ER and transferred him onto a table. A nurse stepped into the room and cut his clothes off, then covered him with a sheet.

A short, slender women in blue scrubs swept into his range of vision. "Colonel Kelly, I'm Doctor Forrest. You have two gunshot wounds, one to your shoulder and the other to your right hip."

"Tell me something I don't already know."

"Oh, so you're one of those wise guys? Well, we're taking you up to the OR to clean out those wounds, dig the bullet out of your hip, then you'll be moved to the recovery room. I suspect the surgery should take about three hours." She smiled. "It appears you will live, although I may have to revise that prediction if you get too smart with me."

"The pain medicine must have done its job. I'm floating in la la land." Zack managed to raise his hand and put it on the doctor's arm. "How is she?"

Forrest leaned down to hear him. "Who?"

"Darcy Quinn? She looked pretty bad."

"Let's get you fixed up before we worry about anyone else."

Quinn must be dead. Damn. His hand slipped off her arm. He fell into blessed darkness.

Zack felt as if he were climbing out of a tunnel, a deep dark tunnel. He climbed up, then fell back again. Finally he saw light. He tried again and managed to open his eyes.

Shelia leaned over the bed, General Hightower standing next to her. "I think he's waking up," Shelia said.

It took a minute for him to form words. What did he want to say? "Ah, pardon me if I don't jump to attention, Sir, but I... "

Hightower's face broke into a grin. "Sounds to me as if you're going to be fine. Shelia told me what she could about what happened with Ms. Quinn. Can you add anything? Why she was there? The press is going crazy."

Zack's head throbbed and he had to think for a minute. "She showed up after I arrived. Apparently...apparently, the two of them had something going. When Lannigan fired at me, I think that...think that Quinn shot him. She probably saved my life. Uh, how is she?"

Hightower squinted, pressed his lips together. "Never had a chance."

Zack's heart sank. Not Quinn. No, not her. Took a minute to form more words. "Okay, what about Lannigan?"

"He's at George Washington Hospital Center undergoing surgery."

Shelia brushed a tear from her eye. "Poor Holly. I don't know how she's going to deal with all this."

Zack tried to focus. "Where am I?"

"You're on the surgical recovery ward at Walter Reed. It took the doctors about three hours to clean your wounds, dig out the bullet from your hip, then sew you back together again. It appears you'll be fine." Hightower started toward the door. "I'd better get with Travis Plank. This press conference is going to be something.

The President wants answers and he's not going to like what I have to tell him. I'll be back when I can."

The door closed and Zack took Shelia's hand. "How are you?"

"Trying to get my act together. I thought Sean Lannigan was my friend. Boy, what a mistake that was."

Zack tried to lift his head off the pillow but nothing seemed to work right. At least not yet. "Tell me what happened."

"I understand the FBI is preparing to arrest him on charges of conspiring to cause prostitution, and I suspect now that'll be upgraded to murder. He must have gotten the word about the charges and called me to come over to his house. When I got there, it was obvious he'd had a lot to drink. Slurring his words, not making much sense. Kept talking about how his life was in tatters. How he'd built up his life from nothing in those slums of Boston and now it was all stolen from him."

"What then?"

"I told him I thought the Irish internship was an awful idea, and I didn't understand how he could trick young women into prostitution. He got upset with me. Yelled that he'd meant this as a chance for the girls to see our judicial system. They were getting a free ride over here. Free room and board. I think he looked on their bodies as barter for that opportunity."

"What a bastard."

"I've always liked Sean. He was like an uncle to me. Stood up for me when my parents booted me out of the house. I always figured he thought I was special, but all the time I suspect he looked on me as another slab of meat."

Zack leaned back on the pillow to get his thinking straight. He tried to move his arm and he pulled on the tube from his IV.

Shelia touched his hand. "Careful, Zack. You're going to spring a leak."

The enormity of what had happened began to settle on Zack. "I think that Darcy Quinn saved my life. If she hadn't shot Lannigan, it could have been lights out."

"Oh, Zack... ." She started to cry.

"And he probably would have taken you as a hostage."

The door banged open. Laura hurried into the room. "Dad, Dad, are you all right?" She stopped next to the bed. "Can I hug you?"

Zack tried to lean up but ended up falling back. "Yeah, just be gentle."

As Laura gave him a hug, Zack spotted Aunt Mary waving from the doorway.

"We've been so worried about you," Mary said. "They wouldn't let us in until a couple of minutes ago."

Zack pointed at Shelia. "This is Shelia O'Donnell. She and I have been working on this case together."

"Are you the medium I've heard so much about?" Laura asked.

"Aye, that's me."

Laura's face lit up. "Cool. I've always wanted to meet a medium."

"Well, lassie, you have now."

"Cool." She stared at Shelia for a moment. "Wow, you're beautiful. And I love your accent."

"Well, thank you, Laura. I'd be glad to tell you what a medium does. And I'd love to hear all about you."

"Don't forget me," Aunt Mary said. "I've always been interested in spirits."

"Hey," Zack said, "what about me? I'm the guy who got shot. Twice."

"Well, that's true." Laura laughed. "But, you're not a medium."

The door opened and Dr. Forrest walked into the room. "I'm going to have to insist that my patient get some rest. I don't want him to fall apart after all my work to glue him back together."

The three turned to the door. "Get some sleep," Mary called. "We'll be out in the waiting room."

Zack waved. "By the way, thanks for your help in getting me away from Spitz."

She gave him a thumbs-up. "I found it kind of exciting."

Laura stepped back into the room. "Guess this means we won't be jogging for awhile. Too bad, because I'll be able to beat you now." She waved. "Love you, Dad."

Zack tried to wave but his head slipped back onto the pillow. A good feeling spread through him. Things were going to be okay with Laura. They'd both have to work on their relationship, but it would get better over time. Yes, it would get better and stronger.

His mind started to drift, then slowly he slipped into sleep, a deep sleep.

47

Gettysburg, October, Four Months Later

Zack and Blake passed the Gettysburg town square in his truck as streams of orange colored the sky from the setting sun. They had talked for a couple of weeks about coming back to the battlefield and agreed it would be important for closure.

When they passed the street with the borough building, Zack glanced down the block. "Wonder how Chief Munson's doing?"

"I don't want to take time to find out," Blake said. "Let's drive out and see Devil's Den. I'd like to take a few minutes and relive the past with you. A past I didn't get to see the first time around."

"Sounds great." Zack couldn't help but wonder what she thought about her father. He'd begun serving a twenty-year sentence after he convinced the jury that Quinn's murder was in self-defense.

Zack flipped on his signal and turned right, up to West Confederate Avenue along Seminary Ridge. "Whenever I come here, I wonder what must have gone through General Lee's mind when he stood on this spot almost 150 years ago."

"It's so quiet," Blake said.

"That's what I love about it and why it pisses me off to think about the state perhaps allowing some contractor to build a casino here. This is hallowed ground and I want them to keep it that way."

Zack slowed his truck and pointed out toward the field. "There's the North Carolina Memorial and over there is what's called the High Water Mark of the Confederacy. Twelve thousand Confederate soldiers tried to breach the Union lines and failed. Once that happened, General Lee had to turn his army south toward Virginia. Ended their last chance for victory."

They passed Pfizer Woods, then followed the road until it turned onto South Confederate Avenue. Zack tightened up a little as they rounded the bend to Little Round Top and Devil's Den. This is where it all started and where Henderson had kidnapped Blake.

Blake looked out through the windshield. "It still makes me angry when I think about Henderson. How he stole all that time from us."

"Well, he'll be in jail for a long time so we won't need to worry about him anymore."

She put her hand on his arm. "Zack, I'm sorry for all that Henderson and my father did to you."

"Ya know what? Let's forget about them and enjoy the moment." Zack pulled his truck into the parking lot down the hill from Little Round Top and shut off the engine. "This is where the Confederate soldiers almost broke through the Union lines. If it hadn't been for the guys from Maine, they probably would have made it."

The two got out of Zack's truck and strolled up the curving path to the overlook that circled Little Round Top. They looked out over the boulders of Devil's Den. Zack thought about Henderson, how he'd misjudged him. How Quinn had saved his life. How lucky he was to still be here and how lucky he was to have Laura with him.

"Hey," Blake said, "I hear you're flying to Ireland to spend a week with Shelia."

Thinking of her made Zack smile. "Shelia was here in Washington a few weeks ago and invited me to visit Ireland. It's such a beautiful country. I didn't get a chance to see much of it the first time I was there. What a time with those crazy clowns shooting at me."

"I bet the fact that Shelia's there waiting for you made your decision easier."

Warmth flowed through Zack. "Well, as Laura would say, there is that."

"Is Laura going with you?" Blake asked.

Zack shook his head. "Her mother is getting out of prison this month. It took a while, but Laura decided she wanted to be there to help her."

"Good for her. What a mature young woman."

"Yeah, I'm really proud of her." Zack hesitated before asking the next question. "How are you dealing with your aunt's death?"

Blake's shoulders slumped. "It's been almost four months and I still can't believe it. I miss her so much. Darcy was a great lady and a wonderful friend."

"Yeah," Zack replied. "Well, I'm glad Garcia is back on her feet. And no ill effects. General Hightower seems delighted to have his team back together."

Zack reached over and took Blake's hand. He cared deeply for this beautiful, talented woman. Most importantly, he knew their friendship would endure.

She looked at him, a hint of moisture in her eyes. "Thanks, Zack. Thanks for all you did to find me. All the things you put up with from my father."

"You're welcome." He squeezed her hand. "That's what friends do for one another."

She turned back to look out across the field, a mist moving in from Devil's Den. "Now, about those ghosts... ."